A.E. NALLE

EVERNIGHT PUBLISHING ®

www.evernightpublishing.com

Copyright© 2023

A.E. Nalle

Editor: Lisa Petrocelli

Cover Art: Jay Aheer

ISBN: 978-0-3695-0840-9

ALL RIGHTS RESERVED

A.E. NALLE

DEDICATION

This one is for the girls that make themselves smaller so other people can be comfortable.
Never be afraid to take up space for yourself.

A.E. NALLE

WICKEDLY INNOCENT

The Wicked Series, 4

A.E. Nalle

Copyright © 2023

Chapter One

When I was in middle school, I made a complete fool out of myself in front of my entire class. I had been walking up to turn in an assignment and face-planted in the middle of the row of desks. Melonie Turner stuck her perfectly manicured foot out, effectively fumbling my forward advance. I promptly tripped over her and the papers in my hands went flying. Of course, kids of such an adolescent age thought the occurrence was one of the funniest they had ever seen. While I was nursing sore elbows and pride, everyone else laughed.

When I looked up at Melonie, she smirked down at me before whispering, "It took your lard ass way too long to stop jiggling after that tumble, Lindsey." She then proceeded to act as though I had intentionally stepped on her foot. I may have broken a bone, she said, just another way to poke at my weight. She limped to the school nurse while I gathered my papers hastily and readjusted my glasses.

I was thoroughly humiliated and coined a new nickname that year, courtesy of Melonie, obviously. *Lardy Lindsey* is what they called me. The creativity of middle school minds was a laughable thing. I had always been on the bigger size of the spectrum compared to most girls, especially girls like Melonie, so that was always the easiest thing for cruel kids to attack. Though it may not have been the most original name a group of cackling preteens could come up with, it was effective in enhancing my mortification.

Up until this point in my life, that had been the single most humiliating experience I had ever gone through. As I had grown, I learned to laugh off any other embarrassing moments. Somehow, I didn't think I would be able to laugh this one off as I stared up at Ian from my spot on the floor.

You know when you drive by a car crash and you get told not to look? And you try, I mean really try, not to look. But eventually, curiosity gets the better of you, and it's almost as if you're forced to look. And then you can't look away no matter what.

That's what happened to me. I remembered I had seen Ian in the crowd of wedding guests and the next I was trapped in the world's most intense staring contest with him. I had been unable to look away from him the moment I spotted him. It was as if his presence sucked me in and wouldn't release me.

****

"You look absolutely stunning, Aunt Jill. And the wedding was perfect," I said as I hugged Jill around her neck. It wasn't an exaggeration when I thought she was the most stunning bride I think I'd ever seen. A lot of women with her petite frame would be gobbled up in all the tulle that came along with a wedding dress. But not her.

The tightly fitted bodice of the dress clung to her every curve and accentuated them even more. Her hair and makeup were immaculate in a way that most would never be able to imitate. I was firmly jealous of her slender body and perfect posterior. Where she was slim and fit, I was soft and what I would consider pudgy.

Even though everyone always told me I held my weight well for my build, it didn't stop that little voice in the back of my brain that screamed I wasn't as pretty as the other girls around me. The one that always spoke too loudly every time I pushed any food past my lips. It yelled I'd never be able to find a good man to love me the way others seemed to be finding without even trying. That voice sounded vaguely like my father's.

That's on Daddy issues, I internally scolded myself as I squeezed Jill. This was no place to think of that monster and what he had done to my family.

"Thank you, Lyns." Her smile beamed my way as she released me and stepped back only to hold my hands. "I'm glad you and your mom were able to talk me down earlier," she mumbled as she gave Damon the side eye. I could almost see her sigh of relief when she realized he hadn't heard her. He was too busy talking with his brothers.

I giggled as I squeezed her hands in mine. "Are you kidding me? Like we would ever let you talk yourself out of keeping a guy like Damon," I said in a hushed tone so as not to raise suspicion. Even though Jill had overcome a lot of her past, her insecurities still shined through under times of stress. And anyone who has ever been involved in one knows how stressful weddings can be.

It's not like she tried to talk herself out of marrying Damon, it's just that she had to be reassured she was indeed good enough for a guy like him. As one of her maids of honor, it was my mom's and my job to kick her ass when she started having doubts.

Jill beamed at me one last time before releasing my hands as Damon approached. The way they looked at each other sparked feelings of yearning I didn't think were possible for me to have.

I'd never had a boyfriend unless you count that one date I went on with Georgie Bluff in junior high. We were barely sixteen at the time and all we did was hold hands at the local movie theater while watching some gory zombie movie. I grinned now when I thought back on the craptastic date.

He had asked me out and I had been so quiet and shy back then that I hadn't had the gall to say I really wasn't interested. He'd picked me up in his mom's old Dodge Neon and we'd split the cost of tickets. I even bought my own popcorn. Why he ever thought I would make out with him in the backseat after the movie was beyond me.

There had been other times in college when I had gone a little further with some guys after a few too many drinks, but it had never been more than some kissing.

That's right, I was going to be a twenty-one-year-old woman in just a couple of days and I didn't have any experience with the opposite sex. How pathetic was that?

It's not like I was saving myself for marriage or anything like that. It's just that I had never met any man that sparked that part of me. Well, all except for one man.

I shook my head to clear my thoughts. Now was not the time to think about Dr. Young. It was a childish fantasy, for one thing. We had only had one encounter but for some reason, I couldn't stop thinking about him. To think a man like that would want anything to do with someone like me was a cruel joke.

I mean, sure, I wasn't completely unfortunate-looking. I had a pretty enough face. I liked my eyes and my long dark hair, but come on. The thought of an older guy like him even having a single fleeting thought about me was ridiculous. But I couldn't fool myself into thinking that when we bumped into one another at the hospital, it hadn't made me feel … something. Just the thought of him sparked feelings inside me I honestly didn't think were possible.

I pushed those inappropriate thoughts aside as I watched Damon envelop Jill into his arms and kiss her like his life depended on it. I couldn't stop the blush from staining my cheeks as his hands wandered lower toward her behind. His smile when he released her lips was enough to make any single woman beg to have a love like that. I couldn't hear what he whispered so close to her ear but whatever it was made Jill throw her head back and laugh.

I looked away from the intimate scene in front of me and watched my mother who looked on toward the newlyweds with such love in her eyes. Heath and Reid flanked both of her sides and were touching her lovingly. It was like they were inseparable. Heath was the first to trail his hand up my mom's neck and nudge her chin in his direction. She grinned before meeting him halfway for a tantalizing kiss. Mom hadn't even fully opened her eyes before Reid was pulling her toward him for their own sensual kiss.

I couldn't keep the smile from my lips as I looked away. I was so happy she finally had found the ending she always deserved.

Emily and Leo were the next in this wedding party. I always thought Emily was a happy-go-lucky person, but I think that may have been a mask all this time. Because as I looked at her situated in Leo's arms, she truly looked happy.

I was surrounded by happy couples and I felt an overwhelming feeling of loneliness. I mean, sure, I was only twenty. I had my whole life ahead of me. Plenty of time to date and meet new people. I could have any life I wanted.

So, why did I want exactly what was in front of me?

I didn't want to party as my peers did. I didn't want to sleep around with a bunch of different people and figure out what I liked. I wanted to meet the person I was supposed to be with for the rest of my life. I wanted to feel like I belonged.

"Hard not to be a little jealous surrounded by all this mushy shit, isn't it?" a deep voice murmured next to my cheek. I flinched and gripped my chest as I faced the person speaking. Damon's brother, Liam. I'd been so busy in the depths of my self-pity I hadn't even seen him come to stand next to me.

"Sorry, I didn't mean to startle you." He grinned down at me and I couldn't help the nervous giggle that rose from my throat.

"It's okay. And yes, even though I'm extremely happy for everyone in this room, I kinda wish they would all get a different one." I winced at my awkwardness. "Room, that is, get a different room." I shook my head to myself. *Good God, Lindsey, get it together.* The first handsome man to speak to me today and I was tripping over my words.

Liam tilted his head back and a deep laugh boomed out of him. I couldn't stop the smile that spread across my face. "I knew what you meant, Lindsey." He smiled.

"Oh." I blushed and then fell silent. This was my problem. I couldn't handle being around the opposite sex, especially if they were vaguely attractive, and not make a fool of myself. And Liam was more than vaguely attractive. He was downright hot. From his perfectly coiffed hair and deep-brown eyes to all those alluring black tattoos, Liam could have any woman he desired. I was sure of it.

Well, except for Emily, I suppose.

I didn't know the whole story of Liam and Emily but I wondered if it hurt Liam to watch her and Leo together. I risked a peek up at him and found him still grinning at all the happy couples, so maybe not.

"Well, what do you say we get this party going?" he said as he turned his attention back to me. I nodded hastily and moved to take my place by the big doors that led to the reception hall.

Liam clapped his hands together loudly to get everyone's attention. "All right, all you perverts, it's time to get in there and get our drink on." His raised voice quieted all the murmuring around us. "I for one need a stiff drink after witnessing this son of a bitch tie himself to one woman for the rest of his life. Poor fucker," he said as he slapped Damon on the shoulder playfully. I covered my laugh as Damon and Jill both raised their happy middle fingers at him. Liam snickered as he sauntered back toward me.

The intro music for the wedding party started to play over the loudspeakers as everyone lined up behind Liam and me. He intertwined my arm with his as the doors sprang open.

The wedding had been beautiful but the reception was where all the real planning had been. The room was artfully decorated with tables on either side of the makeshift aisle we were to walk down. Black tablecloths with beautifully crafted centerpieces dotted the entire area. People that had just come from the wedding sat at said tables with bright smiles. The dance floor had been assembled and waxed to perfection. The DJ had his huge setup at the far end of the building with all the lights and speakers you'd be able to find at a rave. The open bar held all of Damon and Jill's favorites along with top-shelf liquor. This was topped off with tuxed waiters and waitresses to make the evening go off without a hitch.

"Nobody knows how to throw a party quite like a Santos does," Liam whispered into my ear before leading us into the room.

I giggled as he threw his free hand up into the air and started swaying his hips to the beat of the song, "Crazy in Love." He tugged me along with him and I tried to keep the blush from my cheeks as he made a fool of himself.

"Come on, Lindsey. Dance with me," he shouted over Beyonce's famous lyrics. I shook my head but he didn't take that as an answer as he gripped my hand and twirled me in a circle. The giggle that bubbled up was involuntary as he settled his hand at my waist.

Fuck it. How often did I allow myself to act carefree? Never.

I gripped his hand in mine and put my other one holding the bouquet in the air. I swayed my hips and flipped my hair around as we made our way further into the room.

"Yeah!" Liam shouted as we both danced. I waved at friends and family as we continued, grinning like a loon.

The music still beat on and Liam continued to dance when I saw a flash of gray as I looked out into the crowd. I sucked in a sharp breath as piercing blue eyes met mine. His hair was still just as dark with the thick speckling of gray at his temples. His well-manicured goatee was now grown out into the sexiest short beard.

My fingers itched to feel the roughness of that hair. He had ditched the lab coat and was now in a suit that looked specifically tailored for him. The black-on-black suit with his blue tie that matched his eyes only added to the masculine beauty that was him. I could see his lean muscle definition from here and it made my mouth water. The smile on his lips as he watched me, awoke some unknown feeling inside my core. I felt the urge to clench my thighs together as his gaze ate me up like a tiger stalking its prey.

****

I blinked to clear my vision as the image of Dr. Ian Young became clearer. *Please tell me I'm just dreaming.* I didn't remember much besides the fact that I had been dancing one moment and the next I'd been knocked out cold. I shook my head back and forth as though that would help me clear the fog that clouded my brain. I could make out figures standing around me but not the faces. The only face I could see somewhat clearly was Ian's. That was when he wasn't shining that damn light in my eyes.

"Try not to move, Lindsey." His deep, sensual voice seemed to cover me like a warm blanket. I shivered as I felt his hand cup the side of my neck, halting my head from moving.

I half thought that maybe it was my contacts drying out that made it seem like I had tunnel vision. I assessed the man of my dreams with an appreciative glance as my gaze swept across his face.

His medium-length hair was pushed back and to the side in a sexy style. The sides were short but not shaved. I could still see all that glorious grey that speckled those temples and threaded up into the rest of his dark hair. Since he seemed to be kneeling over me, the length of that salt-and-pepper hair that was so perfectly pushed back on top, came loose, and hung slightly over his forehead. My fingers twitched with the urge to run them through the deep inky locks.

His short beard had a thick speckling of grey and perfectly manicured, only enhancing his already plump, sensual lips. I studied those lips as they seemed to frown seriously down at me. I licked mine as if I could ward off the need to taste his by tasting my own.

My confused gaze climbed his face until I reached those ocean-blue eyes. His pupils dilated as if he was ultra-focused on his task at hand. Those eyes told a story of his life for anyone willing to listen. The slight wrinkling around the edges spoke to his happiness and joy from his constant smiles and laughter. The sheer brightness said he was still full of so much life. I felt a smile tug at my lips as I realized those eyes had a bit of green in them as well. So much for being perfect.

Was it weird to be looking for flaws in this man?

"Lindsey, can you hear me?" That voice drew my attention back to his lips as I watched them move. "You hit your head pretty hard. You might have a concussion, I think I should take you to the hospital."

I don't know what made me say it. Maybe he was right and I was truly concussed. Either that or I had sexually deprived myself for so long that my lusty brain decided it had other plans. It was impossible to stop the words from coming out as I smiled up at those lips I wanted to nibble on.

"I could think of a better place I would like you to *take me*," I slurred.

A gasp registered in my foggy brain as Ian puffed a laugh before a broad grin split his lips. I watched with a hungry gaze as he licked those lips before speaking again.

"I would say you're definitely concussed." He

chuckled.

I tried to shake my head again but he held me firm. His gaze darkened and his grin flattened as his thumb started to move against my throat. My pulse leaped as the soft digit grazed against me. I swallowed thickly as my nipples puckered painfully under my dress. I watched his eyes follow his thumb's movements and further still. His nostrils flared as I realized he could see my hardened peaks through my wedding party dress. Damn Jill for choosing a dress that made it impossible to wear a bra.

Shit, I thought to myself. Party dresses, Jill's wedding, I was still at the reception.

Reality crept back in as I pulled my lust-filled eyes away from the all-encompassing man hovering above me. My gaze flew to the blurry figures that surrounded me and I felt my body flush.

My mom stood above me with her hand against her chest, worried. Heath and Reid hovered behind her, each had a hand on her in some way. Emily and Leo stood next to them. Leo's face was written with concern while Emily's eyes bounced back and forth between Ian and me. Jill's white dress finally came into focus as I spotted her and Damon staring down at me. Jill wasn't even trying to cover her smile as she held back her laughter at the scene I had caused.

I remembered then what I had just said to Ian in front of everyone and the gasp that came after. Embarrassment flooded me as I felt a flush take over my chest all the way to my face. I sucked in a startled breath as I tried to sit up, only to be met with searing pain. I hissed and my hand flew to the back of my head. I had a solid knot under my hair that was evidence of the fall I must have taken.

"Try not to move," Ian repeated as he gently

pushed me back down. The lust I found earlier was gone as the medical professional took its place. "Does your neck hurt at all?" he asked as his fingers prodded me gently.

"No," I said quickly as my gaze continued to fly around the room. That's when I noticed Liam. He was squatting next to me on the ground. *How had I not noticed him before?*

I had to smother my huff of frustration as our gazes connected. I hadn't noticed him because I was too busy lusting over someone I shouldn't be.

"What happened?" I asked Liam as concern clouded his eyes. I could tell by his expression that he felt bad for all of this. Why he felt that way, I could only imagine.

"I have no clue," he said with a slight shrug. "One minute we were dancing holding hands and the next you came to a dead stop. It was like you saw a ghost or something."

I winced at his words as it all came flooding back to me. I had been dancing and having a blast when I spotted grey out in the sea of faces. It was Ian, and I had come to a screeching halt in the middle of the aisle. I was a complete moron.

"I'm so sorry, Lindsey. If I had known you stopped moving, I wouldn't have pulled you so hard." he trailed off.

"It's not your fault, Liam. I shouldn't have stopped like I did," I offered to soothe his guilt.

He smiled down at me before smoothly tucking a strand of hair behind my ear. I could see Ian track the movement out of the corner of my eye. If I didn't know any better, I would say those blue eyes flared with some dark jealousy.

I didn't know what he had to be jealous of. Sure,

Liam was handsome, strikingly so. He was covered in dark tattoos that most women would positively drool over. His hair was deep brown as were his eyes. Even his scent drew you in. All around he was the type of dark mysterious man any sane woman would beg for even a slither of attention from.

But he wasn't what got my heart pounding. His touch didn't make me hyperaware of every achy part of my body. His chocolate gaze didn't light me on fire and make all my forgotten girl parts perk up and take notice. No, those parts of me were fine-tuned to sea-colored eyes. Which was silly considering he was more than double my age and nowhere near interested in me like that.

I tried to ignore those very eyes drilling into my soul as I smiled up at Liam. Trying to reassure him I was fine.

"Can I have everyone clear out and give her some air, please?" Dr. Young's booming voice echoed through the room with authority. When I glanced back toward him, I noticed his hard gaze trained on Liam. When I snuck a glance back toward the younger Latino, I swore I saw challenge flare in those dark eyes. I couldn't help the feeling of being a prized toy between two toddlers as he smirked back at the doctor.

"Of course, you want us to leave just as it's getting interesting," Jill mumbled behind her grin. She yelped when Damon pinched her ass before grabbing her hand and leading her away.

Emily was still surveying the three of us as if she was weaving a story only she could read. Leo gripped her around the waist and turned her away from us. She craned her neck to keep watching us until she no longer could.

"I'm staying," my mom voiced before she turned

to Heath and Reid. "I'll be along shortly, I just want to make sure she's fine."

With that, the boys sauntered off quietly speaking to one another. I didn't even want to know what they were talking about.

That left Liam, who was in a rather intense staring contest with Ian right now. I didn't know if he was just trying to ruffle feathers or what, but Liam wasn't budging. I could practically feel anger vibrating off Ian the longer I lay there. When I couldn't take it any longer, I started to sit. That seemed to break their spell as they each helped me.

I looked around the room and my stomach somersaulted. Nobody had moved me from the place I had fallen. I assumed that was Ian who stopped anyone from moving me. It made sense, if I had injured my neck they wouldn't have a way of knowing until I was awake. Even I knew not to move someone who might have a neck injury.

My head swam as I fully sat and I became dizzy. Ian gripped my upper arms with firm hands as if to catch me before I went careening to the side. I hissed as I steadied myself. Liam moved in closer and Ian's hard gaze shot straight to him.

I didn't know what Ian's problem was and I was too busy getting a headache to find out. My mother, as always, knew how to read the room. I watched her as she carefully assessed whatever situation was going down between the two men. She stepped forward and lightly touched Liam's shoulder. "Liam, I think we should let Dr. Young take it from here." Her soft voice seemed to break the tension.

Liam nodded, slowly taking his hard gaze from Ian and softening it as he looked me over. "Are you sure you're good?" he asked.

Sharp pain rippled from the back of my head to my temples as I nodded. I tried to smother my wince as I spoke. "I'm fine. Sorry about all of this," I offered.

He seemed hesitant but stood nonetheless. With one last smile down at me, he turned and headed toward the open bar. Mom stooped down and took his place. She rubbed her hand soothingly down my head as she comforted me. I sucked in a sharp breath as her fingers gently grazed my bump.

"Oof, that's a good one, Lyns." She smiled at me before leaning in to kiss my forehead. "I can get you some ice?" she offered. I instantly felt all the tension leave my body. I may be in my early twenties, but that didn't stop my mom from being my safe space. When you grow up with one parent who didn't really care much about you, you learn quickly to latch onto the one that does.

"I would feel a lot better if you would let me take you to the hospital," Ian said, breaking the moment.

My head screamed as I pulled away from Mom and looked back toward the doctor. The look on his face was laced with worry. He may be right, I probably did need to be seen by someone at the hospital, but did I really want him to be the one that took me? I briefly thought about asking my mom to take me but then quickly dissolved the thought. This was her childhood best friend's wedding. I couldn't let her leave.

But the thought of being alone in the car with this man, made all sorts of feelings flood me. It's not as though I had never been alone with a boy before. Sure, my experience was limited but that didn't mean I lived under a rock. I had never been too scared to leave a place with a boy even if I knew his intentions were pointed toward more than just hand-holding. But the thing was, Ian wasn't a boy, he was a man. The only man, in fact,

21

that had ever sparked this deep yearning I felt every time I looked at him. Could I really be alone with him?

The throbbing in my head intensified further as I stared at him. So much so that I had to squint as the pain assaulted my senses. Even if I didn't think it was a good idea to be alone with him, I was going to listen to my body. *Well, not the whole thing.* I did force myself to ignore that one part of my body screaming at me for the very man I shouldn't have.

I swallowed thickly as I pulled away from my mom completely and held my hand out toward the handsome doctor. A zap of awareness jolted through me as his hand connected with mine. Taking a deep breath, I met his gaze.

"Take me."

Chapter Two

As I sat in the front seat of Ian's Audi, I silently cursed myself once more. I should have just asked Heath or Reid to take me to the hospital. Or anyone else for that matter. Because the moment I sat inside Ian's car I was immediately assaulted with everything *him*. His style, sleek and suave. His scent, clean and masculine. Even his damn confidence as he drove along the busy streets at this time of night. Watching him steer the car with such precision that it would put a professional driver to shame.

Only moments ago, when he carefully placed me in the passenger seat, shivers of awareness slithered up my body originating at his every touch. I took a deep fortifying breath after I sat, hoping he wouldn't touch me anymore. I didn't know how much more I could take of that touch that felt so gentle and caring. But just when I thought I could relax, Ian leaned down and grabbed the seat belt.

He had gripped that belt and smoothly wrapped it across the front of my body. I smothered what would have been an embarrassing groan as his wrist grazed against my breast. Lighting up my still-tightened nipples. I turned my head when all I wanted to do was bury my face in the side of his exposed neck. It wouldn't have been hard as he was mere inches away from me. I thought he took longer than necessary to snap the buckle into place. I could have sworn he stalled at the side of my neck a beat longer than necessary. I had seen his jaw clench before pulling away from me and closing the door, allowing me to release the pent-up breath I'd been holding.

There was something undoubtedly wrong with me, I decided as I watched his every move with the laser focus of a hungry hawk. The way his muscles flexed and released under the black jacket that had to have been made just for him. Every turn we made caused his biceps to move in a different way. The way his hand gripped the steering wheel. I could see his tendons work in tandem with the strong hand muscles there. The way his other hand was resting against his upper thigh. So close to the slight bulge at the center.

I clenched my thighs together as an unfamiliar ache built more and more the closer we came to the hospital. My head was still pounding but that didn't stop the wetness from pooling between my thighs. I nearly whimpered as we hit a bump in the road causing my thighs to move against that achy part of me. I let my head fall back against the headrest as I closed my eyes. I tried to control my breathing, focusing on the inhales and exhales. Tried to ignore the scent of the man sitting next to me.

"We're almost there." Ian's deep rumble filled the otherwise quiet interior of the car. I said nothing, afraid that if I spoke I would sound like a bumbling idiot. "Lindsey?" he spoke my name in the hushed tone of one lover to another. I still said nothing as I kept my eyes closed. My head hurt so bad and everything about being trapped in this small space with him was making me hyperaware of everything else.

I felt the car turn and slow to a stop. I still didn't bother lifting my head until I felt a strong hand grip my thigh. I hissed between my teeth and jerked my head upright. The dull ache at the movement was quickly overshadowed as Ian squeezed the meaty part of my thigh over the silk fabric of my dress. I swallowed thickly before I peeled my tongue from the roof of my mouth.

"Ah, there you are, Little Bambi," Ian said as I

met his gaze. My heart skipped a beat at his term of endearment. *Little Bambi.* It could have been laughable because I was anything but little, but the way he said it almost made me believe it. "Are you feeling okay? Nauseous?"

I shook my head. "No, just a headache now."

His hand never left my thigh as we continued to stare at one another. Even though it was dark in the car, aside from the dim lighting on the dash, I could still see his expression shift to something darker. It was almost as if I could feel my awareness going to that one spot on my body that he was touching. I could see what looked like a flash of challenge in those blue eyes before his palm started to move. I sucked in a sharp breath as it climbed. His lips twitched slightly as we studied one another.

His gaze traveled from my eyes down to my lips as my tongue darted out to wet my parched lips. I could feel myself start to tremble as his hand inched closer and closer to the part of me that ached for him. His eyes seemed to darken further inside the dim interior of the car. I bit my lip to smother it but that didn't stop the moan that wretched from my throat as his pinkie grazed the side of my panties before moving down and away from me.

He cleared his throat as I felt fire lace my cheeks. *I didn't just do that.* "We're here," he said as I heard the distinct sound of my buckle being released followed by a small chuckle, causing me to sag in relief.

I released a hurried breath as my eyes fluttered closed before I looked out the windshield. The bright sign indicating we were indeed at the emergency room came into view. I turned back toward Ian just in time to be met with him stepping out of the car and closing his door.

What was I doing? I was sitting in this insanely

hot man's car after making a complete fool of myself. I was probably concussed and here I was lusting after him like a preteen girl at a Harry Styles concert. I couldn't help the feeling that maybe he wanted me as much as I wanted him when it was probably the furthest thing from the truth. He was a doctor and more than double my age, for heaven's sake. He was probably just trying to be a good guy and help his old patient's kid and how did I repay him? By acting like a sex-crazed idiot in his car.

Before I could compose myself Ian opened my door and held his hand out for me. I hesitated before I placed mine in his. He gently pulled me from the car and my head only swam a little that time. I grabbed onto the side of the car as Ian slid his arm around my waist. I couldn't stop that inner voice I heard every day screaming at me every time I put something in my mouth. She was now telling me that Ian could probably feel every one of my fat rolls on my side. I bet he was used to dating thin supermodels, I wouldn't be surprised if he thought my body was the furthest thing from feminine.

Once my head steadied, I tried to pull away from him but he held me firm. "I've got you, Bambi. Just lean against me." His hushed voice brushed over me like a refreshing breeze. That feeling of being precious to someone warmed my insides again as I did as he asked of me.

He was much taller than me so when I leaned into him the top of my head barely reached the bottom of his chin. His arm that held me tightened before he stooped down and gracefully picked me up, cradling me to his chest.

The squeal that came out of me was loud to my own ears as I fought to grab onto his neck for balance. He didn't even so much as huff a sound of exertion as he started toward the ER entrance.

"I could walk, you know," I said. "You're going to hurt your back."

His chuckle jostled me before he looked down at me. "What? Is that some sort of old age joke?" He smiled.

I couldn't fight the grin of my own as I stared back at him. "No, I don't think you're old. If you haven't noticed,"—I gestured down at myself—"I'm not exactly some little slip of a girl."

His smile vanished as he stopped his forward advance. His hand flexed against my side and under my knees at the same time his jaw did. It was as though he was thinking of his next words carefully before he spoke. "You're right," he said as his eyes bounced between mine and slowly raked the rest of my body.

I would've felt embarrassed at his agreement with my statement had he not been gobbling up the sight of my body with hungry eyes. When his gaze finally met mine again, it took everything in my willpower to keep breathing.

"You're not a little slip of a girl." His sweet-smelling breath puffed across my face. "You're a woman and you have the body of one," he said before dragging his gaze away from me and continuing through the ER doors.

I continued to stare up at his strong jaw as I let his words sink into me. I vaguely heard a nurse rush up to us and Ian started answering questions and making orders.

He called me a woman. Honestly, that was a weird thing to be hung up on. Biologically I knew I was a woman. I was almost twenty-one, I was certainly not a little girl anymore. I left all those adolescent things in the past and grew into a woman a long time ago.

So why did I just now, in his arms, feel like a real *woman*?

I was pulled from my thoughts as Ian leaned down and placed me in a wheelchair. I listened as he rattled off the tests he wanted to have done to the nurse who then started to push me away from him. I glanced over my shoulder as she asked me about my pain level. Ian was still standing there in that devastating suit staring after me. He only pulled his gaze away from me as another nurse came up to him holding a chart, asking him a question I was sure.

"So, on a scale of one to ten, how much pain are you in?" my nurse asked as we wheeled away from the bustle of the ER into a quieter hallway.

"It's just a dull ache now."

****

"You're sure you don't need me to come over?" my mom's loud voice came over the phone I pressed to my ear. The sounds of the reception going full swing in the background almost drowned out her voice altogether. I'd lost count of the number of texts and calls I had received since leaving the hospital. She was worried about me and I didn't blame her. I was her only child after all.

"Mom, for the hundredth time, I'm fine. All the tests came back fine. The doctors said it was just a bump and I should ice it and get some sleep." I sighed as I leaned back onto my pillow. My head was still sore but the pain meds I had gotten at the ER helped a little. At least my headache was gone. I was feeling better except for the leftover ache I was feeling concerning Dr. Ian Young.

No matter how much I tried, I couldn't stop thinking about him and I was about to go crazy. The way he had commanded the room when I was laying in the ER bed was a sight to see. He could so easily swing from being tender to professional, it could give a gal whiplash.

Once he ordered the scans and tests for me, he promptly sat by my side the whole time. I could easily say that had been the fastest ER visit in the history of ER visits. If you ever wanted to get in and out of there faster than a fast-food restaurant, just make sure a prestigious doctor carries you in firsthand. I could tell by the reactions from the staff that he was clearly well-respected around the joint. Nurses smiled brightly and colleagues spoke with high regard around him.

None of it surprised me, though. Even though I hardly knew him, I knew he was a good guy. You didn't offer to take a girl you barely knew to the hospital after she fell at your one-time patient's wedding. Normal people aren't that good.

The ride from the hospital back to my dorm had been less eventful than the ride to the hospital. There were no more touches that I perceived as more. No more sideways glances. No more looks that could be misconstrued as something different than they were. He had simply driven me to the campus and walked me to my dorm.

I found it slightly odd that he knew exactly where to go when I told him what dorm building I stayed in. He had driven straight to it without any other questions. It was as if he had done it a thousand times before. I had shaken off the notion as I told myself he may have just gone to this college back in his day.

He'd smoothly parked the car under the building awning and walked me to my door, even after I had protested. "I will carry you again if I need to," he said. I almost laughed at him until I realized he was being serious. After that I let him walk me right to my door.

The only awkward part of the whole walk was when we made it to my door and he huffed a small laugh. When I turned to him he had a small smirk on his lips. His eyes sparkled brightly as he looked at the collage of photos pinned to the corkboard on the door before glancing down to me. I fiddled with my key card as he grinned at me with a knowing smile. "What?" I asked.

He shook his head and stepped closer to me. My breath hitched in my throat as I craned my neck to look up at him. He was so close, I could smell him again. His heady scent of pine and something else that was distinctly him. "Small world," he murmured so quietly that I barely heard him. He grabbed my key card from me then.

I felt myself getting dizzy all over again as he leaned closer to me still. His throat was so close to my lips that my mouth started to water for just one taste. I felt a rush of air behind me before he pulled away from me. My eyes fluttered a few times as I regained my wits and realized he had opened my door.

He handed me back my card before shoving his hands in his pockets. He looked me up and down with what seemed to be an appreciative gaze. I mentally shook myself as I stepped past the threshold and gripped the door handle. I cleared my throat before speaking. "Thank you … for everything," I said.

Ian shook his head before he backed away from the door and down the hallway we had come from. "Until next time, Bambi," he said. He turned around and sauntered back toward the entrance of the dormitory.

"So, Dr. Young treated you well then?" Mom's voice jolted me back to the present just as there was a knock at my door. I frowned as I looked at the time. It was just past eleven in the evening so I wasn't sure who it could be. My heart thumped in my chest at the prospect of it being Ian. Even though the thought was silly, it still caused me to slip out of bed and head to the door.

"He was great, Mom. Hey, can I call you tomorrow? Someone's at the door," I said as I looked through the peephole. I jerked away when I couldn't see anything at all. It was black as though someone was covering it with their hand.

"Yeah, that's fine, sweety. Get some rest," she said right as I heard Jill's voice sound over the other end. "Did you fuck that delicious doctor yet?" Jill screamed over the thumping music and I flushed. "Oh, you pervert." My mom giggled. "What? Someone needs to take that fine piece of manly perfection off the market, why not let Lyns have a go at it?" Jill sounded like she was having way too much fun. "Red." Damon's voice barely registered before I heard Jill's giggle and then Mom's voice once more. "Ignore her. She thinks everyone should be as sex-crazed as she is. I'll talk to you tomorrow, love you."

I was smiling to myself as another knock came at the door and I ended the call. I took a deep breath and prepared for the worst as I opened the door. To my surprise, Ben came stumbling in the door, as if he had been leaning on it. I jumped out of his way as he regained his footing.

"Ben? What are you doing?" I asked out of breath. I shut the door behind him and walked back over to my bed, crossing my arms over my chest.

I was in my comfy clothes which consisted of sweatpants and a flimsy tank. No bra, obviously, so you could easily see everything I had to offer. I hadn't been expecting visitors so I didn't think I would need to really cover up much.

Ben stood to his full height before he looked me up and down. The grin on his lips vanished when he saw my scowl. "Sorry," he said. "I saw some older guy walking you into the dorm and figured I would make sure you're all right."

"So you thought to listen against my door?" I asked, dumbfounded. I sat down on the bed as he stepped closer to me. "How did you even see that I was with someone else?" His dorm was a few buildings over so I wasn't sure how he would know what I was doing in the first place.

"I was walking home from Delta Pi's party and saw you." He shrugged as he sat on the bed next to me. "And I wanted to make sure you weren't, ya know, getting busy in here before I knocked." He flashed me a goofy smile while humor danced in his hazel eyes.

I couldn't help the laugh that bubbled up. "So you listened for sex sounds?" I laughed as I leaned back against my pillow. "You fucking pervert." I lightly kicked him in the belly.

Ben shrugged again as he grabbed my ankle and placed my foot on his lap. He gripped my sock-covered foot and started to massage the arch. "What can I say, I'll take what I can get." He wiggled his eyebrows at me and I rolled my eyes.

I met Ben when he transferred to my college halfway through freshman year. He was probably one of the nicest guys I'd ever met even if he was indeed a strange one. My roommate, Anna, always teased me that Ben and I would eventually get married with the way he was stuck up my ass. I always brushed her off, Ben was like the brother I never had.

I mean, sure, he wasn't too hard on the eyes. He was lean with an athletic build and quite a bit taller than me. He had a steady stream of thick black tattoos that crawled up his right arm but not his left. He had a strange one on the side of his neck that he refused to talk about when I pointed it out. I always thought it was odd, really. Wasn't the whole purpose of getting a tattoo so you could proudly show them off to people? But when I'd asked him about the sad little wilted flower he'd promptly clammed up and I hadn't asked again.

His classic good looks were enhanced by shaggy inky black hair and hazel eyes. He had just one dimple that showed on his left cheek whenever he smiled at me. He really didn't seem to fit in with other guys on campus. He was different in so many ways. When other boys his age would be out partying almost every night, Ben preferred to stay in, most of the time with me. He got good grades and always seemed to be at the top of any class he was in. He almost seemed smarter than most of the teachers half the time, like he was much wiser than his twenty-one years.

I wasn't so blind as to not see that he was very handsome, downright hot by some standards. He was definitely a catch any girl would be lucky to have. He just didn't do anything for me.

He had asked me out last year and when I politely rejected him, I thought I wouldn't ever see him again. To my surprise, though, he showed up the next day at the library and sat next to me like nothing ever happened. We never spoke about it after that, both of us preferring to act like the occurrence didn't exist.

It didn't shock me that he showed up here tonight. He always had a way of showing up when I least expected him. He had even found a way of showing up at all of my dates, not that I had that many. I never really minded. The boys that had asked me out in the past were always after one thing and one thing only. When they figured out they weren't going to be getting that from me, they quickly moved on. It used to bother me when they would stop coming around and not return my texts, but eventually I moved on with the notion that they weren't worth my time anyway.

It was always odd how it seemed to happen out of the blue, though. I never went on more than two dates with the same guy and then they would just stop communicating altogether. One guy in particular stuck out in my mind—Dillian. I thought we'd had a really good time together the weekend before but the way he'd acted the last time I'd seen him said otherwise.

I'd been walking with Ben to class and having a quiet conversation when I spotted him. I remembered waving at him and watching with confusion as he stumbled to a stop. He nearly dropped the books in his hands as his face visibly paled and he eyed me warily. I thought it strange at the time when he looked at me with what appeared to be fear in his eyes. I liked Dillian but not enough to fret over him. So when Ben had acted just as confused as me but shrugged it off as possible stress, I did too. It made sense in a way, we were in college after all, and there was no shortage of mental exhaustion that came with being there.

I had never felt that attached to any man before so it's not like it hurt too much when they ghosted me. Well, not until … *him.* If Ben had found a way to insert himself between Ian and me, I would certainly have had a problem with that.

Ben stared down at his hands working my foot before glancing at me quickly. "So, who was the old guy?" he asked before darting his eyes back down.

I opened my mouth to give him some form of the truth when Anna came crashing into the room. I sat up on my elbows as I smiled at my clearly inebriated roommate. I giggled as she clumsily fumbled with her key card before kicking the door shut.

"Good night, huh?" I asked around a laugh.

She turned to look at me and scowled when she saw Ben sitting with me. She hissed at him, actually *hissed* like a cat, before staggering toward her bed. "The best night," she said to me before inclining her head toward Ben. "Stalker boy," she said by way of greeting.

Ben's lips flattened in disdain. "Hades," he murmured, his way of poking fun at her hair color choice. Electric-blue this month.

"All right, you two," I said as I pulled my foot away from Ben and sat up. He clenched his jaw in anger as he and Anna stared at one another. It was a well-known fact that these two hated each other. They only slightly tolerated each other because of me. For some reason I couldn't understand, Anna thought Ben was a total creep. When I asked her why she told me, "It was just a feeling." Ben sensed the hostility and reacted accordingly.

"Ben, you better go. Girl time," I said as Anna broke her glare and flopped onto her bed. He looked at me with anger still flaming in his eyes before smothering it with a smile.

"All right, Lindsey Bug. I'll see you tomorrow?" he cooed that godawful nickname, and I tried not to cringe. I didn't want to hurt his feelings by telling him I hated the name, so I just endured it.

I nodded and ushered him to the door. After gently closing it on his smiling face I turned toward my now-sleeping roommate. I sighed as I covered her up and turned off the light.

As I snuggled down under my blanket, I couldn't help but think about the handsome doctor that made me feel like a woman for the first time in my life.

Chapter Three

"Come on, Lyns. We need to celebrate! You only turn twenty-one once, you know." Anna's whining was becoming incessant at this point. She had become relentless this last week, pulling out all the stops to get me to let her throw me a big party.

"We already celebrated. We don't need to make a huge deal out of this," I whispered back. Not that she cared but we were in the middle of the campus library after all. My birthday had come and gone a few days after my run-in with Dr. Hotpants. I didn't see what the big deal was. So what if I could now legally buy and drink alcohol, it's not like that had been my life's mission up till this point.

In truth, I had never been much of a partier. Even in high school when all my peers were out getting slobbering drunk in a cornfield, I was home. I would much rather stay in with a good book than get stupid in the back of a pickup with some boy who would forget me by dawn. I told myself it had nothing to do with the fact that I had rarely even been asked to go to those parties.

I flushed at my memories of high school. It was sad that I tried to justify my refusal to do anything with my fellow classmates, as if it had always been my decision. I shook my head to rid thoughts of the past as I looked at Anna.

"What more do you want? We already went to that bar the other night," I said.

I was pretty sure Anna could see the inside of her brain with how hard she rolled her eyes at me. "Ugh," she moaned loudly. I shushed her as I noticed others starting to glance our way. "Don't shush me, that wasn't a bar," she whined.

I shrugged and looked back down at my textbook. "They served alcohol, what's the difference?"

Out of my peripherals, I saw her jaw drop. I scrunched my face together as I knew what was coming next. "Are you kidding me?" she asked as she grabbed my arm and forced me to look at her. "It was a fucking Chili's, Lindsey," she screeched.

That time others around us started to shush us. I smothered my grin as Anna turned her scowl toward them. She promptly flipped them the finger and told them to fuck off.

Anna reminded me so much of Jill sometimes, it was a little unnerving. I was a lot like my mom in the way that we were both reserved. So, if Anna was my Jill and I was her Kate, why in the world were we friends? I mean, my mom and Jill had grown up together and been lifetime friends. Anna and I only met freshman year when we were paired as random roommates. Even though I felt we had hit it off, I truly hadn't expected her to request me as her roommate again the next year.

I loved Anna for her spunkiness and blatant honesty, but I still couldn't figure out why she put up with someone like me. I was honest with myself, I was a boring person. I was the type of girl to always do my homework *and* the extra credit. I never ditched class in favor of something more fun. I didn't like to go out with a bunch of people, I hated crowds. Even when I did go out, I always ended up being the "mother" of the party everywhere we went.

I mean, sure, I was older than most of my classmates, but only by a year or so. Most people started college when they were freshly eighteen, I had turned nineteen right after high school graduation. But my age never played a hand in our friendship. If I ever assumed she was my friend so I could buy her alcohol, the thought quickly vanished. That girl had a fake ID and knew how to use it.

Anna turned back my way and forced me to look at her again. I tried as hard as I could to keep the smile from my lips as she pushed her palms together as if she were going to beg. "Please, please, please." She pouted.

I rolled my eyes and studied my best friend. "What would we even do?" I asked.

She kept her hands together but arched one brow before answering. "It's almost spring break, I'm sure we could think of something," she said and then continued to beg. "Please, I will pay for everything," she tried.

"You will do no such thing. I can pay for myself," I scoffed as I crossed my arms over my chest. Then I realized my mistake.

A wide grin split Anna's lips before she gripped my shoulders. "So that's a yes?" She beamed.

I couldn't stop the giggle that bubbled up as I watched excitement cloud her features. "Yes," I murmured.

I cringed as Anna squealed and stomped her feet between us. This was her happy dance and everyone in the library was getting to see the show. "I can't wait!" she screeched. More shushes followed but that didn't tramp down her excitement. Soon I found myself smiling with her.

I heard the scratching of a chair being pulled out and I glanced toward it just to have the smile wiped from my face. Melonie K. Turner sat down in front of me as I turned back toward my textbook. The smirk on her face was enough to make me want to run and hide. *Some bullies you could never run away from.*

When I left for college, I told myself it would be different. I said I would make new friends here and never think about those mean girls from my past again. You could imagine my shock when I saw Melonie walking with my roommate a mere two weeks into freshman year. It was bad enough that she was at the same college as me, but she had also befriended my best friend and roommate.

I didn't blame Anna. Melonie was good at hiding her nasty side. It was only when Anna left the room that her true colors showed through. She had dropped my old nickname but that didn't stop her from poking fun every chance she got.

"Can't wait for what?" Melonie's perfect teeth made an appearance as she slapped on a sugary-sweet smile for Anna. I tried not to scoff at the fakeness that was Melonie Turner. Everything from her perfect teeth to that godawful bleach-blonde hair was fake. Sure, she was what most would consider beautiful, but if those people only knew who she actually was on the inside, they would call her ugly.

She had that perfectly shaped nose she probably had picked out in a catalog, her eyes were crystal blue, makeup was always done on point, and she was rail thin but with large perky breasts and an ass you could bounce a quarter off. She was what I would call a real-life blow-up doll. In other words, she was everything I wasn't, including nice.

"Spring break, baby!" Anna was still celebrating when she turned toward Melonie. "Lindsey's birthday was a couple of days ago so we are gonna celebrate big," she said as she smiled up at Malibu Barbie.

Melonie glanced toward me before returning to Anna as if she was going to ignore the part about it being my birthday. "Oh, where are we thinking? Mexico? Oh, oh, what about the Bahamas?" she said as she bounced in her chair with excitement. Obviously, she wanted to go somewhere she could wear as few clothes as she wanted.

Wait, did she just invite herself? I sealed my lips shut, I was going to let Anna handle this one.

"I think we need to keep it Stateside, I don't feel like messing with passports," Anna said. I frowned to myself. *Was she really going to let Melonie invite herself?* As if I had said it out loud, Anna turned to me, worry marring her brow. Just like I knew that she didn't like Ben, she knew I didn't care for Melonie. She didn't know specifics about mine and Melonie's past dealings, I had just told her I thought she was fake. I wasn't the type of person to deter someone from being friends with a person I didn't like. I would let them make their own decisions.

"Is it okay if Mel comes along?" Anna asked me. I didn't have to look at Melonie to know that she was scowling in my direction. If I were a different person, maybe the person I wished I was, I could have said "fuck no" and gone back to my book. I could have told Anna all about the type of person *Mel* really was. Make her see that she wasn't who she thought she was.

But in the end, I wasn't that person. I was just me. I couldn't ruin Anna's friendship with her even if she was an awful human being. "Sure," I said softly. "But I don't really feel like going to a beach." I returned to my book, smiling to myself when I heard Barbie scoff. If I was going to have to deal with this bitch for a week on vacation, then I was going to make sure she had to keep her damn clothes on.

"Who doesn't like the beach?" Melonie whined at Anna before looking at me. I glanced up and made eye contact before she squinted at me.

I nearly jumped out of my skin as Anna slapped the table and stood. "I got it!" She smiled down at us. "My dad owns a cabin in Colorado. We can go there and cut down on costs. We'll have full access to the ski resort next door." She grinned down at me. I flashed her what I hoped was an encouraging smile.

I was less than graceful at anything related to sports. I just knew I would biff it big time the moment I got on the slopes. I was suddenly rethinking my request for no beaches.

But as I looked up at my best friend, I realized I couldn't burst her bubble. Maybe if Melonie did go with us, Anna wouldn't be so bummed out when I decided to stay in the cabin for a day or two. "Yeah, that sounds great, babe." I nodded.

Anna did another happy dance as I felt Melonie's laser focus burn a hole into the side of my skull. "I'm gonna go call my dad and make sure it's okay to use the cabin." She beamed as she practically ran out of the library.

I swallowed thickly as I returned my focus to the book in front of me. Or, at least I tried to. I could still feel Melonie's heated gaze on me. When I couldn't take it anymore, I glanced up at her and immediately regretted it.

She had a nasty smirk on her lips as she crossed her arms in front of her perfect breasts and leaned back in her chair. I knew what was coming next as she opened her mouth.

"What? Are you too afraid you won't be able to fit that big ass into a swimsuit?" She chuckled.

I flushed and wished I dared to say what I really wanted to say. That she was nothing but an attention-seeking bitch and she couldn't find her own friends so she had to try and steal mine.

But I didn't say those things, I just simply ignored her and went back to studying. I'd been told the best way to handle a bully was to ignore them. So that's what I did as Melonie leaned forward to rub some more dirt into the gaping wound that was my pride.

"Hey, Lindsey Bug." Ben's chipper voice surprised me as my eyes flung up to the seat he pulled out for himself next to Melonie. I flashed him a small smile and started to return his greeting when she leaned closer to him.

"Hello, Benjamin," she said in a silky voice that grated on my every nerve. I tried not to gag as she pushed her chest out toward Ben in an obvious to gain his male attention. To his credit, Ben only glanced down at those overinflated balloons before quickly diverting his gaze back to me.

"Hey, Mel," he said quickly before smiling back at me. "Did you sit in on Dr. Henry's presentation this morning?" he asked me.

I opened my mouth to answer but the words caught in my throat as Melonie trailed one of her perfectly manicured nails down Ben's left pec.

It was laughable, really. She needed to have everyone's attention focused on her. I knew Ben wasn't her type. The only reason she felt the need to flirt with him was because she thought she was taking him away from me. She was too dense to see that I had no sexual interest in him whatsoever. She was all sorts of pathetic.

"Do you like my new blouse, Benjamin?" she asked as she gave him bedroom eyes. When Ben's face contorted into something resembling confusion, I couldn't help it anymore. I snorted and tried to cover it up with a cough. Melonie's head snapped in my direction with a scowl creasing her eyebrows.

Then the thought struck me. If I was in for a week of Melonie's tyranny, maybe I would be able to deflect some of her attention away from me. Maybe it was cruel of me to put Ben in that situation but at that moment I didn't care. I just knew I wouldn't be able to survive being around this bitch for that long with her focus solely on me.

I cleared my throat and looked at Ben. "What are you doing for spring break?"

Chapter Four

My head was buried in my textbook as a knock came at the door. I pushed my glasses back up my nose where they had dipped from long hours of pouring over the words. Frowning at the door, I pushed away from my desk before glancing at the clock. It was well after ten in the evening. Anna had gone to yet another frat party. She and Melonie walked arm in arm out the door after I denied the invite to tag along. I had a test coming up in my finance class that I needed to study for.

As I walked to the door, I briefly wondered if it was Ben waiting on the other side again like he had the other night. He always had a way of showing up when I least expected him.

"Ben, I really don't have time for visitors," I said as I gripped the handle and turned it. "I can't fail this test." I swung the door open, revealing the figure on the other side.

My breath caught in my throat as I realized it wasn't Ben on the other end, but Ian. He leaned against the doorframe with that sexy smirk on his sensual mouth. I involuntarily took a step back as he stalked forward.

"Hello, Little Bambi." His smooth voice raked over my body like I was an exposed nerve. Every part of me perked up and took notice of his demanding presence. I stepped further back into my room as he crowded me.

"Ian," I breathed. "What are you doing here?"

His smile was feral as he stepped to the side and closed the door before locking it with a solid click that reverberated in my core. My nipples tightened painfully under my paper-thin tank as his dark gaze assessed me as if I were his next meal.

"I wanted to check in on you, make sure you're

doing all right after the other night." He grinned at me as his stare traveled the length of my body.

I glanced at my threadbare tank down to my ratty, stained sweats. I knew I must have looked like a mess. My long dark curls were up in a haphazard bun, face bare of any makeup. I didn't even have my contacts in so I was showcasing my less-than-sexy plain big glasses.

I was so busy staring down at myself, I hadn't noticed when Ian stepped into my space until his scent surrounded me. I craned my neck to look up at him just as his hand raised to my forehead. I allowed my eyes to flutter shut as his soft fingers collected some hair that had fallen from its constraint. I shivered as he pushed it back away from my face.

"So, how is your head, Lindsey?"

My eyes sprang open at the sound of my name. I liked the way he said it. I swallowed around the lump in my throat as I met his ocean eyes. "I'm a little dizzy," I rasped as his hand moved further down toward my neck. I was sure he could feel the rapid pulse there as much as I could feel it in my core.

I stared at his lips as he grinned. "Dizzy, huh?" he murmured.

I nodded as his hand dipped further still. His palm now grazed the top swell of my breast. He was so close now. All I would have to do was go up on my tiptoes to catch his lips with mine.

"Hmm," he hummed as his other hand gripped my waist. I whimpered as his fingers slipped under the fabric there. He watched his other hand dip down to the side of my breast. I couldn't help but arch into him as his thumb grazed over my puckered nipple. The feeling shot straight to my pussy. He leaned in as if he was going to take my lips with his when he spoke. "I might have to *assess you myself then," he mumbled before sealing his lips to mine in a deep kiss.*

It was as though I was a completely different person when I moaned and stepped into his hard body. My hands found their way into his silky hair as he gripped my ass. He kneaded and rubbed against me there with a long groan. I could feel his hard manhood grind against my belly as he explored.

I nearly melted into a puddle when his tongue flicked against the seam of my lips, begging for entry. When I opened for him he surged in like I was his last breath of fresh air. He ate at me with vigor then as he pushed us further into the room. I hadn't realized how far until the back of my knees hit my bed.

When he pulled up for air the wild look in his eyes told me he was nowhere near finished with me. He bent to kiss my neck and further still as his hands pushed into the back of my sweats. The moment his hands hit my bare ass I could feel a rush of arousal coat my panties.

He licked and kissed his way down my neck until he met the top of my barely there tank. He groaned as his searing gaze took in my hardened peaks. Without a word, he ripped the fabric down and away from my breasts. Exposing me to his view.

I surprised myself by not pulling away from him as he studied me. His hands kept their downward descent, pulling the fabric with them so my whole backside was also exposed. A shiver crawled up my spine as the cold of the room seeped into my skin.

"These are the prettiest tits I've ever seen, Bambi," he groaned before flicking his tongue out to taste me. Pride surged through me at his compliment. When his hot tongue lapped at me I threw my head back as a moan escaped my lips. His hands pushed my sweats and panties the rest of the way down as he continued to

lick me.

I nearly whimpered as he pulled away from me but stopped myself when he knelt in front of me. His hands came around the front of my hips and up as he started to cup my breasts. He stared up at me as his mouth latched around one of my dusty-rose nipples as his fingers tweaked the other. I could feel my pussy getting wetter by the second.

Something was rising within me that I had never felt before. Something I had only ever heard about in movies or read about in those dirty books. The throbbing in my core intensified with each pull of his mouth. I was going to explode and he hadn't even touched my most intimate part yet.

He replaced his mouth with his fingers as he continued to fondle me. "Are you going to come from me just playing with these pretty nipples, Bambi?" he asked with a devious smile. I couldn't stop my nod and sharp intake of breath as he pinched me. So close.

He chuckled as his hands left my breasts and traveled south. "I haven't even touched this juicy little cunt yet. Are you wet for me?" he teased.

His left arm wrapped around my ass again and he held me tight as his right hand reached for my sex. I gasped as he delved in my folds, raking his finger against my engorged clit. His groan of approval nearly had me undone.

"Oh, Lindsey. You're ready for me. This pussy is as wet as a ripe fruit. I think I'll see if it tastes as good as one too." He flashed me a wicked smile and dipped his head to my pussy. I knew one swipe of his tongue would be all it took to send me flying.

I kept my fingers in his hair as I felt his breath fan over the wet flesh he was so close to.

"Lindsey," a far-off voice called but I ignored it.

I was about to experience the one thing I had missed out on my entire adult life.

"Lindsey," the voice that sounded vaguely like Anna said again.

Closer and closer his mouth came to that part of me that craved him more than I craved my next meal.

****

"Lindsey!" Anna screamed at me from her bed across the room. I gasped as I started to push Ian away from me only to realize he wasn't actually there. Panic laced every one of my breaths as I tried to calm my racing heart. The fog of my first erotic dream finally started to lift from my mind.

"Were you having a wet dream?" Anna's chipper voice sounded from across the room.

I started to sit up and nearly moaned as my thighs moved against my sex. I was so sensitive from the dream that felt like a reality. I could feel how wet I had become in my sleep and how easy it would be to finish what my unconscious psyche had started for me.

"What ... no, why?" I lied as I brushed my hair off my sweat-soaked forehead.

"Because you kept moaning the name, *Adrian*. It was pretty hot to listen to, really."

I cringed and sat up on the edge of the bed, ignoring the pulse originating at my core. I watched in horror as she rolled her eyes back and opened her mouth in a mock orgasm. She gripped the sides of her blue hair and really put on a show for me. "Oh, Adrian!" she moaned between heaving breaths.

My face blazed fire red. I wanted the floor to open up and swallow me whole. "Oh my God! Stop!" I screeched as I threw my pillow at her head. She was so busy making fun of me she didn't see it coming until it was too late. It beamed her on the side of the head and knocked her off her bed with a solid thud.

I almost felt bad until she started to laugh so loudly I was sure it would wake up others in the hall. I was completely embarrassed but I couldn't help it when I started laughing with her.

"I can't believe you had a sex dream in the same room as me!" she breathed between laughs.

"Anna!" I screeched. She only continued to laugh as she stood and grabbed my pillow. After throwing it back at me, she walked toward the bathroom.

"It's time to get your horny ass up. We have a flight to catch," she tossed over her shoulder with a mischievous grin.

I groaned and laid back down after she shut the door behind her.

****

"I can't believe you invited John Wayne Gacy," Anna groaned as we grabbed the bags out of the rental SUV. I smiled at my friend before grabbing another bag and placing it onto the snow-covered driveway at my feet. Anna had known since the day we made the plan to come to Colorado that I'd invited Ben, she just liked to complain about it.

The flight out here had been uneventful, to say the least. Anna sat next to me while poor Ben had been forced to sit with Satan herself in the row next to us. I had tried to keep my annoyance to myself every time she made a show of touching him in different ways. It's not like I was jealous, I mean, if she wanted him and he wanted her, then I say have at it. It only bothered me because she was using him to get me riled up.

I had taken a short nap before we landed and I was pleased to announce that I didn't have any more sexy dreams about Ian. One was enough to mortify me for the rest of my life. I was just thankful that Anna was gracious enough not to say anything in front of Melonie.

I was still having a hard time wrapping my head around the dream anyway. It all seemed so real whenever I knew without a doubt that it never would be. The last time I'd seen him I thought I saw vague attraction for me lurking in those sea-colored eyes. But as the days went on I told myself I was just imagining it. I had hit my head hard that night.

"It's fucking freezing," Melonie's shrill voice broke through my thoughts as she rounded the vehicle. *Speak of the Devil and she arrives.* I clicked my tongue while trying to ignore her complaints.

"Whose stupid idea was it to not go to a nice warm beach?" she asked already knowing the answer.

Maybe it was because I'd been interrupted in my earlier orgasm and was sexually frustrated, or maybe it was because I was just tired of Melonie's constant complaining. Whatever it was that urged me to speak my mind, I didn't stop as it came out.

"You know, you didn't have to come. Nobody forced you, in fact, you invited yourself," I snapped before turning toward her.

The look that crossed her perfect features was priceless. She looked as though I had slapped her. Of course, she wasn't exactly used to me sticking up for myself. For the first time since I'd met her, she stumbled over her words.

"Wh–hat?" she stuttered.

When I said nothing and turned back toward the SUV, I could have sworn I saw smoke come out of her ears. I glanced at Anna who was still grabbing ski gear with a slight grin on her lips. Pride surged through me as I gripped Melonie's bag.

"Here…" I held out the bag for her. "Take your bag and go inside if you're too cold to help unload the rest of the car."

Melonie scoffed as she looked between Anna and me. "You're just gonna let her talk to me like that?" she asked Anna, as though she could save her from this altercation. Anna shrugged and tossed some of the ski gear down before turning to grab more.

"Talk to you like what?" Ben rounded the SUV with his hands in his pockets. Everyone ignored him as Melonie and I continued our staring contest.

Although it was unspoken, both of us knew that the first one of us to move was going to be the loser of this battle. I held her heavy bag out and refused to budge. She scowled from me to the bag and back to me again. Also refusing to move.

Ben, oblivious to this, stepped forward and grabbed the bag from my hand. He smiled at me with that golden retriever personality and then toward Melonie. "Here you go," he said happily as he handed it to her.

A beat longer than necessary passed before she finally ripped her heated gaze away from me and toward Ben. As if she flipped a switch, her face went from pissed off to puppy love. "Thank you so much, Benjamin." She beamed at him with that sugary smile that made me feel like I had a cavity. "Some people can just be so rude," she snarked before flipping her hair around her shoulder and stalking off toward the cabin.

I shook my head as I turned back around toward Anna who was barely containing her laughter. "Who knew all it would take to light a fire under you was to intercept your orgasm?" she teased and I snorted. I bumped her shoulder with mine as we both chuckled.

Maybe this trip would be good for me after all.

Ben stooped down to grab the ski gear and headed after Melonie as Anna and I grabbed the rest of the bags. There wasn't that much, as we were only staying here a week, but since it was cold everything we packed had been heavyweight. Meaning there were enough bags for both of our arms to be full.

As we trudged along the snow-covered path, I couldn't help the sigh of contentment that washed over me. All around me was a sheet of fresh white powder. Everything from the trees to the ground was covered in the thick glittery substance. Being from Georgia, I never really got to experience this type of weather. It was refreshing.

I let my gaze wander to everything around me. The cabin we were staying in was more like a large vacation home than anything else. Whatever Anna's dad did for a living must've been lucrative. It had to be at least a four-to-five-bedroom house. It was absolutely stunning. The front of the house was facing the beautiful snow-covered mountains with its floor-to-ceiling windows. The house itself was immaculately styled. The pristine log siding was something you would find in a designer magazine.

I noticed as we walked closer that one of the massive chimneys next to the windows was piping smoke out of it. *Was someone else here?* I looked back toward the driveway and inspected it. If there was someone here, they hadn't left their vehicle outside. That's when I spotted a set of tire tracks leading to one of the garage doors. Whoever was here must have parked inside.

"Anna," I breathed. We reached the front door where Ben and Barbie were waiting for us. The scowl on Melonie's face hadn't slipped as she assessed me from head to toe.

"Yeah?" Anna said as she slid the key into the lock and pushed the door open. She gestured for our traveling companions to head in first. If I thought the exterior had been breathtaking, their faces told me the inside was just as nice.

"Is there someone else here?" I asked as I pointed to the smoking chimney.

Confusion creased her brow before realization dawned on her. "Oh yeah, that's just my dad. When I asked if we could use the cabin he insisted that he be here too. Don't worry, he's totally cool. He will stay out of our way but he can be a worrier sometimes," she assured me. She stepped through the front door Ben was holding open for her.

I nodded as I followed. I'd never met Anna's dad before and I was kind of anxious to. I'd met her mom, Hillary, a couple of times and loved her to pieces. She was a lot like Anna, in looks and attitude, so it was hard not to instantly like her. Anna never had anything bad to say about her dad as I did mine, so it kind of left me wondering what type of person he was. All I knew was that he and her mom were happily divorced but everyone still got along well. Maybe it would be nice to see how a father/daughter relationship was supposed to be.

The heat from the inside of the cabin warmed my cheeks as I stepped through the doorway and turned to thank Ben for holding it. He grinned almost bashfully at me as I did.

"Oh good, you're here. Your flight was all right, then," a deep voice rang out and seemed to echo in my ears. I stood stalk still as I listened closely. The voice that haunted my dreams just this morning had spoken.

I slowly turned around and promptly dropped all the bags I was holding. Causing Melonie to curse and jump back so I wouldn't break her toes.

I couldn't be bothered by it as I stared at the figure in front of me. He was just as imposing as I imagined him early this morning. His hair was perfectly coiffed instead of beautifully tangled in my fingers. Those strong hands were shoved into his pockets instead of gripping my breasts as I'd begged for more. Those blue-green eyes were drilling into my soul as if it were his right to be there. His long powerful legs and tall figure clouded out everything else around me. Those lips, I'd felt as if they were real, smiled as he looked me up and down like I was his next meal.

I swallowed, trying to bring moisture back to my suddenly dry mouth as one word bounced around in my head like a ping-pong ball.

Ian.

Chapter Five

"What the fuck are you doing here?" The words spilled out of my lips before I could call them back.

"Oh my God, Lindsey. Don't be so rude, this is his cabin, after all." Anna laughed off my slip as she walked up to the man I couldn't stop thinking about. "Hey, Dad," she said as she hugged him.

"Dad?" Melonie and I said at the same time. We looked at each other. I knew my face held all the confusion I felt while hers held disdain for me and me alone.

I shook my head. "I thought your last name was Drewer?" I said as my stare bounced between Ian and Anna.

"It is," she said as she threw her bags onto the overstuffed couch.

"You look nothing alike," Melonie said as she raked her gaze up and down Ian like he was some sort of snack. I tried to ignore the surge of rage I felt as I watched her.

"Then how is he your dad? His last name is Young," I murmured ignoring Melonie altogether.

Anna frowned my way. "Do you two know each other?"

"No," I nearly screeched as Ian said, "Yes," at the same time.

Everything fell silent then. Anna's eyes bounced back and forth between us. Ben stood by the doorway, eyeing Ian with the caution of a rabbit looking at a wolf. Even Melonie said nothing as she stared at me.

"I treated Lindsey's mom once after an accident," Ian said as he smiled at his daughter and then returned those bright eyes to me.

I was struck dumb by the situation. He was here. How was he here? If I had known he was Anna's dad I would have never … would have never what? Thought about him inappropriately? Lusted after him like some sex-crazed maniac? Come on this trip?

It took me a while to figure out that everyone in the room was staring at me. As if they were all waiting for me to confirm that I did indeed know who he was.

"Ya-yeah," I stuttered. "That's how we know each other. He's my mom's doctor." When nobody spoke I felt the irresistible urge to fill the silence. "I mean, when you asked if I knew him, I thought you meant did I really *know* him. Which I don't … know him, I mean. We only met one time at the hospital. And even then we didn't really talk. So, no, I don't really know him at all. Just that he's a doctor and his name is Dr. Young … I mean Ian, Dr. Ian Young," I rambled on.

Melonie screwed up her face as she studied me. "Spazz," she mumbled under her breath so only I could hear. I kept ignoring her as I tried to calm my racing heart.

Everything got quiet then as Ian and I stared at one another. I could see a glint of humor in his gaze. *Did he find my awkwardness funny?* My face flamed at the thought.

"Right," Anna broke the silence. She walked up to her dad and looked at him before addressing the room. "Not that I thought I would need to explain this, but Dad here helped raise me. I was like, two, when he married my mom. My bio dad is a shit and didn't want anything to do with me so he stepped up." She grinned up at Ian who smiled back down at her lovingly. I felt embarrassment flood my body yet again. "That's why we have different last names." She laughed as she glanced at me. "Sorry for the confusion." She shrugged before looking back at her dad and smiling. "Just because it didn't work out between him and my mom, doesn't mean he stops being my dad," she said before she hugged his side.

I felt lower than dirt at that moment. What had come over me that I felt the need to question Anna about who her dad was? Even if I had the hots for him, I had been completely inappropriate.

I eyed Ian and said the first thing that popped into my head as an apology. "I'm sorry, sir." I winced at my own awkwardness. *Sir? Who says shit like that!*

Something flickered in Ian's eyes at my words. Something dark and untamed that called to me in a visceral way. I stumbled over my words as I turned away from the imposing male in question and faced his daughter. "Anna, I'm so sorry, I shouldn't have s—"

She waved her hand at me, effectively cutting me off. "It's no big deal, you didn't know. Honestly, if I went on vacation and ran into my mom's doctor I would probably wig out too." She grinned at me before clapping her hands together. "All right, let's figure out the room situation." She practically skipped down one of the halls that led to the bedrooms.

I stood still as Ian and I continued to stare at each other. Melonie seemed to take that moment to embarrass me further by bumping into me as she walked by, causing me to stumble over one of the bags I dropped. "Oops, sorry," she fake-apologized as I regained my footing. *Bitch.*

I watched as she swayed her hips as she walked up to Ian. Even though she had her back to me, I could tell she was giving him a sultry look. To his credit, he never took his gaze off me until she stopped in front of him. I nearly gagged as she tossed her arms around him and gave him a hug. He lightly patted her back in a way that you could see the hug was not warranted on his side.

"Thank you so much for letting us stay at your cabin, Dr. Young," she said as she pulled away from him. I saw a tinge of red as she pushed her tits out for him, held her hands behind her back, and swayed back and forth. "I sure wish I had a *daddy* like you." She pouted and I wanted nothing more than to rip her hair out at that moment. I knew exactly what she was trying to do.

She sauntered off after Anna as Ben walked past me to join them. He eyed Ian warily as he passed him on his way. He halted by the hallway that would lead to the bedrooms as his gaze trailed back to me. "You coming, Lindsey Bug?" he asked.

I could have sworn I saw Ian's jaw clench at the nickname but it was gone before the blink of an eye. I nodded and stepped over the luggage at my feet. Ben turned toward the girls again and stepped out of view.

I tried not to look at him as I passed but it was an impossible task as he stepped in front of me. My breath caught as he gripped my upper arm and pulled me closer to him. I closed my eyes to ward off that ache I now associated with him.

"Hello, Bambi," he growled.

Arousal surged through me as I remembered my dream. I kept my gaze trained forward as my breathing accelerated.

"Don't call me that," I mumbled and he chuckled. He stepped closer to me as his hand trailed up my biceps to my neck, leaving shivers in his wake. He slipped his hand under my hair and gripped me firmly, forcing me to look up at him. I gasped softly as the action sent awareness crackling across my scalp. His gaze flew to my lips.

"Why?" he whispered as he inched closer.

"B-because I don't think you mean the cute little forest animal in the cartoon and it-it's not appropriate," I stuttered. He was so close now I could almost taste him. The pounding between my legs was making it hard to focus. All I could think about was his lips on mine.

I nearly moaned as he stepped even closer now, every breath I took caused my breasts to rub against his chest. He bent down and I thought he was going to kiss me until he stopped and stared into my eyes. "See, that's the thing," he murmured as his lips lightly grazed against mine. Whatever game he was playing, I was clearly losing as I trembled against him. "When I think of you, it's the furthest thing from appropriate," he whispered before he gripped my hip.

"Lindsey, come see your room!" Anna's voice broke through the lusty fog I found myself in and I jumped back away from Ian. He let me go with a devious grin that told me he knew exactly the effect he was having on me.

"C-coming!" I yelled as I tried to skirt around him again. I almost made it when he grabbed me again, causing me to look up at him once more.

"Not yet," he murmured so quietly that I wondered if he had said anything at all. I pulled away from him and practically ran for the hallway.

Once I was out of the room, I exhaled in a rush and bent at the waist. *What in the actual fuck was that?* I thought I had just imagined his interest in me the other night. All the little touches and the looks that told me he would eat me up. Had it all been real?

I leaned back against the cool wall as I composed myself. My skin was too hot, too tight. The aching between my legs had increased tenfold. I was so turned on I was sure a stiff breeze would be all it took to send me off the edge.

I heard talking further down the hall but only half listened to it. It almost sounded like Anna and Melonie were arguing about something. When I felt like I could breathe again, I pushed away from the wall and followed the voices.

"I doubt she will even like it. She's used to sharing a room with you anyway," Melonie whined as I came closer.

"It doesn't matter what she's used to." Anna sounded like she was about at her wit's end with Melonie. "I'm giving her the option," she said before she spotted me and beamed. "Hey! It's your birthday week, you get the big room to yourself if you want it."

I flushed at the offer. I knew she wanted to do this for my birthday but I didn't want the whole week to be about me. "What about you two?" I asked.

"See, she doesn't want it. I'll just put my bag in here and—" Melonie tried to push past Anna but to no avail as she put her arm in front of her in the doorway. I had to stop the giggle from bubbling up as Melonie's face bunched up like she tasted something sour.

Anna kept her squinted eyes on Melonie as she spoke to me. "We are going to bunk together on the other side of the house. That way you have a room all to yourself, Ben has his own room next to ours where he can continue to be creepy." Ben flipped her off and I did giggle that time before she continued. "And Dad has his own space as well," she finished.

It took everything in me not to flush at the mention of her father again. *When did my life become one of those cheesy stories where the girl crushes on her bestie's dad?* I mentally shook myself and nodded at Anna.

"Sounds good, thank you." I cleared my throat before Melonie rolled her eyes and very loudly stalked back the way we came, toward her and Anna's room across the house. Anna shrugged like she couldn't care less and grabbed me for a hug. She grinned at me lovingly as she released me and sighed toward Ben.

"Come on, Bundy. I'll show you your room," she said as she turned away from me. I snorted at her latest serial killer joke but then cleared my throat as Ben looked down at me like I kicked his dog. I glanced into the open room to look anywhere else but at him.

Ben stomped after Anna then, muttering something that sounded like, "Medusa." I couldn't stop the grin from spreading across my lips as they all disappeared down another hallway.

I walked into my room for the week and couldn't keep the awe out of my gasp. The room was gorgeous. It had the same floor-to-ceiling windows that were on the front side of the house. Only these faced a snow-covered forest. The room was painted a dull white with one accent wall in olive green. The four-poster bed with a sheer white canopy was against that wall. The cream-colored pillows and bedding were arranged artfully, practically begging for you to sink into them.

The walls were elegantly decorated with artwork that matched the rest of the aesthetic of the room. The perfectly polished floors were so clean and slick, I could see my reflection as though I was looking into a mirror. Another fireplace arbored the wall opposite the bed where the fire radiated warmth through the room. This was by far the nicest room I would ever sleep in.

I walked on quiet feet toward the window seat and sat down as I stared out at the lightly falling snow. It was still early in the afternoon so I could see all the winter birds flying around and the squirrels still foraging for their next meal. It was absolutely—

"Beautiful." A sinfully deep voice pulled me

from my thoughts and I jerked around to face the delicious figure that filled my doorway.

Ian was lounging against the doorway as if he belonged there. One ankle was crossed over his other foot and his arms across his chest. And he was staring directly at me.

I said nothing as we stared at one another, I didn't know what to say. Just the sight of him had my pulse racing again. What was it with this man making all my good sense leave me? His eyes raked across my body as I sat there. Now that I knew those looks hadn't been just in my head, I could see how much need was there in those eyes.

I watched as he unfolded himself from the doorframe and stood to his full height. He made no other move to come near me and for that I was grateful. "So, you're the friend that had a birthday?" he murmured.

I nodded but said nothing. *Did he really not know that I was the one who would walk through that door?*

"Well, happy belated birthday, Lindsey." The way he said my name sounded like a dirty word. Just the way it rolled off his tongue made me want to clench my thighs together.

"Thank you," I said softly.

He stepped away from the doorway and nodded his head to the side. "If you need anything, I'm just next door." He smirked before he disappeared, presumably into his room. I stared after him as what he said finally resonated in my lust-clouded brain.

Next door.

Chapter Six

The brisk air bit at my cheeks as the chairlift took us higher with each passing moment. I tried not to look down as the ground got further away from my feet clad with hot-pink skis. I preferred to look at the snow-covered pines that scattered around us like someone ripped the image straight out of a novel. Even though it was next to freezing out, the view made the lack of sensation in my fingers slightly more bearable.

Anna sat next to me practically vibrating with excitement the closer we came to the top of the smallest slope. I think it was called the "bunny" or "kiddie" slope. I tried not to get hung up on the wording. It made sense that the instructor would start us out on this slope when I had never been skiing.

Anna had given us about thirty minutes to get unpacked, rested up, and changed before she insisted we "hit the powder," as she put it. She said it had been a couple of years since the last time she came here and we could tell she was overly thrilled to do this again. Apparently, her family had come out here at least once a year when she was growing up. Her dad already owned the cabin when her mom married him so that made it easy for them to do just that.

God, it was still so weird to think of Ian as her dad. I was glad my thoughts regarding the handsome doctor were locked away safely in my mind. I couldn't stop thinking about how bad that blow-up would have been if she figured out I had the hots for him. Or that he seemed to be having the same feelings as me.

As it was, Ian said he would let us do our own thing this week. But he had insisted he come along at least for today. He was currently a couple of rows behind us on the lift. Melonie and Ben were in the seats right behind us and Ian was behind them. He said he wanted to be out here the first day with us just in case his medical expertise was needed since some of us had never done this before. Some of us meaning just me.

I promptly ignored the dark looks he seemed to send my way every chance he got. It was bad enough being trapped in the same car on the way here. I sat in the back seat with Ben shoved in the middle and Melonie on the other side. Every time I felt him look at me in the rearview mirror, I forcefully kept my stare directed out my window.

Everything I thought I'd imagined the last time I was around him was seemingly coming true. All the looks and covert touches he delivered to me that night hadn't been in my head after all. If there was still any doubt in my mind that he didn't want me as I wanted him, the way he spoke to me earlier hammered the final nail in that coffin.

Nonetheless, now that I knew who he was, I would have to shut that shit down. Even though he was the only man that ever made me crave … more, I couldn't let those feelings come between my friendship with his daughter.

"Okay, we're coming up to the drop-off. You remember what I told you?" Anna shouted over the breeze that whipped past my ears. We were both covered in head-to-toe winter gear, including thick scarves that partially covered our mouths, so her words were mumbled.

I tried my best to give her a reassuring smile. I nodded as I replayed her words in my mind over and over again. *"Keep your head up and look forward, stand up, push off the chair, and glide away."* I took slow steady breaths as the turn in the lift approached.

Logically, I knew this would go fast. But as I looked at how the now empty chairs in front of us whipped around the pole, I wasn't so sure I wouldn't be getting a face full of snow just simply trying to get off the damn lift. "Keep your head up and look forward," I mumbled to myself.

The ground lightly touched the bottom of our skis now. Anna had a mile-wide grin on her lips as she took a deep breath and got ready to dismount. She held her hand out for me and I gripped it. I would need all the support I could get at this point. I could feel pressure against the soles of my feet, so it was now or never.

Anna scooted forward and I followed the movement. "Stand up," I whispered as I did just that. Gripping onto the handrail for dear life so I wouldn't slip. "Push off," I said as I let go and pushed away from the moving bench.

"And glide!" Anna shouted next to me as we glided smoothly away from the lift. I couldn't help the surge of pride that coursed through me as I shakily found my feet and continued to glide next to Anna. My smile was the broadest it had been in years it seemed. Maybe it was a small victory for some but to me it was huge. I was completely out of my comfort zone and I was succeeding.

Anna started to giggle as she stared at my expression. I couldn't help my own laugh as I glanced her way. It was silly, but that moment with my best friend felt like it solidified our relationship with each other.

We were so busy giggling and looking at each other that I didn't realize my feet liked to follow my line of vision. Before I could try to stop it, my skis crossed over the top of hers and we both tripped forward. Both of my feet popped out of the boot attachments as I squealed and went head over heels. Anna controlled her fall better than I did and sat down on her ass, the soft powder cushioning her fall.

I pushed my hands out in front of me but it was too late. One moment I was gliding like a majestic swan on a lake and the next I had a face full of snow as I sprawled over my roommate's legs.

I rolled over onto my back and gasped for air as I wiped the cold wet snow off my face. I laid still for a moment as I assessed the rest of my body for injury. When I decided I was okay, I closed my eyes as mortification rolled over me.

That was until I heard Anna start laughing. I swung my head toward her and returned her laugh as I saw her gripping her belly. She was heaving long breaths in and out around her laughs. It was contagious as I found myself doing the same soon. Neither of us noticed Ben and Melonie standing next to us until one of them cleared their throat.

The look of bewilderment on their faces made us laugh even harder. Anna laid back in the snow as if she couldn't keep herself up anymore. My cheeks hurt so much, whether it was from the cold wind biting at the wet flesh there or from my wide smile as I belly laughed, I couldn't tell. The puzzled looks from fellow skiers as they passed us only served to make everything funnier.

"Are you okay, Lindsey Bug?" Ben asked with concern in his voice. Melonie looked at him like he was an idiot and rolled her eyes. I pointed at him and howled in laughter. I don't know why but his concern and Melonie's lack thereof were hilarious.

"You ladies all right?" a deep intimate voice called and a pair of new skis came skidding to a stop next to us. My laughs quieted as I swallowed hard and Anna's died down to a chuckle as she looked up at her father.

"Yeah, we're fine." She quieted the rest of her laughs. I was caught by his gaze as I raised onto my elbows. I couldn't keep the lust from my eyes as I watched him tower over me. *What would it be like to look up at him like this but from a bed instead?* The hooded look he shot my way made me feel like he could read my mind at that moment. I shook my head to rid the thought.

I tried not to think about what he would look like under all of that ski gear. As it was, he looked sleek and delectable in his black ski pants and jacket. Next to the glistening white, the stark black of his outfit was hard to miss. Much like the man underneath it all.

I sat quickly as he helped Anna stand. I looked around me for my skis that had gone flying. I was still wearing my snow boots so I stood when I spotted one a few feet down the hill. I walked down to it and picked it up before I searched for the other. When I couldn't immediately spot it I briefly wondered how I would make it down the mountain with just one ski. There wasn't a shot in hell that I would be trying to get back onto that lift.

"Here you go," Ian said as he slid up to me. I flushed as he held out the bright pink ski. He smiled slightly as I grabbed it from him and started to walk back up to the others. My breath sputtered and stalled in my lungs when he gripped my upper arm to stop me. "You've never done this, have you?" he asked. It seemed he wasn't just talking about skiing.

"Oh, you know, I do this like every weekend. I may as well be a professional at this point," I said, sarcasm dripping from each word.

"I can tell." He chuckled and then looked between my eyes and lips. My pulse spiked at the thought of him wanting to kiss me. "Let me teach you," he said in a hushed tone as if others would hear us. I could have sworn his words had a double meaning at that moment.

I glanced back up to the group who were patiently waiting on us. Melonie and Anna were talking to one another while Ben was watching both of us like a hawk. Ben always seemed to be watching. When I looked back at Ian he was still waiting for my answer.

"I don't think that's a good idea," I mumbled as I started to pull away from him.

"Why not?" He didn't let up. Now I knew from his persistence that he wasn't talking about ski lessons.

I bit my lip and then considered my next words carefully. "Anna," I hesitated then continued. "Anna is my best friend."

He nodded. "All of us are adults, Lindsey. Look..." He leaned into me and lowered his voice. "I'm going to be honest with you. I haven't been able to stop thinking about you since that day in the hospital," he admitted and my breath hitched. "When you came into your mom's room holding that ridiculously huge bouquet of flowers."

Was he fucking with me right now? He actually remembered that fleeting moment?

He grinned fondly at his memory before watching me closely. "You could barely see over that damn thing. But the way you looked up at me with those big grey eyes. You looked so... pure. And maybe I'm twisted for it, but that pureness calls to me." His jaw flexed as his eyes searched mine for a reaction.

"I don't know if I can make it any more obvious for you, but I want you, Lindsey," he growled as his dark gaze drank me in. He was so close it was making me dizzy. "I want to see what makes you tick, want to know what you feel like without the barrier of clothing." I felt that deep pulse forming in my core at his words. "I want to hear all the little sounds you make when you come against my tongue, I want to know what your sweet cream tastes like." The shiver that crawled up my spine had nothing to do with the chill on the mountain and everything to do with this man's words. Nobody had ever spoken to me like this. "I want to feel your wet pussy grip my cock like a vice as you ride me, Bambi."

I hadn't realized how close he was to me but I swear he could hear my heartbeat, as loud as it was to my own ears. I felt dampness gather between my thighs and my nipples tighten under my layers. At that moment, I wanted nothing more than to lean forward and bridge the gap between us. I wanted his lips on mine, I wanted to taste him. All of him. I wanted everything he admitted and more.

I shook my head and leaned away from him before my common sense left me completely. I couldn't do this. Maybe if he were someone else or I wasn't his daughter's friend I could be this person. But he was him and I was a good friend.

"I can't," I whispered as I pulled my arm away from him and started to walk back toward Anna.

"Lindsey," he said between clenched teeth. He flexed his jaw as he looked at me but I pulled my gaze away and kept walking. Ignoring the only man I had craved as I returned to his daughter.

"What was that about?" Melonie sneered toward me as I climbed the hill and came nearer to them.

I shook my head as I sat to put my skis back on. "He offered to help me learn to ski," I muttered as I kept my eyes trained on the task at hand. I could feel all their attention on me and me alone. "I politely declined," I said with a shrug.

Once I strapped my boots back into the skis, I

held my hands up for Ben to help me stand. I caught the look in his eyes but quickly diverted my gaze. His was full of questions and curiosity. Out of all my friends, he would be the one to pick up on something being amiss with me. He was way too observant for my own good.

Anna looked from me to her dad and then back to me like she had questions but didn't bother to ask.

"Well, if you don't want the lessons, I'll take them." Melonie practically bounced up and down as she waved at Ian. I scowled at her as she made a show of bouncing just enough to make this an episode of *Baywatch*.

"Didn't you say you've done this hundreds of times?" Anna asked as she watched the show Melonie was performing just for Ian.

"It doesn't hurt to have a refresher course, Anna," she snapped. Anna flinched back as though she didn't expect Melonie's venom.

I watched as Ian removed his skis and walked back up the hill to us. He stared at me as he trudged through the thick snow. I sucked in a sharp breath as I turned away from him, facing Anna and Melonie. I didn't know what was worse, his heated gaze or her questioning one.

"Will you teach me how to ski?" Barbie pouted toward Ian. I didn't even try to keep the disgust off my face as she stuck her bottom lip out and pressed her chest out toward him. *What a skank.*

I heard Ian chuckle behind me as he agreed to help her. The jealousy I felt surprised me. I cringed as Melonie squealed and clapped her hands together. I shook my head and looked back up at Anna who mirrored the same disgust on her pretty face. I held my hand out for her and she smiled as she grabbed it.

"Can you help me not kill myself going down this

hill?" I asked her as I ignored the *refresher course* going on at my back.

Anna smiled at me before nodding briskly.

Ben went in front of us and made it a few hundred feet before really picking up speed. He had been skiing a couple of times but he was far from a professional. We watched him swing his arms aimlessly to keep his balance.

I couldn't help the giggle that bubbled up as we watched him. Anna snorted and muttered under her breath. All I caught was "Stalker Boy."

She squeezed my hand. "Ready?" she asked as she watched after Ben.

I risked a glance back toward Ian to see him watching me with hunger in his gaze. Melonie was still trying her damndest to get him to look at her chest. I diverted my attention just as quickly. I didn't want to see him *teaching* someone else even if it was just skiing.

I squeezed Anna back and nodded. "Let's go."

Chapter Seven

To say I was sore would be the understatement of the century. I lost track of how many times we had gone up the lift to the top of the bunny hill, just to zoom back down and do it all over again. I had finally gotten the hang of getting off the lift, but I was still far from perfect at going down.

I had fallen so many times today, I would be surprised if I wasn't covered in bruises. Anna had helped me down the mountain a few times but I could tell she was eager to get to the bigger hills. When I told her to go ahead she'd practically vibrated with excitement. Remembering the way she beamed at me made the falls I sustained worth it.

Ben had tried to get me to go down the hill holding his hand more than once. Even though I could've used the support, I didn't want him to think that holding his hand meant more than it did so I'd politely declined. He made sure to stay close to me for the rest of the day, though. It seemed every time I turned around, he was there watching me. I shrugged it off as him just keeping an eye out.

I'd only seen Ian a couple more times while out on the snow. Melonie seemed to be stuck up his ass as she followed him around like stink on a skunk. I tried to ignore the way she touched him at any opportunity. I didn't like the instant jealousy that flared each time I saw them together. Even if his eyes had been glued to me the whole time, that hadn't tramped down the feeling of rage as I watched her flirt with him.

It was ridiculous, really. I shouldn't be feeling any type of way regarding that man. Even if I was still shell-shocked at his revelation to me, I had told him no and meant it. I couldn't jeopardize my friendship with his daughter, she was too important to me. Even if what he said was true, we *were* all adults but that still didn't make it right. But even so, I couldn't shake the feeling that I was missing out on something that could be *so good.* Even if it was doomed to fail.

After what felt like the hundredth time getting a face full of snow, I finally said enough was enough. I very wobbly made it down the hill for the last time, took my skis off, and trekked my way into the lodge. A sigh of relief escaped me as the heat from the building warmed my frozen cheeks.

The inside of the lodge screamed luxury. The floor to the walls and even the ceiling were covered in exposed logs, giving a rustic feel to the whole place. The ceiling was lofted with skylights that let in the midday sun. I counted two fireplaces that warmed the interior of the building. Tables and carved-out seating areas were scattered across the open floor plan. The delicious smells piping out of the kitchen made my mouth water and reminded me that I hadn't eaten much all day. I briefly thought about ordering something to snack on but quickly dismissed it. I was sure Anna had a big dinner planned for us tonight.

I dusted the remaining snow off myself before I made my way to the counter for a hot coffee. After pouring myself a piping-hot mug, I claimed one of the many window seats that faced the slopes. It was an inviting little space with two big wingback chairs and a small table that sat between the two. Both were angled toward the huge windows so you could watch the mountain. I chose the chair that faced the door but also offered a view of where my party was. I sat my coffee down, removed my coat and gloves, and sank into the plush chair. I gripped the mug and let the warmth thaw my frigid fingers and nose as I inhaled the rich aroma.

This was my idea of a good time. Sitting in this cozy alcove with a hot beverage and watching all the other lodge visitors skim down the mountain. I was an introvert by nature so I always felt at home by myself. I could have just as much fun watching others enjoy themselves as I would participating.

I tentatively sipped at the scalding coffee when the little bell above the entrance rang and I glanced over curiously. I immediately sputtered and coughed as the hot liquid burned my throat. Though it wasn't the hot coffee that made me choke, but rather the hot doctor that just walked through the doors.

Ian's gaze burned into me with more heat than the interior of the lodge. It was as though he knew exactly where I'd been before he even entered the building. I gently placed my full cup onto the table in front of me before facing him as he stalked closer. The way he was looking at me right now almost made me think he was angry. He was the type of guy that had probably never been turned down by the opposite sex. So it would stand to reason if he was upset at me because I did just that.

I inhaled sharply as I watched him barrel down on me. *Thirty feet away.* My heart skipped a beat and raced as I watched his intensely blue eyes bore into me. *Twenty feet.* I could feel myself going soft in all the right places at his approach. *Fifteen feet.* I couldn't stop the vision that slammed into my mind of me sprawled naked on a bed for him to devour. *Ten feet.* I nearly whimpered as if I could already feel his soft hands as they roamed my body. *Five feet...*

"There you are, Lindsey Bug." I jumped at the sound of Ben's voice as he walked in front of me, effectively taking away my view of the bulking figure headed my way. I swallowed and squeezed my thighs together as the ache that had built there fought for dominance over my mind.

"Ben," I breathed as he sat in the chair opposite me. "How'd you know I was here?" I asked as I stared at Ian. He had stopped his forward advance as he watched Ben. His eyes darkened as he looked between the two of us. *Was he jealous?*

Ben's mumbled voice was overshadowed by the ringing in my ears as I watched Ian. He was still five feet away from me as if he was rooted in that same spot. I could see anger practically vibrating off his expressive form as he stared a hole in the back of Ben's head. After what felt like hours, he raked a frustrated hand through his hair and turned on his heel. I watched as he receded and slammed out of the lodge and back outside into the cold.

"Lindsey?" Ben's voice finally cut through the fog. I blinked rapidly and shook my head before speaking.

"I'm sorry, what?" I asked.

Ben squinted his eyes as he studied me. His hazel eyes seemed so intense and I found myself having a hard time wanting to make eye contact. His inky black hair was mussed and wild, making him seem more feral than I'd ever seen him. His dark black tattoos stuck out like a beacon around the brilliant white surrounding us. He looked so out of place here. I always thought someone like Ben was a little too intense for a person like me, what with his overall persona and look.

He then turned in his seat and looked toward the door that Ian disappeared out of. "I said, I always know where you are," he repeated as he regarded me seriously. I nodded and brought my coffee back to my lips, taking another sip. "Do you have a thing for Anna's dad?" he asked seemingly out of the blue.

I coughed and choked again, only this time sending piping-hot coffee from the top of my mug, splattering it all over the table between us. I hastily slammed the mug down and grabbed as many napkins as I could, vigorously cleaning my mess as my face flamed in embarrassment. "What? No! Why would you ask me such a thing? That is completely inappropriate," I rambled. "Not only is he Anna's dad but he's also way older than me. I would never be with someone like that," I lied through my teeth as I continued to clean my mess and keep my eyes averted from Ben's criticizing ones. "I mean, yeah, he's not hard on the eyes but I would never..."

I trailed off as Ben watched me, never once offering to help me with my mess. When I risked a glance back up at him he was scowling. *That was weird.* The whole time I'd known Ben, he had never looked at me with anything other than that silly golden retriever expression. In fact, this was the first time I had ever seen him ... angry.

As if I'd imagined it, his scowl disappeared and he moved suddenly. He gripped a handful of napkins and started to help me clean up the coffee. I laughed nervously as we both stood to throw the trash away. When I turned to walk to the garbage can, Ben gripped my elbow, causing me to stop.

"That's good, Lindsey Bug," he said. He smiled at me before it wavered and he got serious. "Guys like him only want one thing and one thing only. I know you're too good of a girl to give it to him, right?" he asked.

I nodded when I realized he was waiting for an answer. His smile returned as he grabbed the coffee-soaked napkins out of my hands. He gripped them in one of his before he bopped me on the nose with his index finger and sauntered off to dispose of them.

I furrowed my brows in confusion as I watched him walk away. Ben had never taken any kind of interest in any other guys in my life. I mean, sure, he always seemed to show up when the date was finishing, but I always chalked it up to timing. There were only so many hang-out places on campus, so when I hung out with other people someone I knew was bound to show up sooner or later.

Still, I found it strange that Ben even knew where I'd been at all. The last I'd seen him was out on the slope. I hadn't told anyone that I was going to the lodge. It'd almost been like he was waiting for me to show up. And he had waited until Ian was almost to me before interrupting.

At that moment the bell for the front entrance rang again and I swung my head in that direction. *Was it Ian again?* I flinched at the thought. *Did I want it to be Ian again?* I couldn't tell if it was a sigh of disappointment or relief as Anna came into view. I waved her over just as Ben returned to my side, sliding his arm around my waist.

I stiffened at the touch before pulling away from him to walk to Anna. I didn't know what was going on with him, but I needed to make sure I wasn't giving him any hints that I wanted him to be anything more than what he was. Ben was just a friend and up until now I thought he knew that. Maybe I was thinking too much into it.

"Are you having fun?" Anna's smile was contagious and I found myself grinning back at her. Her nose and cheeks were cherry red from the brisk winter breeze. Even if skiing wasn't my thing, that didn't stop the joy I felt at seeing my friend enjoy the thing she loved.

"So much fun," I said as Melonie walked up behind Anna. She looked less than thrilled as she joined us.

"Where did your dad go? One minute he was helping me with my form and the next he's just gone," she complained.

I restrained my urge to snarl as Anna told her he was probably in the car. "It's almost dinnertime and I have a whole meal planned for Lyns tonight. We're gonna cook all your favorites." She beamed at me.

I gripped her glove-covered hand as we headed to the door. "Sounds great, Anna. I'm starved."

****

"You cooked, the least I could do is wash the dishes," I complained as Anna shoved me away from the sink.

"It's your birthday. I'll be damned if I let you wash a single dish from your dinner," she tsked as she grabbed the dishrag from me.

"What am I supposed to do then? Sit and watch you slave away?" I scoffed.

Anna shrugged. "You can do whatever you want, just not the dishes." She chuckled. "Why don't you go pour yourself another glass of wine and relax?"

"Anna, there are so many dishes. You made enough to feed an army, let me help." I rolled my eyes.

Anna looked over at Melonie sitting on the kitchen counter with a glass of wine in her hand. She sat there as if she were deaf to the whole conversation as she scrolled through her phone.

"Melonie can help," she said.

Barbie's breath left her in a rush as she slid off the counter and backed away toward the den. "Oh, I would love to but I just got my nails done before we came here." She flashed her bright pink nails toward us and Anna scowled at her. "I wouldn't want to mess them up," she said before taking another sip and vanishing from the room.

I shook my head at her as I approached the sink again. Anna spun around and pointed a soapy scrub brush at me as if it were a weapon. "Back off, Hart," she growled in mock anger.

I giggled at her weak attempt to divert me and put my hands up in surrender. "Come on, Anna. That is a mountain of dishes. Let me help you." I chuckled.

Ben took that moment to walk into the kitchen and smile that dopey smile. Anna looked from me to him and then back to me. "Jack can help me." She smiled as if she'd won the argument.

Ben looked at her in confusion. "Who the fuck is Jack?" he asked and I closed my eyes, bracing for what I knew was coming.

"The Ripper." Anna grinned at me. I snorted and covered my mouth as Ben's lips flattened. He never found Anna's humor as funny as I did.

"Har, har," he fake-laughed. "That's not even clever," he whined.

Anna shrugged. "Doesn't matter. Get your stalker ass over here and help me wash these dishes," she commanded.

Ben threw his head back and sighed as he headed to the sink. I stood there for a few moments, contemplating what to do with myself. I could get another glass of wine and go take a warm bath. God only knew that my body aches would thank me for it. But I couldn't help but feel bad about not helping clean up.

The least I could do was dry the dishes. I searched through the drawers until I found a clean towel and walked closer to the sink. Anna must've known what I was intending because she grabbed the extendable faucet and sprayed me with the warm water.

"Hey!" I screeched as I jumped back.

Anna stopped spraying but kept it pointed at me nonetheless. I couldn't help the giggle that bubbled up at her serious face. "Get out of here, you're not touching a single dish," she scowled.

I huffed and tossed the towel at her as Ben stared between us. "Fine," I said and Anna returned the sprayer to its place with a nod. "I guess I'll go take a bath. I'm ready for some downtime anyway," I muttered as I grabbed the bottle of wine and my glass off the counter.

Anna smiled at me over her shoulder. "Good, go relax because tomorrow we have more activities," she said in a singsong voice.

I tried to hide my grimace as I backed out of the room. Even just the few hours we were out on the slopes left me exhausted, I couldn't imagine what a whole day would be like.

I walked out of the kitchen and into the den. Now that I was no longer in shock about Ian being here, I'd finally been able to take in the beauty of the interior of the cabin. The den that I stood in now was like I'd walked straight into a hunting magazine. The rich light-colored wood of the floor matched that of the walls and lofted ceiling. Large beams flowed from one end of the house to the other, lights strung around the beams in intricate designs. The large black fur rug broke up the continuous color of the light wood. Aside from being in Damon's house, I'd never seen a place as immaculately decadent as this.

The massive den was only enhanced by the huge black sofa that sat in the middle facing the huge hearth that was surrounded by that gorgeous floor-to-ceiling pointed window. What I would give to be able to curl up on that sofa and read a good book. I imagined myself getting lost between the pages while the warm fire crackled in front of me. The matching end tables sported decorative objects that went with the general theme of the room. The whole feel of the room screamed cozy intimacy.

I expected to see Melonie in there curled up on the couch but she was nowhere to be seen. Shrugging to myself, I continued down the hall toward my room. Maybe she went to her and Anna's room for the night.

It was late in the evening now. By the time we left the lodge and made it back to the cabin, dusk had already fallen. Anna had prepared my favorite meal, homemade lasagna with salad and garlic bread. Everything had been delicious.

I'd expected the meal to be awkward on my part because of Ian. But he had surprised me when he'd gotten himself a plateful, kissed Anna on top of her head, and told us he had work to do so he would be in his office. The relief I felt was short-lived as Melonie had offered to keep him company.

"No, thanks," he'd said as he glanced briefly toward me before turning and disappearing down the hallway.

I was surprised when I kept my cool as Melonie pouted at his answer. Anna had looked at her like she was crazy for even offering. Melonie had shrugged at her before claiming she was just "being nice."

I came to my door and glanced toward the one next to mine that I knew to be Ian's. It wasn't quite closed as I could see a dim light shining from the opening. I wondered what he was doing in there and then quickly dismissed the thought. It wasn't any of my business what he was doing.

I slid into my room and shut the door with a solid click. I didn't bother with the light as I padded into the en suite bathroom. This room was just as stylish as the rest of my room. White tiles with sleek black grout paved the way to the huge claw-foot tub that sat against two big windows. I briefly wondered if the outside of the windows were tinted so only you could see outside but no one would be able to see in. Not that it mattered much. We were in the middle of nowhere so I wasn't too worried about prying eyes.

I sat my wine down on the sink and plugged the tub before flipping the water to hot. I poured myself a glass and sipped the cold sweet red liquid before placing it beside the tub and shedding my clothes. Gooseflesh raced across my skin as the chill of the room caressed me. After I tossed my sweater to the floor I unclasped my bra, letting my breasts bounce free.

I avoided the mirror as I slid my thick leggings down my legs along with my panties. It's not that I hated my body, we just weren't the best of friends most days. It seemed that no matter what I tried I was never able to lose those extra pounds I always carried around.

The tub wasn't quite full as I stood there naked. I took another sip of my wine as I glanced at the mirror. It's not like I was ugly, I decided as I stared at my reflection. My face was truthfully quite pretty. I looked a lot like my mom aside from my grey eyes and dark brown hair. Those I had received from my asshole dad.

I let my eyes wander down my body. My breasts were large and not as perky as a lot of other twenty-one-year-olds. They sagged slightly with the weight. Lower I went as I assessed myself. My belly had a solid pooch that no amount of crunches got rid of. I had love handles with just the smallest amount of stretch marks that marred the skin there. My mound was trimmed and kept nicely. Even though nobody had ever seen that part of me, that didn't mean I was lax on maintenance. My thighs liked each other so much that they were always touching. If there was one part of my body I really liked, it was those.

I sighed as I ran my hands down my sides, pinching and pulling on all the parts I didn't like. Body positivity wasn't a thing that lived in everyone's mind.

I pulled my long waves into a messy bun before I turned and shut the water off. I added some sweet-smelling soap to the water and breathed in the steam. Gripping my glass, I stepped into the hot bath with a hiss. It was hot but it felt good as I let the warmth seep into my bones. I took another sip of my wine before placing it on the lip of the tub and sitting back.

I closed my eyes and released a breath I felt as though I'd been holding all day as I relaxed.

I must have fallen asleep at some point because when I opened my eyes my water was chilled and my wine was warm. I yawned as I sat up in the water and looked at my hands. I chuckled at my seriously pruned fingers. I stood on extremely loose legs, not knowing how long it had been. I was like a noodle that had cooked too long.

I stepped out of the tub and grabbed one of the soft white towels. I hastily dried myself before wrapping the black robe that was on the bathroom door around me. I grabbed my wineglass and dumped it down the sink.

I left the bathroom and walked across the room toward the massive bed and tried not to think about the fact that my bed was against the same wall that separated mine and Ian's rooms. Glancing at the clock, I was shocked to see it had been over an hour since I got in the bath. I would bet everyone in the cabin was asleep by now.

I started to turn my bedside light on so I could find something to sleep in when I heard a muffled sound through the wall. I stood stock still like if I dared to move something bad would happen. My breath quieted as I stood there and listened closely for any other sound. Then I heard it again. I squinted at the wall as if I could see what was happening on the other side. It wasn't words that I was hearing but I couldn't quite make out what it was.

Maybe I was a sick person for it or I had more stalker tendencies than I thought, but I didn't talk myself out of it as I stepped forward and placed my ear to the wall. I wanted to know what I was hearing. My heart thundered in my chest and my breath left my nose in labored puffs. It was like my body knew I was doing something I shouldn't be.

I slammed my hands over my mouth and jumped back when I heard it again. It wasn't voices but it was a groan. A deep masculine groan. A sexual groan.

I swallowed around the lump in my throat as I stared at the wall and then the door that led to the hallway. Was Ian with someone in his room? Was it Melonie? Jealousy like I'd never felt flared through my body making me hot and cold all at the same time. As if my feet had a mind of their own, I walked toward the door and opened it. If Ian was really with Melonie I needed to see it with my own eyes. I justified my actions by telling myself that if he was with her then that would end my infatuation with him.

I stepped out into the hall with quiet feet and left my door open. I spied his door a few feet away and padded closer. It was still slightly ajar like it had been earlier this evening, only this time the light was off.

I eased up to the door and took a steady breath. The hall light was off so I was bathed in darkness, and I knew there was no chance he would see me. My heart kept thundering in my chest so hard I could hear it in my ears as I leaned into the opening.

His room was dark with the exception of the moonlight bouncing off the white snow outside. It took my eyes a moment to adjust until I caught sight of his bed. I sucked in a sharp breath as I looked for him.

Then I saw him. He was laying on his bed but nobody else was with him. At first, I thought he was asleep but then he moved. No, not just moved, he jerked. I felt arousal flood my core as I watched him.

By the light of the moon outside I could barely make out his face as it contorted in pleasure. He was naked and the blankets were thrown to the side as he gripped his hard cock in his right hand and jerked it roughly. I felt wetness fill the space between my thighs and my skin tighten painfully.

I stared as he leaned his head up and watched what he was doing to himself. He led his other hand down his body to cup his balls as he rubbed his cock with a firm grip. I gripped the doorframe with white-knuckle force as he tossed his head back and groaned long and deep. He became erratic in his long pulls from his impressive length until suddenly he jerked almost violently. His mouth opened with a gasp as he spilled his release all over his belly.

I barely stopped myself from gasping with him as I watched euphoria cross his features. I'd never seen anything as erotic as the vision he made as his orgasm overtook him. It was a strange feeling having to force myself not to move, not to join him. I wanted nothing more than to be the one th—

"What are you doing?"

Chapter Eight

I yelped as I jumped back and away from Ian's door. Praying like hell that he hadn't just heard me, or worse seen me watching him.

Melonie stood with her arms crossed over her chest as she scowled at me. She had her bright blonde hair up in a ponytail and it looked like she had put makeup on. Why would she put makeup on this late? She was dressed in a skimpy silk nighty that showed way too much cleavage. If I hadn't been so terrified that she had caught me watching Ian, I would have questioned why she was here in the first place. Her and Anna's room was on the other side of the cabin so she had to go out of her way to come over here.

"What are you doing?" she repeated and looked at me as if I were an idiot. She was right, I was such a fucking idiot.

"I, uh—" I stammered as I backed up toward my door. I was what? *Spying on my best friend's dad as he masturbated.* I had no idea what I was going to say.

Melonie looked between Ian's open door and me. I cringed as her eyes got that maniacal look about them. "Oh my God, were you spying on him?" she asked a little too loudly.

I shook my head as I backed up further. "N-no! I thought I heard a noise a-and—" I stuttered as my heart hammered in my ears. *Was this what a panic attack felt like?* My adrenaline spiked and my breathing became rapid. How was I getting out of this?

"You dirty little liar," Melonie hissed at me. "What did you think? That a guy like him would want some fatass like you?" She laughed as she stuck the metaphorical knife in my gut. It was as if she knocked the breath right out of me as I fought to catch it. Just when I thought she was done, she twisted it further. "Someone like him wants a real woman, not some little girl who pretends to be something she isn't—"

"Ladies, is there a problem?" Ian's deep voice cut Melonie off before she could say anything else. He stood in his doorway wearing nothing but a pair of dark grey sweatpants. His earlier actions had been wiped clean from his belly.

If I hadn't been about to throw up, I would have stopped to appreciate his physique. I had seen plenty of guys with their shirts off before. The guys on the football team liked to go on early morning jogs around campus shirtless. I'd never stopped to stare at them as other girls had. But Ian wasn't just another football guy. Ian was different in so many ways.

Melonie had no such problem as her greedy gaze ate up everything Ian was offering. She uncrossed her arms and thrust her chest toward him as she took on the persona of innocence. I wanted to die as he looked between the two of us before settling his gaze on me. Some unknown emotion flared in those eyes.

"Well, I was just walking by when I saw *Lindsey* snooping at your door. I think she was trying to watch you sleep or something," she said in a high-pitched girly voice. If I didn't want to puke before, I sure did now as I watched her fake demeanor.

I stepped forward like I was going to defend myself when Ian interrupted me. "She wasn't snooping," he said as he held his hand out toward me. That's when I saw the bottle of pills he held. I looked from it to him in confusion. His expression never wavered as he waited for me to take the offered container. "She asked if I had any Tylenol because she forgot to pack hers," he lied.

I knew at that moment that he knew I'd been

watching him. He knew I was peeking in on him in an intimate moment. But he was saving me from further embarrassment by acting like I had asked him for something. I didn't know what to say. So I said nothing.

I nodded and muttered thanks as I pulled the bottle of pills out of his extended hand. Melonie watched me with a sour look on her face. I couldn't tell if she believed him or not but right now I didn't care. I palmed the medicine, nodded, and turned back toward my room. As soon as I was back inside I shut the door as quickly as I could and smothered my whimper of embarrassment.

Stupid. Stupid. Stupid. I thumped my head against the door quietly as Ian firmly told Melonie to go back to her room. I could barely hear her response to him as she told him she couldn't sleep. I rolled my eyes at the lame excuse for gathering his attention.

More mumbling ensued until I heard Melonie's bare feet walk past my room and out of the hall. I exhaled in a rush as I sagged back onto the wood. I felt instant relief until I realized I hadn't heard Ian go back into his room.

I jerked away from the door as if it burnt me and turned around. I walked backward with the bottle still clasped in my hand as I stared at the door. The back of my knees bumped into the bed and I blindly sat as I stared at the two shadows underneath. He was standing outside.

When a light tap came against the door I jumped and covered my mouth as though the noise had scared me. It wasn't the noise that frightened me but rather the man that made it. I said nothing as I continued to stare. Maybe if I pretended not to hear him he would go away.

That thought quickly vanished as the doorknob twisted and the door cracked open. I swallowed harshly as Ian stepped into my room and closed the door behind him. He said nothing as his gaze ate me up like a hungry tiger. My breath shuttered in and out of me like I had just gone for a ten-mile run. Silent moments ticked by and I felt the urge to fill them. To say something, anything.

"Thank you," I breathed. When he said nothing I held the bottle out in front of me like a peace offering. "For the Tylenol, I mean."

His smirk made me nervous as he pushed away from the door. When he twisted the lock on the handle I felt the reverberating click in my core.

"Were you watching me, Bambi?" he asked. His voice was raspy with lust.

I flinched back at his question as if he struck me, placing the bottle on my lap before staring at my hands. "No," I lied.

He stalked closer. Each moment dragged out as the quiet of the room became so loud I could hardly stand it. I was still looking down when his bare feet came into view. I don't know why but the sight of those bare feet turned me on. Like I was seeing a part of him nobody else got to see.

I focused on my breathing as his hand grazed the bottom side of my chin and pulled my face up, making me look at him. "Don't lie to me, Lindsey."

I took him in now, all of him. He was immaculate. Even with his bed-ruffled hair, he was perfect. He was tan and lean. His muscular chest was speckled with soft-looking hair. His corded abdomen served as a reminder of his commitment to his body. He had one of those trails that pointed down and disappeared under the low-slung fabric of his sweats. I licked my lips as I tried to pull my gaze away from the growing bulge at the apex of his legs.

I jerked my eyes back up to his to find him still smirking at me. "Did you watch me jerk my cock until I came all over myself?" he asked. I closed my eyes and clenched my thighs together as the vision assaulted my memory. He knew I was there the whole time and he'd wanted me to see.

"You want to know what I was thinking of?" he rasped. My eyes sprang open and I looked back at him. He was letting his gaze travel my body. He released my chin and let his finger graze my neck and further down. I kept my face up toward him as he lowered that finger toward my cleavage. The movement made me aware that I was still very much naked under the robe.

"I was thinking of all the ways I could make you come," he whispered as his hand dipped under the fabric of the robe. I gasped and arched into his touch as his fingers raked over my tightly pebbled nipple.

He leaned down toward me and I braced myself for a kiss that never came. I wanted him to kiss me so much. His fingers kept playing with me as he brought his lips closer to mine. *So close.*

"Were you going to come back here and touch yourself after you watched me?" he asked and I moaned as he pinched my nipple lightly before releasing me. I could feel so much arousal between my thighs now I was sure he could see it. When I didn't answer him he pinched me again only this time harder. I whimpered and inhaled sharply before he grazed his lips against mine.

"Answer me," he demanded.

"No, I-I…" I stammered as his fingers continued to tease their way down. He spread the robe open, exposing my breasts to his hungry eyes. "I've never…" I trailed off.

His fingers stopped moving altogether and I almost begged him to keep going. The thumping in my core was relentless in its need for him.

"You've never what? Come before?" he asked as

he pulled away to look at me. Taking his lips with him.

"I've never … done that," I admitted breathlessly. A hot flush washed over me as he furrowed his brows as though thinking of my words.

"You've never touched yourself?" he asked but it wasn't a question. I pulled away from him as embarrassment flooded me for the second time that night. Why had I just admitted that to him? I felt so stupid.

Before I could think to move any further away, he pounced. He quickly sat on the bed next to me, grabbed me around my waist, and scooted us further up the bed. The bottle of pills bouncing and rattling to the ground was nothing more than an afterthought as he leaned against the headboard and the pillows and pulled me between his legs, my back to his front. He wrapped his feet around my ankles and spread me wide.

I flushed as I felt the cool air of the room rush against my wet folds, sending new waves of awareness through me. I whimpered as his hands untied the knot of my robe and exposed all of me to him. I tried to cover myself again but he stopped me by grabbing both of my hands and holding them against my belly.

"Shhh, Bambi," he whispered in my ear and I stilled. My heart still racing, I tried to calm the labored puffs that rushed from my chest. "I'm going to teach you."

His words excited and scared me at the same time. Was he looking at my body and judging it the same way I did? Did he see the way my breasts sagged as I sat or the pooch at my belly as it lay exposed?

He groaned behind and that's when I felt his hard length press against my lower back. He was turned on from looking at me. The thought sent a wave of pride through me.

He cupped both of my hands in his and made me

touch the smooth skin on my belly. He led one hand up to my breasts and around my nipple. I groaned as he pinched my fingers together on the tender flesh.

"That's it, Bambi. Feel how your body reacts to your touch. Does that feel good?" His husky voice sent shivers down my spine. I didn't think I could speak without stammering so I simply nodded and licked my lips.

He slowly moved my other hand down over the swell of my belly toward my mound. I hummed with pleasure as my fingers met the wet flesh there. I began to tremble as he forced me lower.

"Relax, feel," he murmured. Even though I couldn't see his eyes from this position, I could feel his gaze as he watched what he was making me do.

He pushed my hand further down and spread my fingers with his. The movement spread me wider, exposing all of me now. My clit throbbed and a new rush of arousal leaked out of me. I was so turned on I felt like my body would burn up at any moment.

It wasn't as if I'd never touched myself before, I had. But I'd never done it this way. I'd only ever touched myself in a hygienic way, never a sexual one. And if I was being honest, I'd never even *wanted* to touch myself any other way. That was until now. Now I knew the way I was touching myself was going to lead to a new experience I wouldn't soon forget and I craved it more than I did my next breath.

My hand on my breast moved without him prompting me now. I pinched and plucked at myself as he mimicked the movements on my other nipple. I had hardly touched my pussy but I could feel something earth-shattering building now. My hips churned of their own volition before he moved me again.

I could feel him twitch against me as my fingers

grazed over my sensitive clit. I gasped and arched away from him as he made me rub myself in tight circles. He moved his hand at my breast up toward my neck before gripping me firmly. He turned me, forcing me to look up at him.

"Tell me how that pussy feels," he commanded as lust clouded his hooded gaze.

I moaned as the tightness in my core grew almost unbearable. He moved my hand further down, gathering wetness from my center and bringing my fingers up to circle the throbbing nerve once again.

"Wet," I said in a voice I didn't recognize. He grunted and rubbed himself against my back at my one proclamation. It was like he was getting just as much pleasure from watching me as he was getting earlier by himself.

"That's right, Bambi. That greedy cunt is sopping, begging for a cock. But all it's going to get is your little fingers tonight." His dirty words drove me higher.

My legs started to tremble as I moved my fingers faster. He wasn't even leading me anymore, it was like my body knew what it wanted and exactly how to get it. His hand moved out of the way and squeezed the inside of my thigh as I climbed that mountain I was sure I would fall off soon.

I stared at him as I writhed against him. His hand on my neck never let up as he watched me work myself into a tizzy.

"Yes, Lindsey. Feel that pussy tighten and release. Come against your hand, baby." As if his words were my undoing, everything crashed down around me. I clamped down on my breast and opened my mouth on a wail.

Ian groaned as I came and finally slammed his

mouth down onto mine. He didn't ask for permission and he wasn't gentle as he shoved his tongue into my mouth and drank down my cries of passion. My clit pulsed harshly against my fast-working fingers as he forced my legs to stay open with his hand and feet.

When the waves of my orgasm soothed and I sagged against him he released my lips. I let my hand fall to the side as aftershocks wracked my body.

Ian finally released my neck and moved his hands down my body once more. "You did so well, Little Bambi. I'm so proud of you," he praised as his hands raked down my breasts, plucking the still-tightened buds again. The movement sent new sparks of arousal to my still-throbbing core. I moaned as I leaned against him again, wanting more.

This time I didn't need a guide as my fingers delved through my folds again. I jerked as I circled my clit again. I started to hasten my movements when his hand stopped me. I groaned in frustration as he stilled me.

"So impatient," he murmured. "Not here," he whispered before lowering my hand. He used his finger to move mine around my entrance. I gasped at the sensation it left behind. "Here," he said. "Push that finger into your tight cunt for me."

The way he said it made me want to do anything for him. I would've burnt the world down for him at that moment. I leaned my head back and looked up at him again as I allowed him to lead my middle finger inside my tight channel. The feeling felt foreign but so, so good.

I licked my lips and stared up at him as I tentatively moved my finger in and out of me. My arousal made it easy for me to slide smoothly.

"Feel good?" he asked as his hand left mine. He snaked his fingers under my palm and circled my clit. I nodded my head as I urged myself to go faster. I was already building to another life-altering orgasm.

"Ian, please," I begged, for what I wasn't sure, it just felt right.

"No," he growled. "When we're like this you call me Sir. I like the way you say it." A surge of scorching lust rushed up my body at his command. *Why was that so hot?* "Curl your finger up and rub yourself in firm passes," he rasped.

I did as he asked and gasped as the new sensation overshadowed all the others. I pushed up harder and the pressure I felt in my pelvis was unreal. He rubbed my clitoris in gliding strokes as I fingered myself. I felt like a rubber band coiling too tightly and I was about to unravel.

"Fuck, yes," he hissed as I rubbed against his hand now. "Come, Lindsey," he commanded.

"Kiss me … Sir." I moaned as the first wave crashed over me. He wasted no time as he crashed his lips to mine again. He pinched my clit between his fingers and I screamed into his mouth as the orgasm intensified. I kept moving my fingers as rush after rush of arousal coated them, making everything slick and erotic. The wet sounds coming from me filled the room along with my harsh breathing.

Ian groaned against me as I felt something warm against my back. He had found his own release as I found mine and it was soaking through the robe. My muscles contracted and released erratically as I slowly came back down to earth.

When he pulled his hand away from me and took mine with it, I thought for a second I had done something wrong. That was until he released my mouth and brought my glistening fingers up to his lips. He closed his eyes and I watched him as he sucked my wet digits past his lips. I gasped as his tongue licked at me until my fingers were clean again. The look that crossed his face was pure bliss as he tasted me.

I'd never seen anything like it and second to watching him pleasure himself, it was one of the most erotic things I'd ever witnessed.

When he was done licking me clean, he gently pushed at my back urging me to sit. I did and he slipped from the bed. He walked to the bathroom and returned shortly with a warm wet washcloth. My eyes immediately went to the dark stain on his crotch. I bit my lip and blushed at the sight of it. He looked down at himself and chuckled.

"I got a little too excited watching you." He laughed. He pushed the robe off my shoulders and then pointed to the pillow, indicating he wanted me to lie down. I did just that and shivered as he grabbed the robe and threw it toward the door.

He watched my reaction as he spread my legs. It was still dim in the room but I knew he could still see everything. If the lust in his eyes was any indication, I would say he didn't mind what he was looking at.

He gently cleaned my sex as his eyes gobbled up the rest of my body. He had just come but that didn't stop the tent that suddenly appeared in front of his ruined pants. My fingers itched with the need to touch him but I refrained as he pulled away. He tossed the rag over with my robe before looking back down at my naked form.

"I would like to hold you," he said to me as a way of asking for permission.

I flushed and then scolded myself. As if him holding me would be the dirtiest thing that happened here tonight. I nodded up at him.

The smile that he gave me was worth all the embarrassment of the night. He wasted no time as he hooked his thumbs into the waist of his sweats and pulled the wet garment down, kicking them toward my robe.

His cock sprang free and I couldn't stop my stare. It bobbed between his legs, long and hard. He had a slight curve up toward his belly button. His thick shaft led up to the bulbous head that had a pearly liquid at the tip. I licked my lips as visions of tasting him came to my mind. *That was supposed to fit inside of me?*

As if he could read my mind, Ian's chuckle pulled me from my thoughts. "Not tonight, Bambi. We've had enough activity," he said as he climbed into the bed next to me. He pulled me to his front and covered us both up.

I had never laid in bed with a man, let alone a naked one, so I had no clue how I was supposed to sleep. But as I lay there feeling his hard body pressed against my back, I found my breath syncing up with his. He kissed my shoulder and then my neck as I settled into him. It wasn't long after that we both found oblivion.

Chapter Nine

"Are you having fun?" my mom's chipper voice sounded over the speaker of my phone from the nightstand as I made the bed. She'd called me shortly after I'd gotten dressed this morning. I tried not to flush at the memory of waking up naked.

I'd slept so well the night before, wrapped in a cocoon of warmth that was Dr. Ian Young. And I only panicked slightly when I woke up as the early morning light trickled in through the windows. My eyes immediately sprung open when I replayed the night's events in my mind as I woke up. I thought for sure that Anna would walk into my room at any moment and see her dad lying naked with me pressed against him. But to my surprise, it was almost as if he had never been there at all as I touched the now cold pillow.

I wasn't sure what time he had snuck back to his room but he'd taken our ruined garments with him. I'd whispered a small thanks to the universe for that. I wouldn't have known what to do with them other than to hide the evidence from snooping eyes.

I'd bounded out of bed and rushed to the door so fast it would make a track star jealous. Once I gripped the doorknob, I'd taken a soothing breath before cracking the door ever so slightly. I don't know what I expected when I looked out. If I thought he'd be waiting on me to peep my head out, I'd been sorely mistaken as I came face to face with a silent, empty hallway. I quickly closed the door and got dressed.

As I shook out the duvet I tried to shake away the feeling of rightness at falling asleep with him in my bed. What had happened last night was inappropriate, to say the least. Not only had I crossed a line regarding intimacy with someone I wasn't even dating, but I had done it with my friend's dad. I should feel guilty and gross about what I let happen here last night. I should feel the need to tell him it would never happen again.

So why did I only feel this warmth in my chest whenever I thought of it? Why did remembering the way he made me touch myself only get me hot all over again? Instead of having the urge to beg for Anna's forgiveness, all I wanted to do was beg Ian for more.

Was I sick for wanting him to teach me … *everything*? I wanted to learn what it felt like for a man to touch me in all the ways a man could touch a woman. I wanted him to show me how he liked to be touched too. I needed to know how to make him feel the same way he made me feel. I wanted our hands and mouths to explore each other until neither of us could stand it anymore. I just wanted *him*.

I shook my head as I flattened the blanket out and moved onto the pillows. I could tell myself until I was blue in the face that I wanted everything he offered. But at the end of the day, I was going to say no. I meant it when I said I wouldn't jeopardize my friendship with Anna.

I held the pillow Ian used last night in my hands. It was like I couldn't stop the compulsive urge as I brought the softness of it up to my face. I closed my eyes as I inhaled deeply. His smell of pine and the scent that was just *him* coursed through my nose and fogged my already lusty brain.

"Lindsey?" Mom said, causing me to jump back and drop the pillow.

What the fuck is wrong with me? I'd forgotten I was even on the phone, with my mother of all people, as I'd let thoughts of Ian invade my mind.

"Yeah, sorry … what did you say?" I said as I

picked the pillow up from the floor and tossed it on the bed, slapping it roughly in the process.

"I said, are you having fun?" She chuckled.

I picked up another pillow and gave it the same treatment. Letting some of my frustration flow out of me and into the feathers. "Oh, yeah. It's a regular ol' blast," I gritted behind clenched teeth. I huffed after finishing and plopped down on the side of the bed, staring at my phone.

My mom was speechless for a beat before finally breaking the silence. "You don't sound like it," she said, concern lacing her voice.

I pulled my hair into a haphazard bun on top of my head before flopping back onto the bed. "No, I mean it, I'm having a good time. It's just…" I trailed off as I stared at the ceiling fan whirling around and around, searching for the right words.

Restlessly, I sat up on my elbows and glanced at my phone again. My mom's pretty face lit up the screen along with the bright smiles of Heath and Reid beside her. She looked so happy in that picture. She *was* so happy. And I was being a miserable cow.

I always told my mom everything, so why was I stalling now? *Rip the bandage off, Lindsey.* I licked my lips before continuing. "Did you know that Dr. Young is Anna's dad?" I blurted before sitting up again. It was like I couldn't get comfortable until I got this shit off my chest.

The silence on the other end of the phone was almost deafening as I waited for my mom to reply. I held my breath until she finally spoke. "No, I didn't know that," she said and when I remained silent she continued. "Is that a problem?"

I huffed a humorless laugh as I picked at my sweater. "Yes," I said before glancing at her picture again. "Maybe," I mumbled and then rolled my eyes at myself. "I don't know!" I groaned.

Her chuckle across the line made me less than confident about her lack of knowledge about Ian. Why do mothers always seem to know the answers to questions before they even get asked? "You have feelings for him, don't you." It wasn't a question.

I swallowed hard before I nodded, then I remembered she couldn't see me so I said, "Yes." The urge to share everything with her was too much to bear. "Something … happened with him … last night," I admitted as I winced.

"Heath owes me twenty bucks," she muttered so quietly I almost missed it. My mouth dropped open and I scoffed around a laugh.

"Mom!" I accosted.

"Well, honey, what do you want me to say? You wear your thoughts and emotions right there on your face. All of us girls knew you had a thing for him. *Especially* after what happened at Jill's wedding." She laughed.

"I can't believe you guys bet on whether or not I would hook up with him." I laughed with her now. I was mortified but even I had to admit the whole thing was funny.

"Jill had one with Damon too." She giggled. "Emily and Leo were the only couple in complete agreement about it."

I shook my head in disbelief while her laughs quieted. As we sobered, guilt started to seep back in. When I was quiet she spoke again.

"So you're worried about what Anna will think?" she asked quietly.

"I don't want her to hate me." I sniffed as I bit back the rising emotion clogging my throat.

"Oh, honey, no. I know Anna, she's a good girl with a smart head on her shoulders. I think she would want you to be happy no matter who you decide to be with." Her soft voice soothed the rolling in my gut.

"You think?" I choked.

"Yes, I do. But I think you need to tell her before things get any more serious. It will be better for her to find out from you rather than someone else."

Visions of Melonie telling Anna what she witnessed last night assaulted me. How awful would it be to have her be the one to break the news to Anna? I shuddered at the thought.

A light knock sounded at my door and I glanced at it. I bet it was Anna, ready to start the day.

"Thanks, Mom," I said as I stood. "You always know how to talk me off the cliff."

"Hey, when you get back all of us girls need to get together. We haven't gotten to celebrate your birthday yet," she said in a rush as I grabbed the phone.

"All right, sounds good, love you." I chuckled as I walked toward the door.

"Love you too, be safe," she said.

I ended the call and shoved the phone into my pocket. I smiled as I grabbed the doorknob and twisted. Talking with my mom always helped me put things into perspective. She was usually right after all, I did need to talk to Anna before anything else happened with Ian. Even if I decided not to explore anything with him, I still needed to be honest with her before shit hit the fan.

Fully expecting Anna to be on the other side of the door, I smiled and shimmied as I swung it open. "All right, I'm ready for all of these activities you have planned for the day," I spoke loudly with enthusiasm.

Except, when I opened the door to reveal Anna's vibrant blue hair, I was met with vibrant blue eyes instead. I sucked in and took a quick step back as Ian crowded my doorway. He stood with one hand holding onto the doorframe and the other clutching my robe from last night. I licked my lips as I drank in the sight of him.

He wore a pair of faded blue jeans that fit him as if they were made for him. The thin denim hugged his powerful thighs and left little to the imagination along his impressive bulge. Flashbacks of his thick naked cock jutting my way assailed my memory. I swallowed to bring moisture back to my mouth as I moved my gaze upward.

The way he stretched his arm out to hold the doorframe lifted his dark grey t-shirt just the slightest bit. I could see a hint of golden taut skin peeking out underneath the fabric. I had yet to feel that soft-looking skin with my hands and my fingers itched with the need to see if it was as smooth as it looked.

My eyes traveled up past his broad chest to the biceps that looked barely restrained by his shirt. Up and up I went. To his sensual lips surrounded by that soft facial hair that tickled my lips as we kissed. He smirked at me as my lips tingled with the memory. His expressive eyes were filled with the same need I felt thrumming through my body as he looked me up and down like a hungry wolf. His hair was wet and unkempt as it dangled freely atop his forehead. The thought of him in the shower this morning made my girl parts perk up and take notice.

"Did I scare you, Bambi?" he asked as he released the doorframe and stepped into my room. He didn't bother shutting the door behind him.

I don't know how I managed not to step back away from him, but I didn't move. I stood my ground as he stalked me. I could feel arousal wet my panties as he came closer and I was able to smell the soap he scrubbed himself with. Visions of his wet soapy hands rubbing himself in the steamy shower flashed in my mind before I was able to recall them.

"No." I shook my head as he stepped into my space. I craned my neck to look up at him. *God, he was beautiful.*

He grinned down at me as if he didn't believe me. I couldn't blame him. With the way my heart thundered in my chest, I would be surprised if he couldn't hear it. "Good," he murmured as he dipped his head toward me.

I sucked in a sharp breath as he inched closer. His soft lips grazed mine and I melted into him. He sealed his lips to mine with a tender kiss as his fingers gripped my chin. He ate at my lips with smooth kisses that I felt reverberating through my body. He licked at the seam of my lips and I moaned before opening for him.

His tongue swept in and danced with mine. I could taste his minty toothpaste as if he prepared for this moment. As if he prepared himself just for me. He wasn't my first kiss but damn if I didn't wish he were. When he kissed me like this it made me feel like I was the sexiest woman in the world. He made me feel like ... *his*.

"Good morning," he whispered as he pulled away from me with a grin on his lips. If I didn't know any better, I'd say he enjoyed my inexperienced kiss just as much as I did his.

"Morning." I blushed and looked down.

He released me but didn't step away. He simply held my robe out for me and I grabbed it, my flush deepening when I remembered why he'd taken it. It smelled clean and was still warm from the dryer.

"I need to see you tonight," he murmured before he pushed some hair that escaped my bun behind my ear. I tried not to get hung up on the fact that he said *need* instead of *want*.

Even though I wanted nothing more than to be with him later this evening, I still shook my head. "I don't know if that's a good idea. Anna—"

"Will understand. I know you think it's a big deal that you have the hots for your friend's dad," he said and I felt my face redden further. He chuckled before gripping my chin again and forcing me to look him in the eyes. "But I know Anna. She isn't going to care as long as everything is consensual between us," he said as he searched my eyes.

When I said nothing, he released me and stepped away. "I can tell her if you wa—"

"No!" I spouted a little too loudly as I grabbed his biceps and pulled him back toward me. His smile told me that was the reaction he was hoping for. "I'll tell her," I whispered.

"Good," he muttered as he brought his lips down to mine. He stopped just before he reached them. "It may seem fast but I want you, Lindsey. Mind, body, and soul, I can't think of anything else and it's maddening. I just want you. I need to taste you. I need to worship this gorgeous body. And I need to fuck you, Bambi."

I gasped at his words as he crashed his lips to mine. He groaned against me as I opened under him. He plundered my mouth as his hands roamed my curves, stopping at my ass and pulling me into him. He ground his hardness against me and I moaned in response. I wanted everything he needed but couldn't help my reservations.

What if I wasn't good at sex? What if I couldn't live up to his expectations? Did he even know I was a virgin? Would that turn him off? All these questions clouded my mind as he kissed me.

When he pulled away I was left dazed and

throbbing. As his warmth left me I wanted nothing more than to pull it back.

"Tonight," he said as he backed away toward the door. He never took his eyes off me as I nodded and he disappeared into the hall.

As if his leaving filled the room with air again, I sucked in a large breath and held it. I bent at the waist as I released with a giggle. My cheeks warmed as I smiled broadly. It was silly how happy I felt at that moment.

"You about ready to go?" Anna's chipper voice sounded and I stood upright in a rush. She gave me a curious look as she smiled at me. "You good?"

I puffed a laugh before answering. "Yeah, just give me a few," I said in a rush.

She looked at me curiously before nodding and leaving the room. The giddy feeling vanished as dread took its place. I was in quite a dilemma. I wanted everything and more Ian offered but I didn't know how I was going to tell Anna. Would she accept our relationship or would she hate me? Nervousness flooded me as I feared fucking this up.

Chapter Ten

"Fuck," I cursed softly as I slipped into the scalding bath. Anna was trying to kill me. That's what I'd decided the moment she signed us up for snow biking at the ski resort. *Who in the world had invented such a tortuous activity like snow biking?*

As if skiing hadn't been hard enough, someone had gone and made it all the harder by throwing you a bike and saying, "Here, go down this frozen winding path on two wheels in the slippery snow."

Anna's planned day started with a quick run into town where we ate breakfast in a cute little cafe. At least, *I* thought it was cute. Melonie had complained almost the entire time we were there as they didn't have a low-calorie menu. I had no such quarrels as I ordered the greasiest thing I could. After the activity I had the night before, I was in need of replenishing some of my lost calories. I hadn't even cared as Barbie flashed me a look of disgust when my food arrived.

Being trapped with my worst enemy was proving to be a good thing. The longer I sat and listened to her bemoan everything around her, the more I learned to tune her out. Anna on the other hand was starting to get annoyed with her. I would call this vacation with Melonie a win if Anna finally figured out she wasn't a nice person by the end.

We'd driven back to the resort after breakfast, taking the slow route through town so we could get a feel for all the shops that littered the main street. I spotted a cute little thrift bookstore on the way out of town and made a mental note to visit it before we flew out at the end of the week. You never knew what you could find in those types of bookstores.

Anna had then driven us all to the resort and promptly signed us up for the classes. I feigned a smile and told her I loved the idea. The look of pure joy she'd given me was worth the small fib. But now as I soaked my weary muscles in the Epsom salt bath, I wasn't so sure anymore.

We'd been forced to sit through a dull presentation on how the bikes were not only made to withstand such frigid temps but also how to not kill ourselves on one. A feat I had almost accomplished more than once. When I said I was less than athletically inclined, that's exactly what I meant.

The young girl who was no older than me who taught our class had to have been shocked by the sheer number of times I'd fallen off my stupid bike. No sooner would I get some speed and I would go careening off the path and wind up in a bush. I would be picking pine needles out of my hair for weeks, I was sure of it.

Needless to say, once the excursion was complete, I was thrilled to park my happy ass in front of the fireplace in the lodge while the others went skiing. Anna must have known I was at my fill for the day as she didn't even try to persuade me into going up the mountain with them. That's what I loved about that girl. We were complete opposites but she knew when to back off and let me have a timeout, and I knew when to step back and allow her to be her outgoing self without me dragging her down. Our friendship was easy because of that. And yet, here I was thinking I would ruin all of it.

Between the class today, her exploring the mountain, and not being away from Melonie or Ben, I hadn't gotten the chance to talk with her at all. I thought I would get a chance to speak with her when we got back to the cabin late this evening, but that proved wrong. We had all been so exhausted by the day's activities that when we came through the doors, everyone had gone straight to their rooms.

I plopped the dry washrag into the hot water with a sigh before ringing it out. I was getting ready to place it over my eyes when I saw movement out of the corner of my vision. I moved quickly to look out the huge window next to the tub where the movement had come from. It was a fleeting little movement but still it made me leery of all the things that lurked outside.

I searched the darkened tree line, looking for any sign of life and seeing none. Gooseflesh raced across my body as an intrusive thought of someone watching me bounced around in my mind. I swallowed thickly as I tried to calm my frazzled nerves.

I was being ridiculous. We were literally in the middle of nowhere and I was worried about someone watching me? I shook myself to rid the thought as I moved the washrag to my eyes. I leaned back against the cool porcelain of the tub and tried to relax. The bath was helping with my sore body but not in quieting my racing thoughts. Nobody was watching me, it was probably a deer or something.

Forgetting about sneaky woodland creatures, I contemplated what I would say to Anna. Even if I was still working out all the things I needed to say in my head, she deserved to know that something was up with me and her dad. I was beyond terrified that I was making a huge mistake either way I went. Either I tell Anna how I feel about Ian and she ends up hating me. Or I tell Ian I can't do this and I end up hating myself. Either way, I felt as though I was fucked.

I sighed again as I sank further into the water. Allowing the bubbles that floated on top to tickle my bottom lip. I could feel myself becoming increasingly sedated the longer I sat there. I would need to get out soon before I fell asleep again. I was so tired I half feared I would drown this time.

"You look like my wet dream come true, Bambi."

Ian's voice jolted me out of my thoughts as I squealed and moved to cover myself. I ripped the rag away from my eyes as I sat up to face the bulking man that filled the doorway. It was as if seeing him made me remember I was completely naked and he could see everything. I covered my breasts with my arms and sank down into the water in an attempt to hide under the bubbles. To my horror, most of the frothy water had sadly disappeared, leaving little to no coverage for my naked form.

"What are you doing in here!" I screeched toward him. I flushed when his eyes darkened as his gaze blazed a trail from my face all the way down my body. I sucked in a sharp breath as his scorching stare met my pussy. I quickly moved one of my hands to cover myself. The only problem with that was that my breasts were so big I couldn't cover both of them with one arm. Either way I moved, he would see me.

"Don't you remember our conversation this morning?" he asked. When I said nothing he pushed away from the doorframe and stalked closer to me. I sank further into the water until my nose was barely above the waterline. I could feel heat rising off my chest the closer he stepped. There was no way he wasn't seeing absolutely everything. All my cellulite, my stretch marks.

"We agreed to see each other tonight," he finally said as he stepped up to the tub.

I raised my lips out of the water far enough to speak. "I didn't get to talk to Anna yet," I exhaled in a rush before sinking back down.

Ian chuckled at me before squatting to my level. I tried not to shrink away from the lust he carried in his gaze as he reached for me. His hand dipped into the water before gripping my chin and pulling it up.

"Well, you can try again tomorrow. But that's not going to stop me from being with you tonight, Little Bambi," he muttered as his thumb grazed my bottom lip. I shuddered at not only the feeling of his touch but his nickname for me. The irony of it wasn't lost on me, he could clearly see I was anything but *little*.

I watched his lips as he leaned over the water at the same time as pulling me toward him. When his lips sealed to mine a whimper left my throat. I released the hold I had on myself as I raised my hands. Boldness I'd never felt before overtook me as I reached up and threaded my wet fingers into his hair. His groan of appreciation reverberated straight to my sex as he dipped his tongue inside.

I followed his lips as he pulled away from me. My upper torso now coming out of the water. He stood to his full height in front of me and I couldn't seem to stop my gaze from traveling lower. His jean-clad bulge was right at my eye level. I barely resisted the urge to touch him as the coolness of the room registered in my mind.

I sucked in another sharp breath as I realized he could still see everything. I started to cover myself again when he grabbed my hand. "Come." The way he said it made it sound more like a promise than a command.

I bit my lip as I sat still. I remembered just how big he was compared to me as he towered over me. "I can't stand until you leave," I breathed.

He furrowed his brows down at me and didn't budge. "Now, why would I leave?" he asked.

I blushed further as I looked away. I would rather fall and bust my head open in a room full of people again than sit here and explain to this man that I didn't want him to see me naked with the lights on. Unfortunately, he seemed to be rooted in place and he wouldn't be moved without an excuse.

"I don't want you to see me like this," I murmured under my breath.

His chuckle did nothing to ease my self-consciousness. "I've already seen you naked, Lindsey."

I shook my head and kept my gaze diverted. "That was in the dark," I whispered and cringed. If I didn't say it now, I would never get it out. "What if … what if you don't like me with the lights on?"

The stillness that overtook Ian's body at that moment was enough to petrify me. Had I done it? Had I completely ruined the way he looked at me with my self-consciousness? I slunk into myself at the thought. He was probably used to women who looked and felt confident in their own skin. Now was going to be the moment he decided I wasn't worth his effort.

When the silence dredged on I tried to pull my hand away from him only for him not to relinquish it.

"Look at me, Bambi." His voice deepened with what sounded like anger. I shook my head, I couldn't look up at him just to realize that I ruined everything. "Now," he spoke again when I didn't move.

A shiver snaked down my spine at his harsh command. I didn't know how I found the courage, but I looked up at him then.

His brows were still furrowed like he was looking at the most frustrating thing he'd ever seen. *Was he angry with me?* He moved my hand and I sucked in a fast breath and held it as he placed it on his erection. I could feel how hard and long he was through the fabric of his jeans. My mouth watered as my gaze bounced between my hand and his eyes.

"Does it feel like I don't like what I see?" he asked as he pushed himself into my palm. I swallowed hard as I shook my head. "Every time I look at you I'm painfully hard, Lindsey. Your body is everything and more than I could hope for." His eyes darkened further as my hand twitched against him.

"I can't help but think that I'm not good enough for you," I blurted before I lost the will. "A guy like you can have any woman he wants. You could have someone thinner, prettier. You could have—"

My next words were cut off as Ian bent down and pulled me from the bathtub. Water sloshed over the lip and covered the floor as he sat me on my feet. Before I had time to cover myself he turned me around to face away from him. He gripped both of my wrists and pulled them behind my back, trapping them with one big hand. I could feel the water dripping off my body and soaking his shirt and jeans but he acted as though he didn't care.

"I'm just going to have to teach you how to love your body like I had to teach you how to come, Bambi," he whispered in my ear before moving us. The way he moved my body to his whim should have frightened me. How he spoke harshly and demanded I listen to him would scare most inexperienced women. But for some reason when he talked like this and touched me like he was, it only turned me on.

He turned us around and with his free hand grabbed my throat, turning me to face the huge mirror over the vanity. I felt a deep flush overtake my body but not from embarrassment, from arousal. Wetness gathered between my thighs and it wasn't from the bath. My chest heaved as I stared at the vision we made in the mirror.

His shirt was just as soaked as I was. His eyes were dark with pure lust as his stare gobbled me up in the mirror. The sight of his hand around my throat unleashed an unfamiliar primal feeling deep inside of me. My pussy throbbed and my nipples tightened painfully as arousal coursed through my body.

He turned his face toward me and grazed his teeth against my cheek as he spoke. "What do you see when you look in that mirror?" he said, never taking his eyes off me.

I whimpered as his hand moved down toward my breasts. I clenched my hands together at my back as anticipation rose within me. "I see myself ... naked."

His fingers circled my left nipple before moving on to the right. He was teasing, never fully touching me the way I wanted. "How do you look, Bambi?" he asked.

I squealed as he pinched his fingers around the dusty-rose peak. Pain bloomed across my breast before a deep heat sank into me. Zapping the feeling right to my core. A new wave of arousal dripped from my pussy. My brain was so fuzzy with my need for him that I could hardly think of anything else besides the way his hands felt on me.

He tweaked my other nipple to get my attention and I bit back my scream. "Answer me," he gritted against my cheek.

I whimpered as I really looked at myself. For the first time in my life, I wasn't seeing the frumpy little girl I'd always seen. My face was flush and my eyes were so dark I almost didn't recognize them. I was seeing a full-grown woman as I stared at myself. From my full breasts down to my curvy waist. My needy pussy to my voluptuous thighs. This was a woman's body with a woman's needs. With a beast of a man behind her, willing to give her everything she needed and more.

When I didn't answer right away Ian pinched me again, harder this time. "I see desire!" I whined as I jerked against him. I wasn't trying to get away at this point, I was begging for more. "I see a needy, sexy woman who wants you to touch her in all the ways a person can touch another person." I panted.

His smile was feral as his hand holding my wrists released me. "That's my good girl," he said as his arm wrapped around my waist. Pride at his praise covered me like a thick blanket as his hand moved lower. "Hold onto my waistband," he ordered.

I moved my hands as quickly as I could to do his bidding. I shoved my fingers past his waistband and was met with the course, trimmed hair at his groin. I could feel the root of his cock twitch at my touch as I gripped the denim. "Don't move them," he rasped.

It was hard to breathe as his hands danced against my skin. Gliding from my breasts down further, smoothing over the soft swell of my belly. "You want to know what I see when I look at this body?" he asked and I nodded enthusiastically.

He chuckled as his hand dipped lower. His other fingers continued to pinch and play with my sensitive nipples as he turned his face toward the mirror. All his focus was now on what his fingers were doing to me.

"I see the temptress who looked at me on the mountain like she was going to eat me up. When you were on your back looking up at me like I was your salvation," he said as his fingers slid easily through my folds. I sucked in a sharp breath as he nudged my ankles with light kicks, commanding silently that I spread for him, giving him greater access. He chuckled again at my wantonness as I spread as wide as my position allowed. I didn't even flush that time, I wanted this too much.

"I imagined that's the look you would give me while you're sucking my cock, Bambi," he groaned as he circled my throbbing clit. I gasped not only at his touch but his words too. I'd never wanted to give anyone a blowjob before but I craved it with him.

His fingers worked faster and faster as he rubbed

me. I was winding up so tight, I felt as though I would snap in half soon. "Please, Ian," I whined as my hips undulated themselves and moved of their own accord.

His fingers at my breast tweaked my nipple hard and I squealed at the sharp sting. It felt as though my nipple was on fire before it morphed into something else entirely, something I feared I would come to crave.

"What did I ask you to call me when I'm touching this pussy?" he gritted into my ear. I flushed as I thought of saying it again. I'd felt a way I'd never felt before when I said it the first time. It made me hot all over to think about saying it again.

I must've taken too long to answer because before I could comprehend what was happening Ian moved his hand and gave my breast a sharp slap. I moaned as the sensation sank into my bones.

"Sir!" I screeched. I felt his hardness twitch as if my words had caused him to tighten behind me.

"That's right, I'm your Sir and you're my dirty little slut," he groaned before he tweaked my nipple again, this time not as hard but still enough to light me up.

He thrust himself against my backside as he added another finger. I gripped his waistband so tightly that the button popped open, loosening the tight denim. I held firm as the fabric slipped past his waist. He groaned as the back of my fingers grazed against his thick length. The urge to grip him was almost too much to ignore.

"When you look at me like that, it makes me want to strip you bare and bury myself so deep inside of you I can't tell where I start and you end," he growled as his finger dipped down further, circling my entrance. "Fuck, you're so ready for me, Bambi." His tightly held control was slipping as he rimmed my opening.

I opened my mouth with a cry as he smoothly slid

one big finger inside of me. His other hand traveled up my throat again toward my mouth. I whimpered as he clamped his hand over me, smothering my cries to come.

He dipped his finger in and out before smoothly adding another. My body shook uncontrollably as my orgasm rose. *So close.*

"You're so tight, you're going to strangle my cock when I take this little cunt. Do you want to come?" he whispered against me as his pace quickened. I nodded my head as best as I could with his hand over my mouth. I pushed my hands down, taking his jeans with them. I felt his cock spring loose and slap heavily against my lower back. My eyes flared as I felt its sheer weight against me.

He groaned and pushed himself against me as he ground his palm against my clit and curled his fingers. I threw my head back against him as I screamed my release. My hips moved with his hand as I rode out my orgasm. "Fuck, yes, Lindsey. Come for me," he ordered as if I had a choice. His hand over my mouth held me firmly as I fucked his hand, my arousal coating his thick fingers.

I slumped against him as I came back to earth. My body was languid as he continued to rub me through the aftershocks. "You did so well, Little Bambi," he praised. Pride flooded me at his words.

When I could pick my head back up, I felt his cock twitch at my back. I licked my lips as I stared at him in the mirror. I wanted to make him feel exactly like he made me feel.

With shaky hands, I released his waistband and gently gripped him. He hissed and pushed into my hand at the contact. I watched his eyes as he pulled away to look down at what I was doing to him. Emboldened by the need that was reflected in his eyes, I turned to face him, never releasing him as I did.

He didn't move and simply let me explore. I glanced down and finally got my first real look at him. He was rock hard but covered in velvety soft skin. His length was covered in thick veins that looked almost painfully full. He curved up toward his belly and was so long he almost touched his belly button. My mouth watered as I saw the drop of pearly liquid weeping from his bulbous head.

I swiped my finger against the substance there and rubbed it around the tip. He groaned as I toyed with him. I gripped him timidly at first as I slid my fist from his tip all the way to the root.

"Fuck," he cursed as I tightened my grip. He crowded me and herded me back until my ass hit the cool quartz of the vanity. He leaned forward and gripped the sides of the lip of the counter with white-knuckle force.

He crashed his lips to mine as I smoothly slid my tightened hand up and down his hard length. He shoved his tongue into my mouth and tasted me. I became increasingly curious as I stroked him. I wanted to know exactly what made him go crazy.

I lowered my other hand to the base of his cock and he pulled away from me with a hiss. I almost thought it was a painful sound until I saw the utter euphoria cross his features. My lips twitched with a grin as feminine power thrummed through my blood. I was going to make him crumble in my arms this time.

I slid my left hand down his length and followed it with my right. He shuddered and jerked in my hand. Not that I had much experience in knowing what a man looked like when he had an orgasm but I had a feeling he was getting close. I gripped his base and held my hand firm against him as my right hand picked up the pace at the tip.

His mouth dropped open as he watched what I was doing to him. When he looked back up at me I could physically see when his thin thread of control finally snapped. He crowded me and gripped my ass, pulling me up and sitting me on the vanity. He made a place for himself between my thighs.

I continued to stroke him fast as he gripped my thighs so hard I was sure to have bruises by morning. "You feel so good, Bambi. You're going to make me come," he growled as he thrust into my hands.

I was still riding high with my newfound power as I leaned forward and kissed his neck. I licked and nibbled my way up toward his strong jaw. The way his facial hair tickled my lips would forever be ingrained in my memory. He was so close to me now that I could feel the head of his cock bump against my clit with each pull of my hand. The feeling of his smooth hardness rubbing made me throb all over again.

I thought it would be impossible to have another orgasm so close to the last core-rocking one I'd just had. That was proving to be very wrong as I climbed that hill once again. I knew this time I was going to fall off so fast I might lose my sanity.

My closed fist and his cock knocked against me in a steady rhythm that kept me wound tight. I wanted to come so badly but I needed him with me. I kissed my way toward his ear and he shivered as I did. When I reached his ear, I pulled away just enough to whisper, "Come for me."

As if he were waiting for me to voice it, he exploded. I felt his long-tortured groan in my own body as he thrust forward and rubbed his release onto my pussy. I moaned with him as he fucked my hand. I watched as hot jet after hot jet of cum drenched me.

His last shred of control snapped as he pushed his

hand down to my pussy and circled my clit quickly. He rubbed his release around and around as if he was marking me as his. "You too," he groaned before he pinched my clit and I went flying. I threw my head back and he caught me before I smacked the mirror. He kissed me and drank down my cries of pleasure.

When the waves of ecstasy subsided we both stared at one another. Neither of us spoke as we caught our breath. Words were no longer necessary as something fundamental seemed to settle between us.

Chapter Eleven

What the fuck are you doing, Lindsey? My internal voice kept asking me the same question over and over again as I studied the sleeping figure next to me. Early morning light sparkled through the windows and danced on the bed around us. I'd been awake long enough to hear the birds wake with the morning sun. All of them were eager to start their day. If only I was as overexuberant as they were.

After my impromptu lesson on body positivity last night in the bathroom, Ian used my washrag from the bath to clean us up. First me, with gentle caresses one would expect of a lover. Then he cleaned himself in fast hurried motions as if he didn't want to waste one more second not touching me.

He'd then carried me to my bed, something I would have to get used to. You could drill the idea of someone being the epitome of attraction into their head, but unless they truly felt it then it all meant nothing. One night of looking at myself through his eyes wasn't going to wipe away years of self-doubt.

Not to say what he showed me last night hadn't helped me see myself in a different light, it definitely did that. I have never in my life felt sexy before last night. What he forced me to see in that mirror would forever be ingrained in my memory. I would always remember the time I felt like the most desirable woman in the world.

I couldn't even say that some of what happened last night wasn't still lingering this morning. A kernel of brazenness still smoldered low in my belly. It was silly really, but unmanning him the way I had, boosted my self-confidence enough that I was having a hard time not wanting to see if I could do it again. My inner voice practically screamed at me to make him lose his mind as he did to me. It wouldn't be hard to accomplish since the object of my desire was still next to me and very much naked.

I'd lain here for countless hours watching the very reason I didn't want to leave this bed. Ian looked so peaceful as he slept soundly next to me. Now that the moon's light was replaced by the rising dawn, I could clearly make out each one of his striking features. I had to admit, for a man twice my age, you wouldn't be able to tell just by looking at him.

He laid on his back with his arm over his head as if inviting me to lay on his chest. The sheet was slung low on his pelvis, exposing that smooth golden skin. The sight of his chest and abdomen made me want to run my fingers along the tightly corded muscles that lay there. I wanted to trace every curve and divot. I craved to find out how he liked to be touched in every single way. To see what turned him on.

I inched closer with the urge to touch him. Clutching the sheet to my chest, I curled my arm under my head so I could watch him. I released my sheet before clenching and releasing my hand in self-doubt. *Was this weird? Was I weird for wanting to explore him while he slept?* My gaze shot back to his face where I saw no sign of him waking. His steady breaths were a solid indication that he was still out for the count. *Maybe a little touch wouldn't hurt.*

My hand shook as I reached out for him. When my fingers grazed the warm skin on his side and he didn't move I released a slow breath. I flattened my hand against his ribs before moving it further onto his chest. His soft speckling of chest hair only added to the exquisite feeling of him.

I slowly propped myself up so my elbow held my

weight and I leaned against my arm. I needed to see everything I was doing. I allowed the sheet at my chest to slip down, the soft fabric raked against my tightening peaks. I almost scoffed at myself. I'd barely touched him and I was getting turned on just by the sight.

I delicately moved my fingers up until I reached his nipple, licking my lips before I slowly circled the dusty-pink ringlet. It puckered almost immediately and I smiled to myself before moving to the other. I repeated the same motion and was rewarded when it did the same. But when I moved to do it again, he moved his head.

I held perfectly still as he readjusted himself. He didn't open his eyes and continued his steady breathing while I held mine. My heart thudded rapidly in my chest at the thought of getting caught. *What would he do if he caught me exploring?* I clenched my thighs together at the thought.

I bit my lip and watched his face as I lowered my hand. He made no move to open his eyes as my fingers traced along the ridges of his abdomen. I almost closed my eyes as if my fingers would have a better chance at remembering the feel of him without my other senses hindering them.

I slowly maneuvered my hips so I could get a little closer without waking him. The move made me painstakingly aware of how aroused I was. The inside of my thighs were wet as I had no panties on to catch any of my arousal. I squeezed them together again and closed my eyes as pleasure from the pressure washed over me.

My hand kept its southbound route until I reached his belly button. Just like with his nipple, I rimmed around it with a barely-there touch.

The deep grumble that came from his chest had my eyes springing back open. My adrenaline spiked as I looked back at his face while keeping my hand firmly on his belly. I was surprised to see his eyes still closed but his brows were furrowed. I grinned at the thought of him being frustrated in his sleep. When I pulled my gaze from his face and traveled lower, I realized the reason why.

He was hard. By the looks of it, painfully so. His cock laid heavily against his lower belly, barely poking out of the sheet. My hand was less than a breath away and my fingers itched to explore that part of him next. I circled his belly button one more time as I watched his cock. He made no more noises but I was entranced by the way his length twitched, begging for more.

I swallowed thickly as I moved my hand lower. My fingers brushed over his bulbous head and he twitched again. His heavy length lifted before falling against his belly. I opened my mouth as a breath shuddered out of me before I gently gripped my hand around him. My gaze bounced back and forth between his face and his cock in my hand. His breathing accelerated slightly but his eyes remained closed.

I slid my hand down his hard length and reveled in the way his lower belly clenched as if it had no choice but to react to my touch. I bit back a moan of delight as hot need zinged to my pussy, further dampening my inner thighs. I slowly raised my hand back toward the tip before plunging again. He felt impossibly hard but incredibly soft at the same time. His tautly stretched skin was like velvet against my palm.

I surprised myself by not jerking away from him as his mouth dropped open and a deep groan released from his chest. He was close to waking but not quite there yet. I didn't want to stop, and I wasn't going to. Even if he awoke. I was feeling way too powerful as I brought him the pleasure he didn't have to ask for.

I smiled to myself when I glanced down and noticed a pearly liquid collecting at the tip of his cock.

My mouth watered as I moved down the bed, letting the sheet completely fall away. I never released him as I came face to face with the monster between his legs. I'd never given a man a blowjob and never wanted to, until now.

I moved until I was on my knees between his legs, trying to be as stealthy as I could. His legs moved restlessly as I maneuvered myself, keeping one hand wrapped around him. Maybe it was the pleasure of my touch or just the simple fact that I had moved from my spot, whatever it was woke him from his sleep and we made eye contact.

His eyes darkened and his nostrils flared as recognition clouded his features. His gaze flickered between my hand wrapped around him and my eyes. I could see every muscle in his abdomen and chest flex and release as if he was barely restraining himself from moving. I smirked slightly as his arm above his head started to lower my way.

Without thinking any further, I gripped him tighter, leaned forward, and swiped my tongue against the head of his cock. Lapping up the liquid that wept from the tip.

"Fuck!" he growled. He arched his back and gripped the sheets at his sides, barring the white of his knuckles.

I sucked in a sharp breath and moved away from him quickly. I'd never done anything like this before so I thought maybe I hurt him. I pushed away from him and released my grip as my heart thundered like a racehorse running down the track. I felt a deep flush settle on my chest as he sat up on his elbows and stared at me. *What the fuck am I doing?*

"I'm sorry, I didn't mean … I mean if I hurt you…" I stammered. I leaned away when he stopped me by grazing his thumb along my plump lower lip.

"Why are you sorry?" He looked down at me.

I heated further as I locked gazes with him. "I, ah … I've never done this before," I admitted. He arched an eyebrow and I sputtered. I knew what he was waiting for. "I've never done this before, Sir." I quivered under his intense stare. His eyes flared as he gripped his length. Fresh arousal flooded me as I tried to keep my eyes on his as he rubbed himself.

"You've never sucked a cock, Bambi?" he asked. At the shake of my head, he sat up and grazed his lips along mine. My breath left me in a rush as he spoke against me. "It felt good, Lindsey. You just surprised me. Of all the things I thought I would wake up to, your sweet mouth wrapped around my cock is the hottest of them all. I want you to taste me. I want to shove past your lips so much that you have no choice but to swallow me down and take everything I give you."

My eyes glazed over at his words. The way he spoke to me made me feel things I'd only ever read about.

"But since you've never done this before, I'm going to let you explore," he whispered before kissing me softly and leaning back on his arms again.

I licked my lips as I stared from him to his cock and back again. Timidly, I gripped him and leaned forward. I never broke eye contact as I flicked my tongue out once more. The moment I tasted him, he hissed and twitched against me. I savored his unique flavor as it washed across my tongue.

I scooted forward and kissed the head before pulling him just barely past my lips. His groan of appreciation urged me on and I sucked him further into my mouth. I swirled my tongue around his head before pulling away and diving back for more.

I pulled him further in with each swipe, feeling bolder with each pass. His scent surrounded me and put me in a headspace that was hard to describe. It was as if I was floating above us. I watched myself suck at him like he was the best treat I'd ever had. The woman sucking this delicious man's cock was a woman that held all the confidence in the world. She was the woman I craved to be.

His groan was deep as he threaded his fingers through my hair, lightly tugging and lighting up my scalp. His mouth dropped open as he watched me. Emboldened by his reaction, I sucked him harder.

"Oh, fuck, you suck me so good, Lindsey," he growled and I tried not to smile at his praise. I pulled him deeper and he almost knocked the back of my throat. My mouth was stretched to its limit but I wanted more. I settled in and stared down at what I was doing.

"Use your hand and cup my balls," he coached and I listened. His hand slid into my hair and tightened. The movement caused me to moan around him, and in turn, his lower stomach clenched as if he could feel the sound. I used my other hand to grip his thick base and worked in tandem to reach what my mouth couldn't. He said he would let me explore, but the way he was gripping a fistful of my hair told me he was having a hard time letting go of his control.

I hummed around him as I sucked harder. As much as this was turning him on, it was doing the same to me tenfold. I was sure it would only take one touch to my throbbing clit to get me off at this point.

"Yes," he hissed as he guided me further onto his cock. I gagged slightly before relaxing my throat. Tears pricked my eyes but I would be damned if I was going to stop. "Look at me, Bambi," he grunted.

As if I had no choice in the matter, I obeyed. My

eyes flicked to his and the look of pure euphoria on his face was enough to make me want more.

"I'm going to come," he panted. I continued to slide my mouth along his shaft before swirling my tongue around and starting again. "You're going to take it all, aren't you?" he asked.

I could tell it wasn't really a question but I nodded anyway as I kept bobbing up and down. I hummed against him as I rolled his balls in my hand.

"Fuck, yes!" he groaned as I felt the first hot jet of his release hit the back of my throat. I swallowed greedily as more followed. His release was salty and sweet at the same time. I feared I would forever crave him like this as he washed over my tongue. If not the taste of him, then the way it made me feel watching him crumble for me. I kept eye contact with him as he told me to while I sucked like my life depended on it. "You like that cum, don't you? Suck it all down like a good girl," he growled as he thrust into my mouth.

I took a deep breath and pulled him as far back as I could as he continued to come. He knocked the back of my throat once again and I swallowed around him, savoring his unique essence.

Before I had a chance to lick him clean, he sat up and pulled me away from him by my hair. It shocked me when it didn't hurt but rather lit me on fire. I was throbbing and achy in all the right places.

He leaned forward and sealed his lips to mine. If he cared that he had just come in my mouth, he showed no signs as he shoved his tongue past my lips. He moved us until I was under him and I could feel his semi-hard erection land heavily against my inner thigh.

"You sure you've never sucked a cock before?" he murmured against my lips. I whimpered in response, words completely evading me as pure carnal lust focused on his hard length so close to where I craved it. "Because you sucked me like a dirty little slut. Is that what you are? My dirty little slut?" he teased.

I bit back a smile at his dirty talk. *If he only knew how far I was away from being a slut.* In the back of my mind, I knew the logical reaction to someone calling me a slut would be to get offended. But when he called me a slut it only made me wetter, softer for him.

He kissed my lips, my jaw, and then my neck. When he dipped lower I arched into him, silently begging for him to touch my breasts. He chuckled before gripping the bottom of one and lifting it to his waiting mouth. "I've been wanting to get my mouth on you from the moment I first saw you," he admitted before his tongue darted out from behind his lips and swiped at my puckered nipple.

I moaned as his hot mouth surrounded me and he sucked at me. Each pull from his mouth sent a zap of awareness to my core. It was as if there was a direct link between the two. "Please," I whimpered.

"To show you how proud I am of you, I'm going to reward you," he muttered before nipping me with his teeth. I sucked in a harsh breath and shuddered at the sensation. His hands roamed down my sides before dipping lower. He leaned away from me, taking his heat with him. I groaned in frustration before he gripped my thighs and spread me wide.

The sudden movement surprised me and I squealed before trying to close my legs. I was completely naked and the sun was making its full appearance, bathing the room in brightness. I knew he'd seen me naked last night, but this was different. This was like cutting me wide open and leaving me with no place to hide.

"Now, that just won't do." He tsked as he gripped

my knees and gently tried to pry my legs apart again. "I need to see you, Bambi. I want to see this sweet little cunt before I taste it," he growled.

I flushed as he mentioned tasting me. It was no surprise to anyone that I'd never done that either. The thought of something so intimate always left me so flustered that I had a hard time even thinking about it, let alone allowing someone to do it.

"I…" I said with a shaky voice. "I don't know if I'll like it," I admitted quietly.

Ian went utterly still and his eyebrows furrowed. "Nobody has ever eaten this little pussy?" he asked. When I shook my head he moved his hands down the back of my thighs. I shivered at the feel of his fingers grazing the backside of my exposed ass before raising one hand along my seam. Even though I had my legs closed, he still had no hindrance accessing my pussy with those wicked fingers. He held eye contact with me as he pushed one long finger through my folds and found my clit.

My thighs trembled with the need to open for him. To give him everything he asked for and more. "I'll stop if you want me to but know this, Bambi," he said before his finger circled my entrance, lighting up my nerves and making me want more. "I crave the taste of you on my tongue. I want to eat you like you're my last meal. You will come so hard, you'll wonder why you ever thought you wouldn't like it. I'll bury my face in your cunt so deeply you won't remember a time when I wasn't there," he promised.

I felt my resolve slowly slipping away with each sinfully delicious word he spoke. My knees opened slightly as he pushed his finger inside of me smoothly. My arousal made his ministrations easy. I bit back my moan as he teased me.

"I will lap up all of your sweet cream and beg you for more. This pussy will be mine and mine alone. I want to go to sleep each night with the taste of you on my tongue and wake up each morning just to do it all again," he said as he pushed in further. "Open for me, Lindsey."

I moaned and relaxed into his touch. My thighs spread and he used his free hand to push me open wide. I tried not to blush as he stared down at me with hooded eyes. When he pushed his finger all the way inside and curled it, my back bowed off the bed.

"That's my sweet girl," he murmured before leaning down. He continued to fuck his finger in and out of me before he ran his nose from my entrance up to my mound. I jerked as the sensation wound me tight. When he inhaled deeply I felt a hot flush creep into my face. "This is the prettiest pussy I've ever seen," he said before he laid a kiss right on my throbbing clit. I cried out at the feel of his soft lips against me.

I couldn't help but watch his dark gaze as he stared at me. I let my inhibitions fly away as I braced for what was to come. I truly didn't know if I would like what he was about to do, but the way my body trembled at the thought made me think yes.

I threaded my fingers through his hair and gave over to him completely as he lowered his mouth to—

"Lyns?" A voice at the door jarred us out of the moment. A knock followed and I panicked. I pushed at Ian and scrambled for the sheet.

Anna was at the door while I was getting ready to fuck her dad.

Chapter Twelve

"J-just a minute!" I screeched as I scrambled away from Ian. *Fuck!* I kicked my feet out as I sat up hastily, effectively tangling them in the sheet. I twisted to get out of them and severely overestimated the motion I would need as I started to roll out of the bed. Ian grabbed for me but it was too late. I squealed as I plummeted toward the floor and landed with a thud against the hardwood.

It felt like it took a moment longer than necessary for my body to stop vibrating from the fall. I groaned from embarrassment rather than pain as Ian's grinning face peeked over the bed. I covered my face to stop the blush that was quickly taking over.

"Are you all right?" Ian chuckled quietly as he gracefully slid from the bed and stood over me. I shook my head and held my breath as I looked up at him. He was stark-ass nude and still rock-hard. *How could he still be ready to go while Anna was outside the door?*

"Hide!" I harshly whispered. I sat up and became painfully aware of the fact that I was still naked as well. I could only imagine how I looked right now. Ian held his hand out for me still and I grabbed it reluctantly. He pulled me from my spot on the floor in a quick motion that left me breathless. Before I could turn from him and grab something to cover up with, he slipped his hands around me and grabbed my ass.

I bit back a whimper as he kneaded the now sore area as he pushed his erection against my belly. When I tried to pull away again, he only gripped me tighter. I looked up into his eyes then. "What are you doing, you need to hide. Now," I whispered.

"Lindsey? Are you all right? I heard a thump,"

Anna's muffled voice sounded as she knocked again.

"Yeah—" my voice cracked as Ian brought his head down and nipped my earlobe, making me weak in the knees. "I, ah ... yeah, I'm looking for my robe, just a sec."

Ian chuckled against me as he sucked the lobe past his lips before grinding against me. The overwhelming urge to let him have his devious way with me was almost too much to bear. *Almost.*

I pushed at his chest and dislodged him from me finally. I shoved my disheveled hair out of my face before rapidly searching for my robe. I spotted it slung over the window seat and rushed to grab it. After hastily pushing my arms through the soft material and tugging it around my body, I looked back up to find Ian watching me curiously. I flicked my hair up and out of the robe as I rushed back to him.

"You need to go hide in the b—"

My next words were cut off as he gripped my chin and sealed his lips to mine. I closed my eyes and went on my tiptoes against my will as I sunk into his touch. He released my lips but didn't step away completely. "You know, this would be the perfect time to tell her about us," he murmured.

I sucked in a sharp breath and started to protest when he kissed me again. His tongue slipped between my lips in a tantalizing way that silenced me and made me dizzy. His hands held me firmly at my hips and all of my being zeroed in on the contact. When he pulled away from me again my lips followed as if they knew exactly where they wanted to be.

"But I understand you want to tell her in a different way. As long as you hear me when I tell you that I will have you soon, Little Bambi. With or without Anna's blessing," he whispered as he searched my eyes seriously. "I want this, Lindsey. I want you, and not just in a one-time, fuck-your-brains-out-and-never-see-you-again way. I thought maybe I would need to have you a couple of times and then be able to walk away after. But now..." he trailed off as his hands flexed against me. "Now there's no walking away for me," he finished before pulling away from me completely.

I stood stock still as I watched him back away from me before turning and disappearing into the bathroom. The soft click of the door closing behind him echoed in my brain as I stared at the plain wooden door. I hadn't ever expected to hear the words he just said to me.

If I was honest with myself, I never really knew where this was all headed with us. I just knew that I personally wanted him in a carnal way. I hadn't looked much past the *now* in regard to him. All I knew was that he was the one I wanted to play out all the lustful, primal urges that coursed through my mind the moment I laid eyes on him.

Another knock at the door jarred me from my thoughts. I shook my head and released a breath I hadn't known I was holding as I strode to the door. I calmed myself before swinging it open to reveal a very curious-looking Anna.

"Hey," I breathed as she brushed past me.

"What took you so long?" she asked as she stepped into the room. I turned to follow her as my mind raced to think of an excuse.

"I, uh, was just looking for my robe," I offered with a shrug.

Anna walked further into the room and I followed her line of vision right to my bed. I cringed as I took in the sight of rumpled blankets and threw about pillows. The sheet I'd gripped on my tumble out of the bed was strewn half on, half off the bed. From an outsider's viewpoint, it looked like some seriously inappropriate things happened in this room.

I scrunched my face up and hoped Anna wouldn't put two and two together as she stepped up to the bed. She ran her fingers over the rumpled sheets before turning to face me and plopping down. She leaned back onto her hands as she smiled at me mischievously.

"Were you masturbating?" she asked suddenly.

I choked on thin air as I blustered at her question. "What? No!" I sputtered as I gripped my robe tightly around myself.

Anna rolled her eyes before picking up one of my pillows and tossing it my way. I barely caught it before it smacked me in the face. "You were totally diddling your skittles, weren't you!" She laughed and I reddened further.

I tried to defend my innocence when she held her hand up to stop me. "Dude, look at your bed. Don't get me wrong, I get it. We all need to act like a DJ with a turntable sometimes. It's okay to make a little music with yourself," she teased before making the universal sound for porn. "*Bow-chicka-wow-wow.*"

"*Anna!*" I screeched with a smile on my lips as I tossed the pillow back to her. She caught it before gripping it to her middle and barking a belly laugh.

"First you have a wet dream about someone named Adrian and now you're masturbating," —she made a *shame-shame* motion with her fingers—"We're going to have to call the church soon, you're turning into quite the little slut!"

"Oh!" I huffed as I rushed her and pushed her onto her back as I tumbled down with her. She giggled madly as I punched her upper arm and lay next to her. I couldn't help the smile that formed on my lips as I listened to her laugh. Soon I was giggling with her.

Once she quieted to a chuckle she sat up and slapped my hip before standing. "If you're done touching your delicates, you need to get dressed. We're going into town for some shopping after breakfast," she said as she sauntered toward the door.

I sat up and gripped the pillow to my lap as I watched her. I was still smiling when she reached the door and turned to face me again. "Don't forget to wash your hands, pervert," she teased. I scoffed before chucking the pillow at her again. She smiled as she dodged it and went on her way down the hallway.

My cheeks burned as I shook my head and stood. Anna's sense of humor would forever embarrass the shit out of me but I loved her all the same for it.

I walked to my door and poked my head out into the hallway before declaring it safe for Ian to come out. I quickly walked to the bathroom door and gripped the handle. Before I could twist it, it jerked open from the other side and Ian gripped me around the wrist. He pulled me into the bathroom and shut the door with a solid thunk before pushing me against it.

I barely had time to catch my breath before he captured my lips with his. I sighed as I sank into him. His hands gripped my arms and placed them around his shoulders. He pushed himself flush against me as he explored my mouth.

"Who's *Adrian*?" he asked between scorching kisses. I couldn't help my grin against his lips at his question. *He was jealous.*

That brazen feeling I seemed to associate with him made another appearance as I decided to tease him. "Just a guy I had a dream about," I said before I licked his lower lip. His resounding growl rumbled through my core.

"You shouldn't tease me when I'm this close to

the edge, Bambi," he threatened deliciously before gripping my ass and pushing me up the door. My robe opened below my breasts, exposing my naked lower half.

I had no choice but to put my legs around him as he held me snuggly to him. I gasped as I felt the head of his thick cock prod my entrance. I was still so wet from our earlier activities that he slipped in just the slightest bit.

I sucked in a harsh breath at the foreign feeling. He was so big that it would be a fight when he actually fucked me. Though, I had the feeling it would be a beautiful struggle I would forever remember. I wiggled against him as if tempting him to push further.

His eyes closed and his chest heaved as if the slightest feel of my pussy was enough to unman him completely. When he opened his eyes again, the fire I saw burning there should've made me run.

I'd yet to tell him I was a virgin. I was still mulling over whether I needed to tell him at all. Wouldn't it be better to just get it over with than to talk to him about the fact that I was still so innocent? I bit my lip to keep from spilling my guts. Sharing that intimate detail with someone when I didn't know exactly where our relationship was headed didn't make much sense to me.

"Who?" he gritted as his hands moved restlessly against my ass.

Rather than tease him even further, I relented. "You," I said as I delved my fingers into his hair. When he looked at me curiously I continued. "I had a dream about you and I guess when I said *Ian*, it sounded like *Adrian*," I admitted and to my surprise, I didn't blush when I did. Something about having a dick posed to fuck you took away the shame that would normally come with such an admission.

Ian's grin was barbaric as he stared down at me. "You had a wet dream about me?" he asked but didn't wait for me to answer before continuing. "What was I doing to you?"

His hands moved from my ass to my hips and further up. As they did, he slowly allowed me to slide down the door. I tried not to dwell on the crestfallen feeling I got in my chest as he dislodged himself from me.

"You were..." I trailed off as I stared at his chest. He was a good half-foot taller than me so I was at eye level with that impressive part of his anatomy. I tore my gaze away from it before forcing myself to look up and match his heated stare. "You were getting ready to lick ... my pussy," I said before immediately biting my lip.

I would've gotten red and flustered had I not seen the visceral lust cloud his expression. The way he looked at me seemed to embolden me to say things I would've never said before him.

"Oh, Bambi..." He crowded me again before gripping the doorknob and twisting it. He braced his other hand on the doorframe above my head as if it would stop him from touching me. Our time together this morning was coming to an end. He knew I needed to get ready to meet the others soon. "I like listening to those dirty words come out of your innocent little mouth. Don't you worry, I plan on eating you up and fulfilling every dirty fantasy you could ever have," he murmured before kissing me one last time.

I flashed him a sultry grin before nipping his lower lip. His eyes flared before I ducked under his arm and twisted away from him. He was still gloriously naked and sporting the biggest erection I'd ever seen when I slid out of the bathroom. I watched him as I retreated with a giggle. He looked ready to pounce on me and I was ready to let it happen.

I thought briefly about shutting and locking my door again just to have a few more minutes with him. I turned around to do just that when I gasped and came to a screeching halt.

"Ben?" I spoke breathlessly.

Ben jumped from his spot in front of my open suitcase and turned to face me hastily. His face flushed red as he gripped his hands behind his back. His eyes looked wild as if he hadn't expected me to be in here.

"H-hey there, Lindsey Bug!" he said overenthusiastically.

Panic lodged in my gut like a ball of lead as I looked over my friend. He was dressed for the day in jeans and a red sweater that looked too hot. He had a fine sheen of sweat that coated his forehead and upper lip. His chest rose harshly as his eyes darted between me and my bathroom door.

Was Ian still hiding? I knew the door was still open but I didn't dare turn around to see if he stood there. If I looked and he wasn't there, then Ben would only be suspicious. *Fuck.*

"What are you doing?" I spoke loudly as if Ian would hear me and stay put.

Ben moved his hands behind his back and I saw his shirt move slightly before he spoke. "I was just looking for some Tylenol, Mel said you might have some," he said. He moved his shirt back into place and his hands toward the front of his jeans. He nervously wiped his hands down the dark denim. "I have a … killer headache."

I frowned at him before stepping closer. A nagging feeling at the back of my brain told me he was hiding something from me. But I was also hiding something as well and I needed to get him the hell out of my room.

"You should've knocked," I said as I walked toward my suitcase. I clenched my hands around myself as I stepped closer to him, making sure all my bits were covered under the robe. "I could've been in the middle of getting dressed."

I looked from him to my suitcase and back again. He smiled sheepishly before stepping to the side. "Right, I … the door was open so I didn't think you were here," he said as he stared down at me.

I looked down at my open bag then. The clothes looked like someone had gone through them to find something, which made sense because he said he was looking for Tylenol. What *didn't* make sense was the fact that I could plainly see the travel bottle of pills through the mesh compartment along the top of the case. I'd packed it right beside my other toiletries. If he'd been looking for pills then he should've been able to see them as soon as he opened the bag. *Why would he rifle through my clothes if what he was looking for was clearly in another place?*

I unzipped the compartment and shakily grabbed the bottle. "It's right here," I said as I handed it to him. Ben looked down at me and shrugged his shoulders before glancing toward my bathroom. I swallowed thickly while resisting the urge to look behind me. *If he saw Ian he would say so, wouldn't he?*

"Huh," he huffed before he turned toward me. The look he gave me confused me. He had a secret gleam in his eyes as he smiled down at me like he knew something I didn't. "Sometimes things can be right in front of your face and you still don't see them for what they are." He cocked his head to the side. Something darker flashed over his features but it was gone in a flash. If I'd blinked I would've missed it.

He grabbed for the bottle and his hand lingered longer than necessary. I sniffed and pushed the bottle into his hand before taking a step back. Ben had never made me uncomfortable before but that's exactly what he was doing right now.

"I hope your headache goes away," I murmured as I hugged my middle again.

His brows furrowed as if he were confused before shaking his head and smiling down at me. He palmed the pills and stepped into my space. I avoided eye contact, choosing to stare at the wilted flower tattoo on his neck, as he stared down at me. When he pulled his other hand up and toward my face, I flinched away from him. He chuckled to himself but it sounded almost humorless. He stepped away from me, then.

"Me too, though that's not the only thing that pains me lately," he said as he headed toward my door. I stared after him as he walked away. His head swiveled toward my bathroom again and he kept his gaze locked on the open door as he exited my room.

The back of my eyes burned as I rushed after him. I grabbed the door and slammed it while pulling in harsh breaths. I felt as though I'd just run a marathon and my heart was refusing to calm down.

What the fuck was that?

I'd been around and alone with Ben a million different times and he had never made me feel like this. Like I was guilty of something dirty. Like he knew exactly what I'd been doing in the bathroom. I had the overwhelming urge to lock the door as soon as he left me. I felt … threatened.

"He's in love with you," Ian's deep voice sounded in the bathroom doorway and I jumped around.

"Fuck!" I yelped.

"Exactly what he wants to do to you, Bambi," he

said as he pushed away from the door and stalked my way. He'd wrapped a towel around his waist while he'd hidden from sight. At least now when I looked at him my brain wouldn't completely short circuit.

"Did he see you?" I asked as I calmed my wild heart.

Ian stepped into my space and kissed my forehead before pushing my hair behind my ear. "No." He shook his head. "But he knows something's up with you. He can sense the change in dynamic. I don't like it," he warned darkly.

I swallowed again before I pushed away from the door. I shook my head, I didn't know what was up with Ben but that didn't make me less of a friend to him. "He's harmless," I said as I stood in front of my suitcase again. I blindly fingered through my clothes to find something to wear. Anna wouldn't wait forever so I needed to get a move on.

"Hmm," Ian hummed before opening the door. "We'll see about that. I realize he's a friend to you, but know this, Bambi…" He paused, waiting for me to look up at him. "If he touches you, 'll kill him," he promised before stepping into the hallway and disappearing.

It should've scared me, the way he was staking claim to me as if I were some sort of prize to be won. Or even the fact that this was still new, still fresh, and he was already having strong inclinations toward me. I should be ending this before it got even more complicated.

So why did I crave him even more now?

Chapter Thirteen

"What about this one?" Anna asked for what felt like the thousandth time. This time she held up a bright neon-yellow, cold-shoulder blouse. She held it against her coat-covered chest and posed ridiculously with the garment. I couldn't help but giggle at the silly face she plastered on as though she were posing for a photo shoot.

I had to admit, she would've looked stunning in it. The bright yellow complimented and really pointed out the bright blue in her hair. "I think you would rock it," I said before she placed the shirt in the ever-growing pile of try-ons.

We'd been at this now for the last two hours. After a very tense breakfast at the cabin, we'd come straight to town. The meal had been made awkward in my eyes because of the staring match that happened between Ian and Ben. Nobody else seemed to notice their pissing match besides me.

I'm not sure what had gotten into Ben all of a sudden, but it was as though he was marking his territory, with me being the territory. I'd known him for a long time and he'd never acted like this when it was any other boy from school that was interested in me. I thought Ian and I did a well enough job at hiding our attraction for one another but it was obvious Ben had picked up on it. He'd even made a point to sit right next to me while I picked at my waffle this morning.

The morning was made even more awkward when Anna laid out our itinerary for the day. We were to spend most of the day shopping in town and exploring the little businesses that littered the main street. When she was in the middle of explaining that we would drive down the mountain as soon as breakfast was done, Ian cleared his throat and announced that he would drive us.

My face flushed bright red as he stared between a scowling Ben and myself before smiling at his daughter. Anna was none the wiser at the display of dominance as she smiled brightly and thanked him for playing chauffeur.

The flush I felt was quickly replaced by an angry heat when Melonie clapped her hands together in excitement before saying how happy she was that he would be tagging along. "I need a man's opinion on some of the outfits I'm going to try on," she'd said. I'd nearly gagged at the innuendo laced within her words. It was only the fact that Ian had ignored her that kept me from jumping over the table and ripping out her extensions.

His ignoring her obvious attempt to gain his attention only further drew me back to what he'd said to me this morning. *"There is no walking away for me."* His words should have been a claim of ownership. I should've been offended that he would have the audacity to even make such a claim on me.

But I felt no such way when he'd spoken the words. If anything, I'd felt butterflies in my stomach. It was odd, but when he spoke to me like that I hadn't felt as though he was trying to control me, I felt turned on at the prospect of belonging to someone for the first time in my life. Even though his proclamation had stirred up some questions I was now forced to ask myself.

What did I want after this week was over? What was my plan when we got back to Florida? Did I really think I could have this amazing experience with him and then just go back to normal like it never happened? It had to be terrible that I had no clue what I wanted from him after I let him take my innocence, and I needed to figure that out.

I was a virgin, for fuck's sake. Didn't normal girls want to start a life and marry the first guy they ever slept with? I was so past the point of knowing what a normal person expected from the first person they were intimate with.

I glanced over to Anna, who was still perusing the racks and throwing more items on her ever-growing pile of clothing. *She would be able to tell me what was normal, wouldn't she?* I shook my head as the thought popped into my brain. I couldn't ask her the burning question bouncing around in my head. Especially when the question was directly related to her father. I frowned to myself. *It's not like she would know that you're talking about her dad,* I reasoned.

I fingered through the clothing next to her mindlessly as I gathered the courage to finally speak. "So…" I cleared my throat as I glanced at my bestie. She was still fully immersed in her task of finding a new outfit, she never looked up at me as she grunted my way. "Can I ask you something?" I blurted before I lost the guts.

She grinned up at me briefly before returning her gaze to a sparkly top she held in her hands. "What's up?"

I swallowed thickly as I pretended to be deeply interested in the pair of jeans in my hands. "Who was your first…" I trailed off as I tried not to cringe. When I glanced up at Anna she was eyeing me curiously. "You know, your first…" I said as I gestured to my body. I wanted the floor to gobble me up as Anna started to giggle at my childish display.

"You mean who was the first guy I had sex with?" she said and I wanted to hide my face between the clothing. She noted my reaction and chuckled again before looking deep in thought. "Seth Harvey," she said as a look of nostalgia crossed her beautiful features. "We were both sixteen and neither of us had a fucking clue what we were doing in the back of my piece of shit Toyota Camry. Foreplay was not a word in that boy's vocabulary." She cringed at the memory before returning her gaze toward the rack.

I nodded as I pretended to look through the sweater collection. I forged on before I lost the nerve. "Did you think you would end up together ... forever?"

"Fuck, no!" Anna snorted before she threw another blouse into her pile and faced me. "We were just two stupid-ass kids playing at being adults. I was desperate to prove I was just as cool as all the other girls in my class and he was an idiot that couldn't find a clit if I put a neon sign above it pointing directly at it." I flushed before snorting at her joke. Anna always did have a way with words.

"I don't think that happens as often as you think it does," she allowed. "I think if it's meant to be then that's great, but I also think you should feel free to let your freak flag fly too, if not." She stared at me as curiosity creased her brow. I nodded and turned back to the clothing rack as if the conversation was over. Anna was way too smart for my own good as she forged on. "I think it's rare to find the person you're supposed to be with the first time you have sex. But, just because it didn't happen for me doesn't mean it isn't possible or even something you shouldn't hope for." She stepped closer to me. I tried to avoid eye contact with her but I could feel her inquisitive gaze against my temple. "What's this about anyway?"

A breath shuddered out of me as I stammered and faced her. "Wh-what do you mean?"

"You have never asked me about anything sex-related. Normally you grit your teeth and bear my slutty-time stories. Are you seeing someone I don't know about?" she asked.

Shear panic laced my blood at her question. "I was just curious, that's all," I breathed quickly. Trying to feign nonchalance, I shrugged. "You never know when the opportunity might present itself." I shrugged.

I watched Anna's eyes flicker to me and then further behind me as if putting together a puzzle. When her eyes widened and she opened her mouth with a gasp I fought against my rising panic. "Oh. My. God. You're not planning on fucking Ben, are you?" she screeched loudly.

I shushed her and slapped my hand over her mouth as quickly as I could. Like if I silenced her quickly enough it would recall the words spoken.

I looked between her and the rest of the store shoppers nervously. I flushed bright red when I spotted Ben and Melonie staring at us like they were trying to listen in but couldn't quite hear us.

"No!" I whispered harshly. Anna visibly relaxed while my hand was still over her mouth. Rather than move away from me, she licked my palm.

"Yuck." I grossed as I pulled my hand away and wiped it down the back of my jeans. Anna shrugged like she couldn't be bothered one way or another.

"Well, thank God for that," she muttered as she continued to browse through the racks. "So, is it this Adrian guy then?" she asked without looking at me.

"I'm never going to live that down, am I?" I smiled.

"Not in a million years." She giggled.

At that moment I was overcome with such love for this girl. She was always there for me no matter what I was going through. Anytime I had a problem, she always pushed everything to the side to make room for our friendship. Even when all the shit with my mom and dad was going down, she'd sat by my side and let me cry on her shoulder. And how was I repaying her? By sneaking around with her dad and not having the balls to say anything to her. I was the worst type of friend.

"Anna, I need to tell you something," I blurted as I grabbed her by the shoulders and spun her to face me.

A bewildered expression clouded her face as she looked at me. "Okay," she murmured.

I licked my lips to bring moisture back to my dry mouth. I could feel my heart pounding in my chest as I stared at my best friend. *What if she ends up hating me? What if she never wants to speak to me again? Could I really survive without her in my life? All because I had feelings for her dad.*

"I—" I swallowed as I stared into her expressive eyes before shaking my head. "I just wanted to tell you..." I sighed before I hugged her to me. *I can't do this.* I squeezed her tight and buried my face in her shoulder. "I love you and I couldn't ask for a better best friend," I whispered and clenched my eyes closed. *I'm such a fucking coward.*

Anna giggled against me before wrapping her arms around me and hugging me tightly. The back of my eyes were burning as she spoke. "I love you too, Lyns," she said and then pulled away from me. She looked at me with a soft smile on her lips. "You know, all you have to do is tell me that you don't want to shop for clothes. I know you hate this."

I laughed as Melonie and Ben approached us. "I hate it so much." We both giggled as I tried to hold back my tears.

"Well, that sucks for you because I'm not done shopping." Melonie sneered my way as she held her arms full of clothing.

I rolled my eyes at her before looking back at

Anna. "I saw a little thrift bookshop down the way, I think I'll take a walk down there and look around for a bit," I said.

Anna opened her mouth but before she could say anything Melonie spoke again. "Typical, Lindsey. Why can't you be like other girls and just shop with us? Your attire could use some updating anyway." She smiled at me. The longer we were together this week, the more her pleasant mask she kept on around Anna slipped. "I mean, really, some new clothes might make you *appear* less frumpy," she snorted. "Lord knows you need all the help you can get," she said under her breath.

Anna snapped her head in Melonie's direction. I could tell she was going to lay into her but I held my hand up for her to stop. I squinted my eyes at my bully and for the first time allowed the words that always flew through my mind out of my mouth. "When was the last time you read a book, Melonie? I mean, really, you would be surprised how much smarter it would make you *seem*. Maybe you wouldn't act like such a stupid bitch all the time." I smiled a sugary smile as she dropped her mouth open wide in shock. She wasn't used to me biting back at her. "Lord knows you need all the help you can get." I copied her earlier words, not bothering to speak under my breath.

Anna's eyes widened before she busted up laughing. When Melonie scowled at her she didn't even try to quiet her giggles. Her joy was contagious and I found myself laughing with her. Melonie's red face only made the whole altercation funnier.

"I'll meet you guys at the restaurant later." I smiled at my friend before turning on my heel and bumping into a solid slab of warm muscle. I stumbled back before big hands gripped me around my upper arms to steady me. I inhaled sharply as I looked up at Ian. His warm smile told me he'd heard our exchange and found it humorous.

"I've been wanting to go to that bookstore too, I'll walk with you," he said before tearing his gaze away from me. He tossed the keys to the vehicle to Anna and she caught them without a problem. "You drive everyone to the restaurant later and we'll walk."

"Sounds like a plan," Anna said as she pocketed the keys. My head swung back and forth between them as if they were playing a tennis match.

"Let's go," he said as he grabbed my hand. I was dumbstruck as he dragged me toward the door. Any protests that I may have had died on my lips as my feet moved.

"I'll go with you too!" Ben suddenly spoke as he stepped closer to us. I immediately felt tension radiate off Ian as he twisted to face Ben. He covertly pushed me behind him as if to protect me and then the two of them squared off. Ian never dropped my hand in the process, a fact that apparently only I noticed.

"Jesus, Dahmer, why don't you let up just this once? Leave her alone and stop being a fucking stalker," Anna growled as she stepped up to Ben and grabbed his wrist. Ben snatched his hand back viciously before glaring at her. I'd never seen him look so angry.

"You know, I'm getting pretty tired of you acting like I'm a fucking psycho serial killer," he gritted behind clenched teeth as he balled his fists up.

"Maybe you should stop acting like one, then," Anna scowled up at him, not letting him intimidate her. Ian's hand flexed and released in mine as though he was getting ready to pounce on the person that looked threateningly at his daughter. I couldn't help the upsweep of nerves that fluttered through my belly at the possible altercation.

I was getting ready to step away from Ian and defuse the bomb that was Ben when Melonie whined and grabbed his hand. "Ben," Melonie pouted in that girlish voice that ground on my last nerve. "I want you to stay. I need your help picking out some outfits anyway."

I rolled my eyes at the obvious display of her trying to take what she thought was mine. If only she knew he could be hers at the drop of a hat. I held no inclination of my own toward him. If anything, the way he acted this morning made me leery of him.

Ben ignored Melonie as he kept his scowl directed at Ian. I needed to stop this before they made a scene and Anna figured out the hard way that I was a terrible friend. "It's fine." I wiggled my hand away from Ian and stepped around him. I could feel the annoyance from his stare as I did. "I'll just meet up with you guys later," I said to Ben, gaining his attention. He looked down at me but the same hard look he threw at Ian was now directed at me for a split-second before he calmed. If I had blinked, I would have missed the way his expression shifted from utter rage to a smooth smile. He gave me the chills.

"Have fun," he murmured quickly around that sweet smile before twisting on his heel and grabbing Melonie's hand. He pulled her behind him toward the dressing rooms and she had to rush to keep up. He twisted and gave me one more odd smile before pulling Melonie past the door of the dressing room and slamming the door behind them.

I looked at that closed door and felt a shiver crawl down my spine. Ben was starting to scare me with how he'd been acting since coming to Colorado. He reminded me of someone who was becoming unhinged. Like he was slowly having a mental breakdown.

"What the fuck is his issue?" Anna murmured as

she watched the closed door as well. She shook her head and looked back toward me. "What are you still doing here? I can handle them, go." She waved me away before resuming her shopping.

I swallowed harshly before looking up at Ian who was staring at me with curiosity written on his brow. I forcefully shook myself before I skirted around him and headed toward the door.

Chapter Fourteen

The brisk winter air bit at my cheeks as I stepped out of the warmth of the store. I welcomed the cold after the way I felt like I was on fire inside. Nothing about today was going as I'd planned. I just wanted to be able to sit down with Anna and tell her exactly what was going on with me and her dad. I hadn't been able to do the one thing I needed to because I was a fucking coward.

I walked fast as I swerved around other shoppers. I needed to get as far away from the others as I could. I needed to clear my mind and figure out exactly what I was going to do. The most fucked-up thing about this whole situation was that I didn't even feel guilty anymore. I should feel like the scum of the earth for messing around with Anna's dad behind her back but I didn't feel like that at all.

Ever since last night in the bathroom with Ian, I felt … different. Something had shifted inside of me like I was becoming a different person. The type of person that refused to act embarrassed about the things that happened last night. This new person didn't feel the need to explain herself to anyone when it came to what she wanted. And what she wanted was Ian.

I shook my head and scowled at myself as I tightened the sash around my waist that held my coat together. Maybe if I squeezed myself tight enough there would be no more room for the anxiety building in my gut.

The old Lindsey would have never even thought about deceiving her best friend the way I was. She would have never bitten back at Melonie the way she did in the store either. And when Ben offered to go with her to the bookstore, she would've happily let him tag along even if all she wanted was a little alone time. I couldn't recognize this new person I was becoming.

"Lindsey, wait," Ian's deep voice shouted from somewhere behind me as I quickened my pace. I had no idea what I was going to say to him right now. He was expecting me to tell Anna exactly what we were to each other and I'd failed miserably.

I spotted the bookstore up ahead and rushed for the entrance. I slammed into the quiet shop and made a beeline straight for the back of the building. I didn't want to deal with Ian right now, I had enough on my mind as it was.

I hastily made my way past the tall rows of books. I normally would stop and gawk at all the different selections but I had one thing and one thing only on my mind at this point—*escape*. It was a good thing there weren't many people in the store, otherwise they would've thought I was a madwoman with the look I'm sure marred my face.

I didn't realize how close he was to me until I felt his hand circle my waist and bring an end to my power walk. I hissed and tried to pull out of his embrace but he didn't relent as he brought me flush to his front. "Where are you running off to, Little Bambi?"

I'm not sure why, but his nickname really rubbed me the wrong way at that moment. Maybe it was because of Melonie's *frumpy* comment or maybe it was because I was already feeling so frustrated by how this day was going. Whatever the reason, I snapped.

I whirled around in his arms and pushed at his chest. A look of pure confusion crossed his handsome features before he released me. "Stop calling me that! I'm not little if you haven't noticed. I'm clearly in need of a diet and you just keep reminding me of it," I seethed as I stared up at him.

Once again, this new Lindsey made an appearance as I watched anger flare in his eyes. I didn't move or back down from him as he crowded me. He gripped me around my waist and hauled me to him as he stepped forward. I didn't even realize he was moving me until my ass hit the edge of a table. It was darker in this part of the bookstore as it was so far away from the sunny windows in the front. There were no prying eyes back here with us.

Ian threaded his hand into the back of my hair and pulled. I tried to ignore the flood of arousal that zapped to my core as he forced me to look up at him. I kept the scowl on my lips as he hovered over mine. He stared into my eyes with that dark look I'd come to crave.

"Hear me now, *Little Bambi.* I've been extremely gentle with you because I didn't want to scare you off but if I ever hear you talk about your body like that again, I won't hesitate to bend you over this table and spank that nasty self-hatred out of your ass."

I gasped at his words. Nobody had ever spoken to me like this. I had a feeling the old Lindsey would've feared his dark promise. But this person I was becoming craved everything he said and more.

His other hand moved to the knot of my sash and skillfully untied it. He slipped past the thick garment and blazed a trail down my belly toward the top of my jeans. "If you're angry about something I did, then by all means rip me a new asshole," he growled against my lips as his fingers unbuttoned the top of my jeans. I whimpered from the coolness of his touch as he met my overheated flesh. "But don't you talk about this body like that ever again," he threatened.

I gripped his coat as his fingers pushed past my

panties. He stared at my lips as my breath shuddered out of me rapidly. The moment his cool fingers brushed over my throbbing clit my knees buckled.

"I want to worship this body," he whispered as he slid his fingers through my wetness. I bit my lip to squelch the moan I felt raising. *Was I really going to allow this to happen here?* "I want to love this body the way it deserves to be loved." He groaned as if he was getting the same pleasure I was from his touch. "I want to own this body. And I don't let anyone talk badly about my belongings," he said before he removed his hand from me.

I nearly whined as he released my hair and pulled away from me. He stared at me with such heat in his eyes, I thought I might melt under the scrutiny. He kept eye contact as he raised his fingers that were just playing with me to his waiting mouth. My mouth fell open on a breath as he sucked the digits inside and groaned as if the taste of me was a delicacy.

He stepped further away from me and I became mesmerized watching the way his body worked to shrug off his heavy coat before throwing it on the table behind me. He wore a tightly fitted grey long-sleeve shirt underneath that I wanted to remove for him. I was on the verge of begging him to keep going when he turned from me.

He gripped a thick black curtain and slid it closed, sealing us off from the rest of the store. That's when I realized we were in a research cove at the back of the building. I'd only ever seen these rooms in libraries. This store must double as one and I just hadn't realized it.

"This is how this is going to go," Ian's deep voice sounded thick with lust as he turned back toward me. My heart pounded in my chest mightily as I watched him raise his sleeves up his tightly corded forearms. "You are going to ride out that anger coiling in your gut and then we are going to talk about where we go from here on out."

My chest labored as I watched him prowl closer to me. I leaned heavily against the table with each step he took. Said anger coiling inside of me was slowly fizzling into something much deeper, much darker. "How exactly do you expect me to ride out anything when you're still near me?" I breathed as he stepped into my space.

The grin that spread over his lips made my pussy clench in anticipation. He gripped the sash off my coat and pulled it through the loops holding it in place with a snap I felt echoing in my core. "We're going to finish what we started this morning, Bambi. You're going to ride out that anger against my tongue," he growled. He pushed my coat from my shoulders and it slid silently from my body, sending a shiver down my spine. "Lose the jeans," he demanded as his hands slid toward my breasts.

I stared up into his eyes to see if he was being serious. *He had to be joking, right?* We were in a bookstore with others in the same building. There's no way I could allow this to happen.

When I opened my mouth to protest he gripped my breasts in those big hands before tweaking my hardened nipples. I hissed as the pain flashed through me and quickly turned to heat. "Now," he ordered. His fingers moved to graze over me now where he'd just pinched. His softness after the harshness of his pinch made me crave more.

I trembled from the adrenaline coursing through my body as I moved my hands to my already undone jeans. I leaned into him and kept eye contact as I shoved the denim down my thighs, leaving my panties in place.

The heavy fabric gathered at my ankles before I slipped my shoes from my feet and stepped out of them completely.

Ian's smile was feral as he raked my body in an appreciative gaze. "That's my good girl," he murmured and I felt my whole body flush from his praise. My lips twitched with the grin I tried to hide. I didn't know if it was his praise or the fact that he called me *his*, but I wanted to do anything I could at that moment to earn it again.

"Sit on the table," he said and I immediately obeyed. I pushed myself up and scooted back until my feet were no longer touching the floor. It was as though I was watching myself from far away as I waited for his next command. "Spread them," he ordered as he stepped away from me, taking his heat with him.

Unlike this morning, I didn't hesitate as I spread my thighs. In the back of my mind, I knew the vision I was making for him. I knew when I sat like this my thighs looked bigger than normal and my belly hung lower. I knew I didn't look skinny. But for some reason, I didn't care. Because the way he was looking at me made me feel like the sexiest woman in the world.

I spread myself wide and immediately felt the chilled air brush against my wet panties. I pushed my chest out and leaned against the table with my hands behind me. His hooded gaze ate up every inch of my body and it was like I could feel every place he looked at me heat under his scrutiny.

"Beautiful," he said before he gripped the back of a nearby chair and slid it over. He carefully placed it right in front of me as he kept his eyes plastered on me. My heart thundered in my chest as he stood next to me.

I turned my head to look at him just before he brought his lips to mine. His kiss was short and left me wanting more as he pulled away. He held my coat's sash in his hands in front of me and I suddenly realized why he took it. "Open."

The one word was not misconstrued as something else as I opened my mouth for him. He grinned at me as though my knowing exactly what to do pleased him greatly. He slipped the sash past my lips and gently pulled it around my head. My breath left me in labored pants as he tied it firmly. He leaned into my ear as he finished. "So you aren't too loud, wouldn't want anyone to know what we're doing back here, would we, Bambi?" he whispered before nipping my earlobe. I jerked and moaned from the sharp ache he inflicted.

He rounded in front of me and smoothly slid into the chair. His hands glided from my knees up my trembling thighs. I watched every move he made, I wanted to memorize this moment. The moment I let go of my inhibitions completely and just … felt.

His eyes were trained on my pussy as his hands met the apex of my thighs. He hummed his appreciation as his thumb grazed over my clit covered in the soft cotton of my panties. "You're so wet, Lindsey. For me?" he asked but I knew there was only one answer he was looking for.

Since I couldn't speak with the sash in my mouth I simply nodded. Hoping I conveyed my unspoken words with my eyes. *Yes, Sir.*

He flashed me a devious smile as his fingers slid against the seam and delved inside. I whimpered as he spread me under the fabric before pulling it out of the way. The cold air of the room hugged my slick folds as he exposed me to his view. Something about him not taking the time to fully remove my panties made me feel like I was in an inferno.

He used both of his hands to spread my thighs

impossibly wide as he stared at my pussy. I refused to allow my insecurity to shine through as I watched his heated gaze gobble me up. He kept one hand on my inner thigh, holding the side of my panties while his other hand wandered. He rested his palm against my mound and allowed his thumb to rub tight circles around my clit. I felt myself clench before jerking against him. I was already wound so tightly, I didn't think I could last much longer.

His resounding chuckle had me pulling my gaze back to his blue eyes. It felt as though he were boring a hole straight into my soul as we stared at each other. His thumb moved up and down from my entrance to my clit in a rhythm I tried to match with my breath. I felt my hips start to move of their own accord and that seemed to please him as he smiled up at me. "That's it, Bambi. You like the way I touch you?" he asked.

I nodded my head vigorously as I bit down on my gag. I was going to come and it was going to be explosive.

Ian moved then and smoothly slid a finger into my drenched channel. I moaned and rolled my head back at the sensation. He fucked into me softly a few times before adding another digit. He moved his other hand to my clit and continued to rub me there, keeping me right on the edge. My hips moved faster as if they knew exactly what to do to get me to the finish line.

"Fuck, you're squeezing me so tightly. I can't wait to sink my cock into this tight little cunt." I moaned at his words as I felt the wave that was my orgasm crest over my head. My legs trembled and I became too weak to hold myself up as I slid down onto my elbows. "That's it, Lindsey. Fucking come for me," he rasped as he curled his finger inside of me. "Now," he demanded at the same time as he pinched my clit and I went flying.

I bit my gag so hard that I was surprised I didn't break a tooth from the pressure. I tried to keep my whimpers quiet as my body convulsed around his working fingers. He was staring at himself fucking into me as I felt a flood of arousal coat his fingers. I could've sworn I heard him groan as he watched me fall apart for him.

Before I could comprehend what was about to happen, Ian pulled his fingers out of me and gripped both of my thighs. He pulled me to him before his mouth latched onto me. I laid back and immediately thrust my fingers into his hair. Either to push him away or pull him closer I had no idea. I was wound so tightly that when he sucked my clit into his mouth and groaned I exploded again.

My back arched and I throbbed as I came. Ian held me tightly against his mouth as my orgasm ensued. He lapped and sucked at me with such vigor that it prolonged every feeling. Just when I thought I was almost done, he twisted his tongue a new way and I started all over again. Before I knew it my hips were moving against him of their own accord, fucking his mouth.

My vision became blurry around the edges before he finally came up for air. He crawled up my languid body before settling between my still-open legs. I felt his denim-covered erection prod at my entrance as I looked lazily up into his eyes. He pulsed his hips against mine, the roughness of his jeans so at odds with the softness of his lips.

"I was right, your cream tasted like the sweetest dessert," he whispered as he pulled the sash from my mouth. I breathed deeply as I stared up at him and licked my lips. "Here, taste," he rumbled before crashing his lips to mine.

He shoved his tongue inside and I tasted the taboo flavor of myself mixed with the taste of him. I moaned as fresh arousal flooded me. He groaned as he pulled away and brought me with him. I sat on the edge of the table and tried to catch my breath as he held me firmly.

He pulled my panties back into place before sitting again in front of me. He then pulled me to him and I slid easily onto his lap. I felt his hard length press against my ass as he curled me against him. His arms wrapped around me and I allowed my head to lay against his chest in contentment. My earlier anger fully dissipated.

"Now, what's the problem?" he asked as he kissed my hair. After the harshness of his ministrations, his softness with me now made me melt a little more.

I took a couple of breaths as I mulled over what to say to him. I figured the best way would be to just forge on. "I feel like everything is moving too fast and I'm losing myself along the way. I feel like I'm deceiving my best friend as I try desperately to figure out how I'm feeling for you. I don't understand what exactly you want from me or what I want from you. Where is this going, what happens when we get back home, how is thi—"

Ian cut my words off as he gripped my chin and kissed me softly. His lips gently ate at mine and all my ramblings ceased. "That's better," he murmured as he gazed at me with some indiscernible emotion in his expressive eyes. My heart fluttered from the warmth I saw there.

"Let's do this one question at a time, okay?" he said and I nodded. "You feel like this is moving fast and the truth is, so do I," he admitted and my brows creased. For the first time since I'd met him, he looked like he didn't know exactly what he was going to say. "I've never felt this way for another person before. Not even when I married Anna's mom. That felt like something I was supposed to do so I did. This feels like something that I *need* to do … like I don't have a choice." He swallowed as he continued to search my face.

I willed him to continue with my eyes. "That leads to your other question. What I want from you, the answer is … everything." His admission took my breath from me. I didn't know this was that serious for him. He huffed a laugh as he rubbed his thumb against my bottom lip, his gaze following the motion.

"When I first saw you, I knew I wanted to be with you in a physical way, Lindsey. Then I couldn't stop thinking about you and I realized I wanted to be with you. Especially after last night. I know it's fast, but I want to get to know you not only physically but in every way one person can know another person. When we get back home I want to keep seeing you. This isn't a one-and-done for me, Bambi. This is real."

He was silent for a moment as I allowed his admissions to sink in. Somewhere deep down I knew he felt more for me than in a visceral way. The way he acted toward me wasn't the normal way you acted toward someone you only wanted to sleep with.

He cleared his throat and swallowed heavily before continuing. "As for you not knowing what you want from me, I can only hope that you want this as much as I do. I want to give you absolutely everything this world has to offer. I want to take care of you. I'm sorry if you feel like you're losing yourself, that's not my intent. I just want you to be open to the possibilities of this relationship. The only thing I can offer in a way of making you feel better is to say that maybe you feel like you're losing yourself because you're finding exactly who you want to be," he said. He kissed my forehead and pushed me back to his chest as if he didn't just drop a bomb between us.

"You don't need to give me answers right now. I just need you to know where I stand. And as far as Anna is concerned..." I tensed at the mention of the elephant in the room. "We can tell her together if you want," he said and I pulled my head up to look at him again. He pushed my hair away from my face. "Tonight, if you w—"

"No!" I cut him off. "Not tonight, I need time to figure out what to say to her first," I said and he nodded. "Tomorrow?" I asked.

"Tomorrow," he said with finality before sealing his lips to mine again.

As he kissed me I felt a nagging feeling tickle the back of my brain. I hadn't told him about the extent of my innocence and now it felt like I was outright lying to him. The fact really hadn't made much sense to divulge to him until now. When I thought he only wanted me in a physical aspect it didn't seem relevant to tell him anything.

I needed to let him know exactly what he was getting into before we took another step. I pulled away from him and looked him directly in the eyes.

"I'm a virgin," I blurted a bit louder than necessary.

Ian's eyes widened and his mouth dropped open when someone cleared their throat. I jumped in his arms and he gripped me tightly to him as someone spoke outside of the curtain.

"I don't know what's going on in there and I'm not going to ask questions if you two leave without making a scene. I'll give you five minutes," the firm feminine voice sounded before the sound of retreating footsteps.

I know my face flushed bright red but I said

nothing as I scrambled off Ian's lap and quickly put my pants back on. I tried not to look at him as he helped me into my coat and quickly tied the sash in its proper place. I said a silent thank you to the universe when he grabbed my hand and led me out of the bookstore without another word.

Chapter Fifteen

I followed Ian with my hand firmly grasped in his as he pushed the door open and pulled me out with him. The still cold air took my breath away for a moment as my lungs adjusted. At least I was pretty sure it was the frigid breeze that took it away and not the scolding man in front of me. Everything was happening so fast that I didn't even get the chance to gauge his reaction to my admission.

Was he mad? Surely he wasn't, what was there to be mad about? It's not like I'd outright lied to him or anything. I just hadn't felt the need to divulge the truth with him. Although, some people thought that a lack of transparency was the same as lying.

I frowned as he kept pulling me along, as though he was in a hurry to get as far away from that bookstore as possible. *Or maybe he's just in a hurry to get away from you, you idiot,* my inner voice taunted me as my feet struggled to keep up with his long-legged strides.

The sidewalk was still very much full of other shoppers but I paid them no mind as I focused on the looming presence in front of me. I thought once we exited the store he would pull me aside somewhere and talk to me. He was proving me wrong as he continued to lead me to the restaurant we were supposed to meet the others at.

"Are you going to say anything at all?" I questioned in an all-too-small voice. Ian said nothing but I saw his shoulders bunch up as if my words made him tense.

I felt an unfamiliar anger coil low in my gut with each step he forced me to take. This was extremely childish of a grown-ass man. He was ignoring me and acting as though I hadn't divulged such personal information to him. I'd just about had enough of people ignoring me or treating me like I wasn't worth the waste of breath.

In the back of my mind, I knew that wasn't what he was doing. I knew logically that I'd thrown him for a loop and he was probably just processing that information before saying anything. That's what mature people did—took in info and expressed themselves in a calm way. But right now I didn't want a mature conversation. I wanted him to communicate with me even if I hadn't really given him the time to digest what I'd told him.

I could see the restaurant just up ahead when I dug my heels into the sidewalk and halted our forward advance. I wasn't going to sit with his daughter at the table and act as though everything was fine when it clearly wasn't. I ripped my hand out of his and tried not to pay attention to the immediate loss of his warmth. "Is this what we're doing then?" I gritted behind clenched teeth as he turned to face me. His heated gaze bore into me like a laser but I stood my ground. "What? I tell you I'm a virgin and suddenly you don't want to have anything to do with me anymore?" I seethed as I stalked closer to him.

His hands squeezed and released as he stared down at me like it was taking enormous restraint to keep his hands to himself. Random people along the busy sidewalk veered around us, some outright scowling as we effectively made a roadblock for them to go around. *Let them look.* I didn't care what they thought of me. If this week had proven anything to me it was that I didn't really care what *anyone* thought of me anymore. This was the only life I got to live and I was done making myself smaller for others.

"Did my admission make you not want to *fuck* me anymore?" I held my hands out gesturing to myself. Ian's eyes flared at my curse and I tried to ignore the tightening in my core as my arousal spiked. I stepped up to his chest and looked into his heated gaze. *No more backing down.* "Because you were singing a different tune this morning with your cock in my mouth," I said proudly.

I saw the moment his restraint snapped and felt a grin tug at my lips. *Was it terrible to be turned on by that wild look in his eyes?* He gripped the back of my head and slammed his lips to mine. I went up on my tiptoes as his tongue forged its way past my lips. I'd broken the last of his restraint and reveled in the way he demanded his dues. This new version of myself loved the dominant man he'd suddenly become.

Without taking his mouth from mine, he shoved me backward and crowded me. I stepped back blindly until my back hit the cold brick wall of a nearby department store. I never opened my eyes as his hands traveled lower until they gripped my ass. I felt the vibration of his deep growl as he thrust his erection against my belly.

"Does it feel like I don't want to *fuck* you anymore, Bambi?" he grumbled against my lips. I whimpered as he squeezed me and kissed me again. Our breaths melded into one as I focused on those lips. I nipped his bottom lip and was rewarded with another deep groan before he ground against me again. He felt impossibly hard under all his layers.

He moved one hand and traveled up my coat-covered back until reaching the back of my head. I emitted another whimper as he dug his fingers into my hair and pulled hard. My scalp lit up at his rough treatment and turned into an odd heat that sank into my core. I could feel myself becoming needy for the very part of him that pressed firmly against my belly.

"I'm only going to say this once, so listen well," he growled as he released my lips. "Look at me," he ordered and my eyes sprang open. I wondered if my eyes mirrored the same carnal lust he displayed.

"You caught me by surprise just now but that does nothing to cool my feelings toward you. If anything it makes me want to plunge my cock so far into your tight little cunt you will be able to taste it. I wanted to bend you over that table and show you just exactly what it means to be fucked by someone. Maybe it makes me the villain to want to be the one that takes away your innocence, but so be it. I want to be your first *and last* in everything, Bambi," he admitted.

Maybe it made me stupid, or immature. Maybe it made me a bad friend and needy. But I didn't care anymore. I wanted everything he offered and more. I wanted *him*.

I pushed my hands between us and gripped the seam of his jeans, allowing my fingers to dip in and feel the coarse hair there. I stepped up on my tiptoes as high as I could before I grazed my lips against his. "Please," I whispered before kissing him lightly.

I could feel his smile against me as he gripped my hair tighter. I swear my eyes rolled into the back of my head as pleasure raced down my body straight to my sex. "That won't be the only time you utter that word tonight, Bambi," he promised.

When I thought he'd kiss me again he did the opposite and pulled away. My chest deflated as the cold of the winter day replaced where he'd been moments ago. I tried not to look as crestfallen as I felt as he stepped away from me.

"I can't fuck you in the middle of the street,

Lindsey." He chuckled as he held his hand out for me to grasp. I looked between it and his face as a smile creased my kiss-swollen lips. *Maybe this new Lindsey wasn't so bad after all.*

I clasped my hand in his and he pulled me to him. I could've swooned when he tucked me under his arm and pulled me snuggly to his side. I smiled up at him and he returned it before I looked at the others walking around us. Nobody paid us any mind now as we made our way to the restaurant.

We were still somewhat early as we entered the warm cafe. The bell above the door dinged as Ian held it open for me. I smiled and flushed slightly as I ducked past him. Why did the simple act of him holding the door for me make me blush when I all but fucked him outside?

We gave the waitress the number of people for our party and she led us to a back corner booth. Ian helped me out of my coat and I couldn't help my grin as I watched his expression flicker to something darker. He pulled the sash on my coat until the knot came free as he locked gazes with me. "I'll never be able to look at this coat the same way again," I muttered. He flashed me a devastating grin as he removed his own coat then. His tight-fitting shirt and jeans were now fully uncovered for my hungry gaze. I'd seen him naked but that didn't stop me from getting turned on by looking at him fully clothed.

He took our coats and hung them up before gesturing for me to slide into the curved booth. As I settled in the vibrant red round seat, I pulled my phone from my pocket and sent Anna a quick text letting her know we were here. As I pocketed my phone Ian slid in beside me. He wound his arm around my shoulders and pulled me into his side. I sighed a sound of contentment as he kissed the top of my head. *This felt ... normal.*

I pressed my hand against his jean-clad thigh before glancing up at him. He was staring down at me with some indiscernible emotion flashing in those sea-colored eyes. He leaned down and kissed me softly before pulling back up. He rubbed his thumb against my shoulder as he searched my eyes. A warm feeling expanded in my chest at his gentle caress.

"I like this," he murmured.

"Me too," I whispered. It was only the truth.

He moved his other hand and pushed my hair away from my forehead before trailing his fingers down my jaw. He swallowed thickly before he spoke again. "I can't wait until I can finally make you mine. Like legitimately, no hiding, mine," he murmured.

I mimicked his swallow as a kernel of dread roared to life in my stomach. *Anna.* "Tomorrow," I whispered.

He gripped my chin and brought my lips closer to his. "Tomorrow," he agreed before sealing his lips to mine in a gentle caress.

I was left breathless as he pulled away. He smiled down at me with those pearly whites and I was reminded again of how strikingly handsome he was. I flushed and grinned as I turned my face away from him. I could get lost so easily with him if I allowed myself.

The bell above the entrance dinged loudly and I glanced up. I sucked in a startled breath as I was forced back to reality. Anna stood there looking the opposite way as I sat up straight. I removed my hand from Ian's thigh and he moved his arm up to lie on the back of the booth instead of my shoulders. I immediately wanted to ask him to lay it back down. A chill snaked up my back at the loss of his warmth.

I shook myself as I flagged down Anna. She glanced my way as I waved toward her. My smile turned into a frown as I watched my best friend head our way. Her usually beautiful face was marred with worry as she stepped up to us. Her lips were sunk in and her normally honey-colored skin looked pale and not just from the cold.

She looked over her shoulder before removing her coat like she was searching for someone. "Hey, what's wrong?" I asked, worried. Ian removed his arm from behind me and sat forward on alert. He sensed something was wrong with her too.

Anna flung her gaze back to me and that's when I saw confusion laced through her eyes. She slid into the booth and sat next to me, shivering as she turned toward me.

"Anna, what is it?" Ian's deep voice sounded from behind my turned body.

Anna shook her head and eyed both of us before finally speaking. "I don't really know," she said shakily. I furrowed my brows and willed her to continue. She licked her lips and looked back toward the front entrance before locking eyes with me again. "I think Ben and Melonie hooked up in the dressing room."

I felt my jaw drop before I had the common sense to catch it. "What?" I questioned louder than necessary. Anna nodded as our waitress stepped up to our table and deposited five waters. She muttered a quick thank you as she picked hers up and took a big gulp. I stared at her like she'd grown two heads as our waitress left again.

"Yeah, I mean, I can't be sure but they were in there for a *really* long time. And then before I knew what was happening Melonie burst out of the room. She was jerking her coat on like she was pissed off and it looked like she was about to start ... crying?" Anna screwed her face up in confusion.

I was left reeling and I didn't even feel Ian place

his hand on my knee under the table until he squeezed me. "Wh—" I stuttered. "What happened then?" I asked in a rush.

"That's the weird part." Anna seemed to finally be calming down as she gripped her menu in front of her while still looking at me. "Melonie mumbled something about catching up with us later and Ben—"

"Ben, what?" a familiar voice spoke, causing Anna and me to both jump.

Ben stood in front of our table with a sugary-sweet smile as he stared down at us. He even flashed Ian the same smile before unzipping his coat. I felt Ian tense beside me as he scowled at him.

Anna, ever the one to ruffle feathers, spoke first, "You tell us. What happened with Melonie at the boutique?" she asked with a pointed glare.

Ben shrugged before removing his coat and hanging it next to ours. He said nothing as he slid into the booth next to Anna and grabbed his menu. We all sat stock still as he glanced over the lunch specials like he didn't have a care in the world.

"Ben," I was the first one to speak. Ian's hand on my knee flexed and released as if to hold me back from speaking further.

Ben looked up at me and I swore I saw anger flash in his hazel eyes before it disappeared completely. "I don't see how anything I do with Melonie is any of your business, Lindsey," he said firmly before smirking. "You certainly don't take my feelings into account before *you* fuck other people."

I flinched back at his words as though he'd struck me. *Did he just insinuate I was a whore?* I felt Ian tense before he moved to get out of the booth. I slapped my hand down on his thigh to stop him but it did nothing of the sort. He was about to stand when Anna blustered at my other side.

"You know I put up with a lot of shit from you and I'm just about fed up with it, *Ben*. If you want to show your ass and make a fool of yourself then that's your prerogative. You want to fuck Melonie in a dressing room as some sort of sick way to punish Lindsey for not returning your affection, go ahead." She leaned into his space as she quietly uttered her next words. "But if you ever think to insinuate that Lindsey is a whore ever again, I will cut your balls off one at a time and shove them so far down your throat they come out your ass, and I will make sure you're forced to fucking watch as I do it." I couldn't see the look she was giving Ben but he had common sense enough to slide further away from her.

Ben's eyes flickered from my seething bestie to an equally as pissed Ian and then finally to me before nodding. "I–I didn't mean … I'm sorry, Lyns," he stammered as he shook his head. It seemed like he was coming out of some sort of trance as he looked confusingly down at his lap.

The bell above the door rang again and I looked over in time to see Melonie marching our way. Ian and Anna kept their gazes locked on Ben as she approached.

For the first time since I'd met Melonie, she looked disheveled. Her hair was falling out of her perfect ponytail, her coat was buttoned incorrectly, and she looked fidgety. Worry marred my brow as she looked at Ben like she was half frightened by his presence. She stared at the side of his head and back toward the door like she was contemplating running away.

"Are you okay?" I asked as she stood in front of the table. She jumped as if she just remembered there were other people at the table. When she realized I was the one that spoke her fearful expression was pulled into a look of annoyance.

"Why wouldn't I be?" she scoffed and rolled her eyes as she climbed into the booth next to Ben.

Both refused to make eye contact with one another as they thumbed through their menus. Silence ensued as Ian and Anna both relaxed next to me. I released a breath as I tried to process how this day was panning out.

I was still confused as to why Ben was acting the way he was but I decided to shelve the feeling for now. Maybe when we got back home and into our normal routine things would calm down. *Well, almost normal.* I smiled to myself. One thing would be changing when we got back and that was that Ian and I would be together.

I wanted to experience all the things that made my heart flutter with him. Not only that, I wanted to experience what it was like to be in a fully committed relationship. For the first time in my life, I didn't feel awkward or uncertain about the possibility of having a love life. It was both exhilarating and frightening.

"Well, this is awkward," Anna stated loudly. I snorted at her obvious description of how this shopping day had gone. She smiled at me before nudging me with her shoulder. "What do you say to hitting the slopes after lunch? You almost made it down the entire bunny slope last time without falling," she teased.

My eyes widened at the thought of skiing again. It was abundantly obvious that it wasn't my forte. "Actually, would you hate me if I just stayed at the cabin and relaxed for the rest of the day?" I winced.

Anna clicked her tongue before smirking at me. She knew I was so far past wanting to learn to ski. "Of course, that's fine. It's your birthday trip, you get to do whatever you want," she said. I turned away from her before she could see the red staining my cheeks. *What I wanted to do was her dad.* I smothered my erratic giggle at the thought.

"You wanna go?" She turned toward Melonie. She jerked slightly as she looked at Anna. It was like she'd been startled out of her own little world.

"Oh, yeah, fine, whatever," she said as she set her menu down and looked at Ben. Whatever had been riding her when she walked into the cafe quickly disappeared as she flicked her eyes from me and then to him. "You'll go too, won't you?"

Ben nodded absentmindedly and she accepted that as an answer before shooting me another nasty look. *Was she trying to keep Ben away from me?* The way she kept looking between the two of us made me feel as though she were threatened by me.

I frowned at her as the waitress stepped up to our table. Whatever questions I felt the urge to ask died on my tongue as she recited the day's specials.

Chapter Sixteen

"Are you sure you have to work?" Melonie pouted to Ian as we entered the cabin. "I could use some more lessons." She held her hands clasped in front of her in a way that thrust her chest out. Whatever had been riding her back in town was obviously gone as she shamelessly flirted with Ian. I had to bite my tongue as red flashed before my eyes. Couldn't she tell by now that he clearly wasn't into her like that?

Ben slid past all of us, making eye contact with nobody as he disappeared toward his room. I tried to ignore the pinch of guilt I felt at his turn of mood.

Ian, being the gentleman he was, was kind in his letdown. "I have reports I need to catch up on and phone calls to return," he said before glancing at me as I stood in front of the fireplace to warm my hands. Anna stood next to me with a scowl marring her features. She knew exactly what Melonie was doing and it looked like she had just about enough of it. Ian must've seen my annoyance with Barbie at that point as he looked back toward her. "I'm sure you can find another instructor for the day, Malinda," he said.

I slapped my hand over my mouth to smother my snort and Anna outright howled with laughter. She gripped my arm as she cackled, causing me to look at her. The moment we made eye contact we both erupted into hysterical laughter.

Melonie huffed and crossed her arms over her chest. "It's Melonie," she seethed at Ian before scowling at me. Ian held his hands up in defeat as he apologized but he and I both knew he'd done it on purpose. He's seen my jealousy and acted accordingly and I liked him all the more for it.

Melonie stomped past Anna and me on her way to their room with a nasty look twisting her lips. She wasn't used to not gaining the male attention she so desperately sought.

"Oh, man," Anna breathed before wiping a tear out of the corner of her eye. "That was fucking hilarious, thanks for that one, Dad." She chuckled as she looked at Ian who had the decency to at least try and look innocent. He said nothing as he grinned at us before shoving his hands in his pockets.

"Anyway, I'm going to get ready to go. Are you sure you don't want to go with us?" she asked the question directed at me. I tried not to let my eyes wander to Ian as I answered her.

"Are you kidding?" I scoffed. "This fireplace has been begging for me to curl up with a nice long book since we arrived here." I gestured to the huge hearth in front of us and the large black sectional behind me facing the fire. For once I felt like I wasn't outright lying to my friend, I really had wanted to sit and just enjoy a good book in front of that fire.

Anna rolled her eyes at me before flouncing toward her and Melonie's room. "All right, but just remember, we only have a couple more days here and it doesn't snow in Florida," she sang as she disappeared down the hall.

"Oh, believe me, I know!" I called after her with a chuckle. The snow was beautiful to look at but I was so over the frigid temperatures and ready to get back to warmer climates.

I was so busy looking after Anna that I didn't see Ian invade my space until he was tugging at my coat sash. I sucked in a startled breath as I swiveled my eyes in his direction. He was staring into mine with such intensity I felt as though I'd burn under his gaze. His fingers worked with precision as he pulled the knot free for the third time that day. As he slid the coat from my shoulders, I couldn't help the vision that flashed before my eyes of him slipping other clothing from my body. I flushed at the thought.

Would he forever have this effect on me?

He gripped my coat before it fell to the ground and tossed it on the couch at my side. When he returned his hands to me I felt myself leaning into him against my will. The sheer magnetism he emitted seemed to pull me in at every given chance.

After our impromptu groping session on the busy sidewalk, I was ready for everything he promised me. I wanted to know what it felt like to have someone make love to me. I wanted to know what it was like to be joined as one. I simply *wanted*.

"Looks like we'll have the house all to ourselves, Little Bambi," he murmured before his hands drifted to my hips. His fingers danced their way under the hem of my shirt, teasing the flesh that lay underneath. I shivered and licked my suddenly dry lips, his eyes followed the movement hungrily. "Whatever will we do with ourselves?"

I allowed my eyes to flutter closed at the sensation of his thumb dipping below the seam of my jeans just to come back up and repeat the process. *Up, down, up, down.* When I heard him chuckle at the effect he was having on me my eyes sprang open.

His sea-colored gaze held challenge as if he were begging me to play along in his sexy little game of cat and mouse. I felt a grin tug at my lips as I moved my hands to surround his neck. I leaned forward to give him the impression that I was going to kiss him, only to pull back slightly before our lips were sealed together. I hoped my eyes reflected the same provocation as I spoke.

"I hope you'll teach me a few things I've been dying to learn," I said in a voice much huskier than I'd ever heard. I leaned in then and ran the tip of my tongue along the seam of his lips. When he opened for me I nipped his bottom lip. His hand flexed against my hips as a deep rumble emitted from low in his chest. When his eyes met mine again I knew I'd awoken the dominant beast I'd gotten a taste of earlier. *Good.*

"Oh, Bambi, you have no idea what I have planned for you," he admitted deliciously before kissing me lightly. When he nipped my lip I couldn't hold back the whimper that rose. The sharp pain zapped straight to my pussy before settling in my core as a steady thrum. His smile was animalistic as he pulled away. "I'm going to shower. Will you join me when everyone leaves?" he asked.

I swallowed my anxiety as I nodded. He sauntered from the room and I found myself nervous. *Are you really going to do this?* my inner voice screamed at me as I watched the hallway Ian had disappeared down.

"All right, we're out of here," Anna's chipper voice sounded loud as she appeared behind me. I jumped at the sudden surprise at her appearance before recovering quickly. Melonie and Ben followed, dressed in their thermal wear.

Melonie's face still kept the same shrewd look of disgust as she glared at me while Ben looked simply unfazed. Ever since the cafe he hadn't said much at all. I caught him looking my way only once since then and I got the weirdest feeling from it. His gaze had held confusion, anger, and oddly enough resolve. Like he'd decided something and failed to clue the rest of us in on his plan.

Since he wasn't speaking I only had to assume he was trying to work our new dynamic out in his mind. I'd thought that when I told him I didn't see him the same way he saw me, that would've been the end of it. I honestly thought he could go back to seeing me as a friend but after today I began to wonder if that was even a possibility.

Even if he insulted me today, I still cherished our friendship and wanted to continue it. Besides Anna, he was my only other friend. I made a mental note to sit him down when we got back home and discuss where we were to go from here.

I meant what I told Ian, I wanted to be with him when this week was over. I knew everything was happening super fast for us but I couldn't help but think this was the way it was always going to pan out. I wasn't making any proclamations of love, but I wanted this. For the first time in my adult life, I was going to fight for something that made *me* happy. I wasn't going to let other people's perceived opinions cause me to lose out on something that could be great, perfect even. Even if one of those people was a close friend of mine.

Let's just hope that Anna is okay with this when the dust settles. I honestly didn't know what I would do if she wasn't.

Anna led the others toward the door and opened it for them. When they were out of hearing range she smiled at me. "I'm going to make them stay with me at the lodge for dinner tonight so we will be out of your hair until at least eight this evening," she said and I was taken aback. When I meant to ask why she held her hand up, halting my words. "I can tell you need a break from people. I know you, Lyns," she admitted.

I flushed slightly. "You don't have to do that," I said softly.

Anna beamed at me now. "I know but I'm going to. Consider it your birthday gift."

I snorted at that. "And what would you call *this*?" I gestured to the room we were standing in.

"Also a gift," she said and shrugged. "What can I say, I'm an awesome friend." She giggled and I did too. "And don't worry about my dad, he'll be locked away in his room for most of the night. You won't see him at all."

God, how I hope you're wrong on that one, I thought to myself and then immediately had to stifle a giggle. I was acting like a horned-up teenager.

"Thank you, Anna," I said

"You're welcome," she said as she backed out the door. "Okay, love you, bye!" she yelled before closing the door, and suddenly I was alone.

I took a deep breath as if to breathe in my solace before what was about to happen. The only sounds in the room were the crackling of the fire in the hearth and my own rapidly rising heart rate.

"All right, Lindsey, let's do this," I murmured as I rubbed my suddenly sweaty palms down the front of my jeans.

I forced my feet to move and I headed toward the hallway. It felt as though time slowed down the closer I came to his door. He'd left it slightly ajar, his way of welcoming me in. I took a deep breath as I pushed it open and slipped inside.

My feet padded quietly against the dark hardwood floor as I turned and shut the door. The resounding click made my anxiety tick all the more. I forced myself to breathe as I twisted the lock. When I turned to face the room I was taken aback.

I'd only seen his room the night I'd caught him pleasuring himself. The room had been bathed in darkness that night so I had no idea what I'd find when I ventured here today. His room had the same floor-to-ceiling windows mine had, though this room seemed almost darker. It vibrated with a cozy vibe with the dark fabric that lay strewn on top of his bed. I smiled to myself as I stepped up to the unkempt bed. It was nice to see he wasn't perfect after all. He was a bit messy by the looks of his room.

His bedside table was littered with a couple of empty water glasses as well as a few medical journals with the pages marked in various places. His laptop sat above the mess, half open, half closed as if he'd been in too big of a rush to finish what he'd been doing.

I allowed my eyes to drift to the opposite side of the room where a plush seating area sat facing an equally messy desk. I could picture him sitting behind that desk sifting through papers and scrawling hasty notes as he went. I walked toward one plush armchair with a few shirts thrown carelessly atop it.

My fingers danced along the soft fabric of one of the t-shirts before I picked it up. It was a plain charcoal grey shirt with a modest V-neck I just knew he would look delectable in. Without thinking, I brought the smooth material to my nose and inhaled deeply. His masculine scent coated every fiber of the shirt and I found myself wanting to be surrounded by it. Just the smell of him sent hot arousal flooding my panties.

I turned to face the en suite bathroom where I knew him to be. The light was on and the door left slightly open as though he knew I'd come for him. The steam permeating from the room indicated that he was enjoying his hot shower.

I placed his shirt back onto the chair before I slowly walked closer. My pulse jumped in my throat with each advancing step. My nerves were starting to get the better of me the closer I came. *Am I really going to do this?*

It was obvious I wanted to do this, with him no

less. I couldn't think of any other person I would rather do this with. But I couldn't stop that little voice in the back of my mind that screamed I was making a huge mistake. I would never be able to go back to the girl I used to be after this day.

I stopped outside the door and closed my eyes. Placing my hand on the door but not going any further, I hardened my resolve and quieted the voices telling me this was a terrible idea. I wanted Ian and he wanted me, so how could this be wrong? When I opened my eyes I told myself it was okay to never be the girl I used to be. That was a part of life. One day, we all had to decide if we wanted the same we'd always had or if we deserved new things for ourselves, better things.

I shoved the old Lindsey down, the one who was always insecure and cared too much about what others thought of her. The Lindsey who always took everything given to her and never dared ask for what she wanted, what she *needed*. I said goodbye to the girl of my past as I pushed that door open and welcomed the woman of my future.

"There you are, Bambi."

Chapter Seventeen

It took a moment for my eyes to adjust to the sudden fogginess of the room, but when they did my breath stalled in my chest. The object of my desire stood under the hot stream of water looking like he stepped straight off the set of a porno. He was in the middle of washing himself when he saw me enter the room. I was too stunned by the sight of his soapy body to bother with shutting the door behind me as I stepped closer.

"What's the matter?" He chuckled as his lathery hands roamed down his washboard abdomen, heading further south. "Cat got your tongue?" he teased.

Something like that.

His hair and beard were sopping wet, making the normally light grey color look darker. His longer hair on top of his head was slicked back as if he'd shoved it out of his face while he rinsed the shampoo from the silky locks. His eyes flickered with lust as he stared me down, begging wordlessly for me to join him. As if my body had a direct link to his thoughts, I slipped my hands under the hem of my top. I kept my eyes on him as I lifted the material up and over my breasts before pulling it over my head. I dropped it to the ground in front of me before pulling my hands toward my back to grip the clasp of my bra.

His gaze became hooded as he drank in the sight of me. The heated look he gave me emboldened my every move. I smiled slyly as I released the tight clasp and my heavy breasts sprang free of their constraint. I'm not sure where I'd gotten this surge of bravado but I teased him with slow tantalizing movements as the fabric slipped slowly down, uncovering my achy nipples one at a time before letting it fall from my body.

My eyes blazed a trail from his face down further where he was still rubbing his hands over his torso. I became mesmerized by the way his biceps flexed and relaxed as his hands worked the masculine-smelling soap over his body. I licked my lips as his hands dipped lower to that part of his anatomy I wanted to become more familiar with. The suds from his abdomen seemed to follow his hands as he slid them down to his thick cock, which was proudly pointing my way.

I unbuttoned my jeans before slowly sliding them down my hips. I didn't care that it was daytime and he could see all my curves for what they were. This was my body and I needed to start loving it the way I knew Ian did, cellulite and all. My eyes never left his cock as his hand wrapped around the impressive length. My eyes flared as my jeans coiled around my ankles at the same time he gave himself a long stroke, his soap making his hand glide effortlessly.

"Do you see something you like, Bambi?" he growled. He slid his hand back up to his bulbous head just to descend again. His chuckle had my eyes darting away from his manhood and up to his scalding eyes. "If I'm not careful I'll come in my hand. The way you're looking at me like I'm your favorite snack makes me want to shove my cock past your lips and give you everything I have."

His words sent a fresh wave of wetness to my already soaked panties. I wanted that too. Without a word, I pushed my panties down until they met my ankles right alongside my jeans. I toed out of the fabric and stepped closer to the shower. I could feel his scorching gaze on me as I stepped under the hot spray.

He still stood in front of me stroking himself with a deep hunger set in those sea-colored eyes as he rinsed the soap from his body. I found myself shaking with either nervousness or excitement, which one I couldn't be sure. I just knew I wanted everything this man had to offer.

"Show me," I said as I stepped up to him and sank to my knees. The heat from the shower spray had nothing on the way he looked at me at that moment.

He said nothing before he threaded his hand into my now wet locks and stepped closer to me. I stared at that monster between his legs as he held onto the base. He pulled my hair, and pleasure mixed with a hint of pain crackled along my scalp as I looked up at him.

"You want to suck my cock like a good little slut?" he asked almost harshly. He was on the edge and I was about to shove him the rest of the way off.

"Yes, Sir," I whimpered. The word no longer felt foreign coming from my lips, it felt right.

His eyes flared before he stepped closer and tapped the head of his dick against my chin. "Then open," he gritted behind clenched teeth.

I obeyed immediately and he fed me his thick length. I kept my eyes trained on his as his mouth dropped open and he pushed past my lips. I swirled my tongue around his head and nearly moaned as the taste of him washed over me. He held his hand in my hair so firmly that I had no choice but to take what he had to give me and I loved every second of it.

I flicked my tongue and teased the V under the head of his cock as he pulled out. My mouth made a popping noise as he withdrew completely before pushing back inside. With each thrust, he pushed himself deeper and deeper.

"I'm going to take you to your limits, Bambi. You will swallow everything I have to give you. If it becomes too much, tap my thigh. Do you understand?" he asked.

I hummed my agreement before he loosened his hand in my hair and gripped the back of my head in his big hand. He tunneled in and out of my mouth and I focused on my breathing. He groaned above me and sang my praises as I sucked him as hard as I could. My pussy was throbbing so much that I squeezed my thighs together to ward off the ache. It didn't work.

"Oh, Lindsey, you feel so good. I like the way you look with my cock in that pretty mouth. Spread your legs and show me that little cunt," he ordered. I did as I was told and shuddered as the cool air caressed my slickness. "Is that pussy ready to take me?" he gritted as he pushed further into my mouth. I gagged as he knocked the back of my throat but I refused to lose him. I nodded as I stared up at his pleasured expression. "Touch yourself for me, Lindsey."

Yes, Sir.

I wasted no time as I thrust my fingers through my slick folds. I moaned as I circled my thumping clit and Ian took advantage, sliding further into me. My legs trembled as I rubbed my clit just like he showed me. I was going to come but I wanted him with me.

I spread my thighs as much as I could and used my other hand to grasp his heavy balls. He gasped and his grueling pace quickened further. "That's it, Bambi. I'm going to come and you are going to swallow it all," he groaned as I felt his balls tighten.

I pushed down against myself and saw stars as I exploded. If my mouth weren't full I would have screamed. As it was, he tunneled down my throat as hot jets of cum shot out of him. He held himself in as far as he could as he groaned his release. I was still thrumming with my orgasm when he pulled out of me and pulled me to my feet.

He hastily shut the water off before picking me

up. He seemed to be in a hurry as he completely skipped drying us off and walked us to his bed. He slammed his lips to mine as soon as my back hit the soft bedding. I could still taste his release along my tongue so I knew he could too but he groaned against me nonetheless.

I expected him to thrust into me and was shocked when he lowered himself between my thighs. He gave me no time to get ready for him as he sucked my clit into his mouth. I screamed and gripped my hands into his sopping-wet hair. Cold water droplets dripped from his hair onto my overheated skin as he ate at me.

The orgasm took me by surprise as he wrapped his arms around my thighs and forced me to feel everything he had to offer. My legs shook as my release overwhelmed my body.

He slowed his hastened movements and lapped me softly while my body twitched with aftershocks. Just when I thought he was done he latched back onto me as his thick fingers thrust inside of me. My arms flung to my sides as I gripped the bedsheets with white-knuckle force.

My orgasm blinded me that time as it ripped through my body. I felt my hips move with his mouth, fucking his face as much as he had mine.

"Oh, God! I can't take anymore!" I screamed before I tried to push his mouth away from me. His fingers pumped into me as he stretched me from within. I could feel his fingers scissoring inside of me and it took me a moment to figure out what he was doing to me. *He's preparing me to take something much bigger.*

I could feel another climax rising as he curled his fingers inside of me. I trembled as his mouth rose from my sensitive bundle of nerves and he grinned at me. I didn't blush that time as I saw my arousal glimmering on his plump lips. I was too turned on to be embarrassed. He blew a gentle breath against my slickness before speaking.

"What do you want, Lindsey?" he asked, fully knowing the answer.

I felt a new pressure build inside my core as his fingers worked that magical spot inside of me. Something explosive was about to happen. I gripped the sheets beside me as my breath left me in sharp pants. Under normal circumstances, I would have blushed and shyly averted my gaze. I would've never begged for what I needed. But this was anything but normal circumstances as I felt my body burn up with carnal lust.

"Fuck me!" I begged.

He chuckled before lapping at me again. I could feel his devious grin against my cleft. "Say please," he growled before moving with quickness.

The unbearable pressure at my core became too much as I felt a burning wash of arousal bombard me. My pussy clenched down onto his fingers right before he clamped his hot mouth back to me. I cried my release and felt a rush of fiery liquid soak his fingers and chin. He groaned against me as wave after wave of ecstasy crashed over me.

"Please fuck me, Sir!" I screamed.

Whatever tight restraint he had left snapped as he grabbed for me. He pulled us up the bed and rolled us quickly until he had me situated on top of him. He leaned against the plush headboard as he pulled my hips to his. I could feel his pulsing cock against my slick core and I wanted nothing more than to put his hot length inside of me. I needed him to mark me as his in every single way.

"I had a vasectomy twenty-something years ago and I'm clean, but if you don't feel comfortable taking me raw there are condoms in the nightstand," he stated with urgency as his hands roamed my body.

I gripped his cock between my thighs and raised onto my knees. "I trust you," I said as I stroked him. I felt as though I was going to die if I didn't get to feel him inside of me.

He stilled my hand before crashing his lips to mine. I could feel my release still coating his beard and it only served to heighten my need for him. I sighed against him as he ate at my lips. I was ravenous when he pulled away enough to speak. "You decide how fast this goes, Lindsey. We go at your pace," he whispered against my lips.

I nodded against him and felt a sudden flood of nerves rush to the surface. If I was finally going to have sex, I was glad it was with Ian. I released my breath slowly and tried to relax.

I gripped him with a shaky hand as I lined him up with my entrance. My slickness made it easy for him to slide in inch by inch. Pure desire sparkled in his sea-colored eyes as he pushed into me the slightest bit. I gripped his shoulders and focused on his softened features as I slowly dipped lower with each pass.

I knew he wasn't even halfway inside of me but I felt as though I were being stretched to my breaking point. Reality dawned on me the moment he hit that place inside of me that marked me as a virgin. The thin little piece of flesh we would have to rip through protested painfully as his thick length throbbed against it. I moaned an uncomfortable sound as sweat broke out along my brow. I didn't know how I would be able to take all of him. *Maybe this was a mistake.*

"Hey," he murmured as he gripped my chin between his fingers. I'm sure my face mirrored my discomfort as he soothingly rubbed my thigh with his free hand. I focused on that hand going up and down from my knee up to my hip over and over again.

"I ... I don't kn ... what if I c—" I stuttered as I trembled.

"Shh, it's all right," he said soothingly as his hand dipped to my sex. I sucked in a sharp breath as his thumb rubbed my clitoris, making me needy all over again. "Relax and take a deep breath."

I did as I was told and took a shaky breath in before releasing it. He breathed with me and we took a few more calming breaths. His thumb never stopped rubbing me and I could feel myself building up just to crumble back down.

"You look so fucking beautiful, Lindsey." He palmed my breast with his free hand and lightly grazed his thumb over my hardened nipple, lighting me up. "I'm so goddamn proud to call you mine, Bambi. You were made to take me," he murmured and I preened at his loving words. "I can feel that little cunt throbbing around me. I'm only halfway in and I can feel you squeezing the life out of me. I'm going to make you come for me while I'm inside of you." He upped his thumbs' movements and I could feel my hips start to move again. "Yes, Lindsey. I want to feel you pulse around my cock, be a good girl and come on your Sir."

His words were my undoing as I came crashing down and I braced myself. When the first wave crashed, Ian grabbed my hips and slammed me down onto his cock, fully sheathing himself. My orgasm ripped through me at the same time blinding pain tore at my core. The pleasure mixed with the pain blended so perfectly that it took my breath away.

I wailed as I leaned forward to his shoulder. He wrapped his arms around me and held me to his chest as I adjusted to him. I could feel tears prick the back of my eyes from the pain but as I sat in his arms I could already feel it melting into something else entirely.

Ian rubbed my back and sang soft praises as he kissed my hair, neck, and shoulder. I sank into him, soaking in the entire experience for what it was. Loving every uncensored, raw feeling that surrounded the moment. I could feel him throbbing inside of me and I knew he was withholding his own pleasure just to make sure I was all right. My chest expanded with a warm feeling at the thought.

"Are you okay, Lindsey?" he murmured against my hair.

I nodded as the pain in my core dimmed into a dull ache. I sat back slowly but his hands never left me, he simply slipped them back down to my legs. I released a shaky breath as I slowly pulled myself up, sliding up his thick shaft. I gasped at the sensation of nerves firing that I didn't even know existed until that moment. Ian flexed his hands against my thighs as pleasure morphed across his beautiful features.

"Fuck!" he growled as I sank back onto him slowly. "This isn't going to last long," he gritted behind clenched teeth. I could feel his abdomen flex with restraint against my palms as I rose again. That time when I moaned it was with pleasure. I could feel myself winding up all over again.

I felt my body start to shake as new sensations fired deep within my core. "Ian," I whimpered. "Please."

As if my words broke the chains that restrained him, he pounced. He gripped my lower back as he pulled me under him, never taking his cock from me. I yelped as he fit his hips between my thighs and fucked into me with urgency. Every twist of his hips ground against my throbbing clit, driving me to the brink of insanity.

"You are mine. This pussy is mine, say it!" he growled.

"I'm yours, all of me is yours!" I screamed as my

orgasm loomed over my head. I wrapped my legs around him and gripped his muscled back with my fingers.

"That's right. No one else will ever have this tight little cunt. I'm your first and your last." He gripped my breast and pulled it up toward his mouth. "Now, be a good little slut and come all over my cock," he commanded before his hot mouth latched onto my achy nipple.

As if I was waiting for his command, I exploded around him. My back arched and I dug my nails into the smooth skin on his back as I screamed my release.

"Oh, fuck!" he growled as he slammed into me one last time. I felt his hot release spew deep as he pulsed inside of me. His mouth dropped open as he rubbed into me with a long groan. I didn't think I would ever get tired of seeing that ecstasy contort his features.

When his orgasm subsided he collapsed on top of me. I welcomed his heavy weight as if it were a blanket. He kissed my neck and I rubbed his back. He stayed inside of me for long moments as we soaked in the last moments of my first time. A swell of pride surged through my body as I realized I was no longer a virgin and I had made the correct decision to let this man take that precious part of me.

Chapter Eighteen

"I met Hillary at the hospital I used to work at," Ian spoke in soft words as my fingers played in his chest hair. "She was a nurse and I was the attending physician," he said matter-of-factly. I tried to tramp down the instant jealousy that flared at the mention of his ex's name, Anna's mom. I was the one snuggled up to his side after our romp in the sheets hours ago, not her.

When he finally pulled himself from me earlier and cleaned us both up, he'd simply grabbed me to his side and hadn't let go. It felt natural to lay like this with him.

As it was, we'd lay like this while he talked about his past. He talked briefly about his marriage to Anna's mom. I felt a wave of relief when there was no hint of sadness in his voice about the divorce from his ex. Apparently, the whole situation had been mutual and there were no hard feelings. "I will forever be grateful to her for bringing Anna into my life," he said with a small smile playing on his lips.

It was obvious that he and Anna had the type of father/daughter relationship some would never get. He loved her like she were his own in every single way possible. It was something I found myself envious of.

I laid with my head on his chest as he relayed story after story of Anna growing up. And when he ran out of stories about her he moved on to stories of his own youth. Everything from his father teaching him to play baseball to him getting a scholarship to Harvard Medical School.

I was stunned and intrigued to listen to him talk about his life. It was moments like this that made me remember our age difference. I was basically new to adulthood and here he was having lived a whole-ass life. Complete with college, marriage, and a kid. "Wow, you've had a full life," I muttered, my voice dull to my own ears. The thought of us being in completely different phases of our lives caused my chest to deflate some. "Sometimes I forget that there's such a large gap in our ages," I admitted.

I knew that when we went back to our real lives we were going to try and make this relationship work, but I still held onto my reservations. Even just replaying what he said to me before we had sex got me thinking about the future. He'd had a vasectomy twenty-something years ago and I was just entering my twenties *now*. Sure, I didn't want babies at this point in my life but that wasn't to say I would never want them. Would he be okay with that or would he opt out completely? The thought of putting so much effort into a relationship just to see it fail scared the shit out of me. Maybe I was childish, but I wanted a lifelong partner. Not someone to just pass the time with.

He shocked me with his intuitiveness when he realized my thoughts had turned dark. He rolled me over and kissed me senselessly with the promise that everything in our relationship would work itself out. "No, Bambi. It hasn't been full because I haven't gotten to spend any of it with you," he said and I melted at his words. "I want this badly enough that I'd never let something as silly as an age difference come between us," he promised quietly.

By the time he let me up for air, I was needy all over again. I took a deep breath as he pulled me back to his side and stilled my wantonness. As it was, I was starting to get a dull ache in my core from our earlier activities. Not that that stopped my mind from wandering to dirtier things.

My hands itched to move the blanket that covered his hips. My eyes wanted nothing more than to gobble up the sight of him again, hard, and ready to take me. My sex clenched with the anticipation of a possible round two. I smothered a giggle as I shook my head to myself. *Down girl. What? You get great sex once and now you're addicted?*

"Enough about me, what about you?" Ian's voice rumbled in his chest under my cheek, effectively halting my kinky thoughts.

I lifted my head and curled my arm over his chest. I tucked my chin against the bend in my elbow and looked up at his handsome face. "What do you mean, *what about me?*" I asked.

The grin that split his lips made me want to grin right back up at him. *Will I ever get used to his charming good looks?* He tucked one hand behind his head and leaned against it as his other tangled in my mass of dark curls. He lovingly finger-brushed my hair before he spoke. "I mean, what have you been up to these last twenty-one years?" he asked.

I tried not to flush at the lack of wonder my life was composed of. I had a mediocre childhood followed up by a mediocre young adulthood. All in all, it was nothing to ring home about.

"What do you want to know?" I asked.

His chuckle bounced me lightly. "Let's start with your college major."

I curled my nose up at his question. "Economics," I stated factually. He raised a regal eyebrow at me eliciting a giggle to bubble up from my belly. "Boring, I know, but I'm good with numbers. When I started college I didn't really have that much of a clue about what I wanted to do when I grew up. It always seemed crazy to me that people expected a bunch of eighteen and nineteen-year-olds to know exactly what they wanted to do for the rest of their lives." I frowned to myself before shaking my head. "Anyway, Aunt Jill said she may have some strings to pull when I graduate. Apparently, she knows some people that could use a good financial manager." I shrugged.

"Sounds like you have it all figured out." He grinned.

"Hardly," I laughed. "But everyone has to start somewhere."

"Okay, so now I know where your future is going, what about your past? How was growing up in Georgia?"

I scoffed with a smile. *"Well, my Mr. Big City Doctor Man. I fancy it was just grand growing up in my dinky little town,"* I spoke in an exaggerated southern accent.

Ian tossed his head back and laughed before returning his eyes to me. Humor sparkled in his eyes as he tugged a piece of my hair. I laughed again before I laid my head back down against his softly rising and falling chest. "It was fine." I shrugged.

His hand kept playing with my hair. "Just fine?"

I nodded. "There isn't much else to say. I grew up in a small town where everyone knew everyone else's business. I went to the same high school my mom and dad went to so every teacher thought I was going to end up just like my mom. Pregnant at sixteen with a loser baby daddy." I winced as the words flew out of my mouth. The way I spoke of others' preconceived notions of my mom made her sound like a loser too when she was the furthest thing from it.

"I think that's partially why I never wanted to have sex with anyone," I admitted quietly and Ian's hand stilled in my hair for a moment before continuing. "That, and I was just never interested in anyone in that way," I reasoned while drawing meaningless swirls against Ian's chest. His hand kept playing with my curls as I continued talking.

"When my dad cheated, everybody in town knew," I said quietly as if I were quiet enough my mother would never have to relive that humiliation. "And with everything that came after their divorce, I'm sure our family drama was the talk of the town."

Ian was quiet for a moment as if carefully navigating the fragile topic of my father trying to kill my mother. "He's in prison, right?" Ian asked, a hint of concern in his voice.

I nodded. "Fifty years, though that's too little as far as I'm concerned." I liked to say I was a person that never hated anyone. Hate was such a strong word and it was hard to come back from that place. But I *hated* my father with every inch of my soul. For what he put my mom through. For what he put *me* through.

"Were you close with him?" he asked.

"Ha!" I barked a humorless laugh. "That's a joke," I said, realizing how bitter I sounded. I moved my head again to look up at him. His hand moved from my hair down to my shoulders where he continued to delicately run his fingers, gently tickling the skin there.

"I never really knew the guy, not in any sense that mattered anyway. I know he loves me but he never treated me the way you treat Anna," I said before searching his eyes. When I thought I'd see pity in those sea-colored eyes I found nothing but empathy. "I think he blamed me for the way his life turned out. As if I was the one that asked to be born. He was always just a fixture in our house that my mom and I had to put up with. And believe me, that was a feat in and of itself." I looked away from Ian and disassociated from the world around me.

"He treated my mom like shit for their whole marriage. Maybe that's why I always steered clear of boys in general," I muttered almost to myself. "You always hear that you tend to date men who are a lot like your own father. Maybe on a subconscious level, I saw how shitty he treated Mom and knew I wouldn't allow that to be me." The back of my eyes burned with tears I refused to let fall. I wouldn't shed any more tears for that bastard.

Ian rubbed his thumb against my lower lip at my admission, bringing me back to the now with him. "When I found out he shot her," I swallowed thickly. "It was the scariest day of my life." My voice wobbled as I spoke. "How could someone you built your life with not only ruin your self-esteem, but also cheat on you and then try and take your life? It's all so fucked up."

Ian pulled me up his body then. He kissed my lips as he crushed me to him. Before I knew it, I was underneath him. He held onto me like I was a lifeline as he nuzzled his nose against mine.

"I have no idea, but I promise you I will never be that way with you, Lindsey. I know this is all going really fast but the way I feel for you … it's hard to put into words," he whispered. For the first time since I met him, he seemed at a loss for words.

I felt unhashed emotion clog my throat as I left the past where it belonged and brought myself back to the now with him. I knew exactly what he was talking about but I didn't want to be the one that said it first. I was afraid if I did then I would look like a starry-eyed child in his eyes and not the lover I wanted to be.

"If you let me, I will show you what a good man is supposed to act like. I'll teach you all the ways a man is supposed to treat a woman. With respect and dignity and … love." He spoke the word against my lips in a hushed tone as if he'd scare me away. "We are supposed to build each other up and help the other strive for greatness. We're supposed to love them no matter what. I will give you everything you've ever wanted and needed. Will you let me do that for you, Lindsey?"

I had no words left to speak at that moment. I watched the emotion swirling around in his eyes and knew without a doubt that he was telling me the truth. He would give me the moon if I asked for it.

I wrapped my arms around his neck and nodded before sealing my lips to his. I still didn't know how everything would pan out with our relationship in the long run or with Anna when this was all over. But I did know that I wanted everything he offered and more. It was no longer just about sex, it was about that and so much more. The future may be uncertain, but I wasn't.

Chapter Nineteen

The soft crackle of the fire seemed to soothe my soul as Ian and I sat adjacent to one another on the oversized couch. My feet were propped on his lap with a soft blanket covering them up to my hips. My book between my fingers was almost all but forgotten as I tried to catch little glances at the immaculate beauty next to me. I smiled behind the pages as I glanced over the binding at him.

He looked so at odds with the man that had taken my innocence only hours ago. As it was, he sat with his laptop on the side of the couch staring intently at the screen. When he pulled his computer up into position, I promptly tried to move my feet so he could have the use of his lap. He'd simply grabbed onto the souls of my fuzzy-socked feet and refused to let me move. It was a small movement but I melted nonetheless. Something so domestic as having my feet on his lap shouldn't cause me to have this foreign warm feeling in my belly, but it did.

We'd ventured in here eventually after spending hours in his bed. After we talked about our pasts and my apparent fear of abandonment, we'd spent time just being in one another's company. It had been nice to just lay with him and enjoy the moment without feeling as though we had to fill it with words.

We reluctantly left the privacy of his bed when my stomach made it apparent that it was time to eat. We both dressed in our comfiest PJs and ventured into the kitchen. Ian had tried to convince me to let him cook but I politely declined. It would be silly to cook a whole meal for us two when there was still Anna's leftover lasagna in the fridge.

I allowed him the small courtesy of warming the

plates up, though. He seemed determined to spoil me and wait on me hand and foot so who was I to turn him down? It felt way too nice to have someone take care of me for a change.

The dining table seemed way too big for just us two to sit at so we opted to sit at the bar in the kitchen. We sat side by side but as if our bodies gravitated toward each other, we ended up facing one another. Our legs tangled together as we ate our meal. It seemed that with every bite I took Ian would stop and watch me as I pushed the fork past my lips. I would blush each time I caught him and he would just grin at me. Both of us could feel the unspoken sexual draw toward one another. It gathered around us so thickly it was hard to breathe.

Eventually, both of our meals lay half-eaten in front of us as we found other ways of entertaining our mouths. I wasn't sure how it happened but I ended up straddling his hips while he remained on his barstool. I used the height of the position to my advantage as I boldly explored his lips with my own.

I thoroughly enjoyed taking my time to learn his every nook and cranny. The way his facial hair tickled my lips with each kiss was something I wanted permanently ingrained in my memory. I learned that he really liked it when I nibbled on his bottom lip before plunging my tongue past to taste inside. The subtle flex of his hands on my ass urged me on as I explored. He also liked having his hair tugged and pulled on just as much as I did if his groans were any indication. I could almost feel the way his heart raced against my lips as I kissed the pulse point on his neck. He skillfully restrained himself as I kissed up to his ear before softly breathing into it as I sucked his earlobe past my teeth. That move made his cock jump against my ass through his thin pajama pants.

Both of us were panting by the time we came up for air. I could still feel deep twinges of arousal in my core from it hours later. The way he had felt pressed up against my seam made my mouth water. He was hard and just as needy as I was.

In the end, it was him that pulled away first. "You'll be too sore. You need a break from me," he murmured as his hands slid up my sides toward my breasts. In the back of my mind, I knew he was right. I was already feeling the achiness from our earlier activities. But I didn't care. I wanted him at that moment as much as I wanted my next breath. The thought of fucking him in the kitchen topped the list of the things I wanted to do this evening. It seemed taboo and the new Lindsey wanted to explore all taboo things with Ian.

As much as I wanted to shove the bitch down and take him right there in the kitchen, logical Lindsey won out in the end. I nodded quietly as I slid off his lap. A twinge of regret flashed in his eyes briefly before he cleared his throat and stood with me. I grinned at that. I was glad I wasn't the only one under the lusty spell I found myself in.

We'd cleaned up our plates and he led me into the den shortly after. After grabbing his laptop and my book, he sat me on the couch and covered me up as if I might catch a draft without the soft blanket. Though I had the blanket and I sat in front of the fire, those things had nothing to do with the heat I was feeling. No, that feeling came from the man next to me.

He had a little crease between his eyebrows as if he found the contents on the glowing screen extremely interesting. Now and again he would twist and type a few sentences on the keyboard before returning his hands to my feet. The way he rubbed his thumbs against my arches was doing wicked things to my libido.

It was ridiculous really. We'd just had mind-blowing sex and I'd been fully satisfied, but I still found myself craving more. I thought it had nothing to do with the way he was rubbing my feet and just the fact that it was him doing it. I really didn't know if the newness of this relationship would wear off eventually but I couldn't help the feeling that maybe it would always be like this. A girl could only hope so.

My mind replayed how barbaric he was when he slammed into me hours ago. The way his face contorted with pleasure was like a painting my mind memorized. I could still feel the ghost of his tongue against me as he ate me like I was his last meal on death row.

The words on the page in front of me blurred together as sexual tension surrounded me. My nipples puckered and my core clenched as all of my being focused on his working fingers. I wiggled my toes at the same time I clenched my thighs together. I could feel fresh dampness coating my panties as I tried to quiet my need.

My heart pumped viciously as I stared blankly at the pages between my fingers. *Was he feeling the same tension I was?* Curiosity won out as I glanced over my book once more to meet a devious grin flashing my way. My breath hitched at the same time I felt his hard cock throb against my heels.

We stared at one another for a long moment. Neither of us said a word as the thin string of restraint became thinner between us. I could hear my heartbeat in my ears and wondered if he could hear it too. When I saw the flicker of heat in his darkening eyes, the string snapped.

I tossed my book to the side as he lunged for me. His laptop crashed to the floor with our sudden movement but neither of us cared. The moment his lips sealed to mine I whimpered my need as I tore at his clothes.

He was just as desperate as me as he roughly grabbed the blanket between us and tossed it to the side. The sound that emitted from his throat as he sat up was almost primal. He gripped the opening of my button-up top and ripped it open, exposing my naked breasts. Buttons went flying and scattered along the floor around us but I didn't care. I was desperate in my need for him as I clawed at his t-shirt-covered torso.

I sat up and helped him rip his shirt over his head. I leaned forward and licked the warm flesh along his abdomen and gripped him through his pants. He was commando underneath the fabric and it would take no time at all to get him in my mouth.

"No," he barked as he pushed me onto my back once again. "Need to be inside of you," he spoke in broken sentences as he yanked my bottoms and panties down. I helped him as best as I could from my position. I was so wet and needy that I didn't even bother taking both legs out as the material gathered around one ankle.

Within the next breath, he lowered his pants just enough to release his cock. It jutted out proudly before he laid down on top of me. He sealed his lips to mine as he lined himself up with my sex and pressed in.

I cried out into his mouth at the mixture of pleasure and pain. I was slick enough that it made his entry easy but that didn't ward off my earlier soreness. He grunted as he sank in to his root and my core trembled around him. I was so impossibly full and it felt so fucking good.

I churned my hips against him, needing the friction it would create. When I threaded my fingers into his hair, he sat up abruptly and gripped my wrists in his hands. He hauled my arms over my head, the position thrusting my breasts out. He held me captive with one big hand as his other hand roamed downward.

He slowly thrust in and out of me, building me higher with each slick inch. His fingers tickled the sensitive flesh of my inner arm before dipping toward my throat and up to my mouth. My eyes flared as he forced two long fingers past my lips. I moaned and swirled my tongue around the digits before sucking them further inside.

"You look like a fucking goddess wrapped around my cock, Bambi," he growled from above me as he fucked me slowly. I felt a flush take over my body at his compliment. I whimpered as I tried to churn my hips again. I loved what he was doing to me but I wanted more. I *needed* more.

He pulled his fingers from my mouth and moved down toward my breast while still keeping the same pace. He swirled his wet fingers around my nipple, making it pucker painfully from the coldness of my saliva.

He teased me a little longer before leaning down and taking my nipple into his hot mouth. I arched into him as much as I could with my arms restrained. My pussy was throbbing with the need to release when he moved to the other nipple.

"Please," I whimpered.

I felt him chuckle against my breast before returning to his previous position. His slow ministrations never changed as he moved his hand down my belly toward my mound. I jerked and a moan ripped from my throat as his thumb rubbed over my swollen clit. Not enough to send me flying but enough to tease me with the possibility of release.

"Please, what? Does my little goddess slut want to come?" he asked in a deep voice as he continued to circle my clit. My legs trembled uncontrollably as I nodded. He pinched down on my clit before he slammed into me then. I screamed as my body was shoved further up the couch by his powerful thrust. "I need to hear it, Bambi," he gritted as if he were still restraining himself.

"Please, Sir! I want to come!" I screamed.

Whatever restraint he had left vanished at my words. He released my hands and grabbed onto my hips. He yanked me back to him and forced me to meet him pound for pound.

"That's right, Lindsey. Take this cock like a good girl and come all over me," he ordered harshly before slapping the outside of my thigh.

I yelped as the pain turned to molten heat and sank into my core. My pussy clenched down on him as he twisted his hips just enough to send me over the edge. My muscles convulsed around him as my orgasm blinded me.

He grunted above me before covering me with his big body. I dug my nails into his back and rode out wave after wave of euphoria as he pumped viciously into me. His thrusts became erratic as he pressed his forehead to mine.

"Yes, squeeze me, gonna come," he groaned as I felt his hot release flood my core. I could feel every twitch of his cock inside of me as he spilled himself. Something about letting him come inside of me turned me on to no end.

When his orgasm subsided he went lax on top of me. He brushed my hair away from my face as he peppered me with kisses. I rubbed my hands up his muscular sides and shivered when I felt his still slightly hard length twitch again inside of me.

The way he was laying with his pelvis against mine, put the most delicious amount of pressure against my clit. I was soaked with his release but I could feel myself getting wet all over again. The mental image of him fucking me again with his cum covering his cock turned me on more than I'd like to admit. *Am I turning into a sex addict?*

Ian chuckled against me as his hips started to move again. He pulled out a fraction and sank back in, lighting me up. "So much for taking a break," he mumbled before feasting on my lips.

Chapter Twenty

After our romp on the couch, Ian had been gracious enough to be the first to get dressed again and go get me a new top. As I'd only brought one pajama set with me, I had to opt to wear an oversized t-shirt. The thin material did nothing to hide the fact that I wasn't wearing a bra. Something he zeroed in on almost immediately.

It had been nice after we'd been intimate again as we snuggled on the couch. He sat closer to me after and slung my entire legs over his lap that time. He'd forgotten about his laptop and we'd just lazed together. It was as if we were magnets to one another and couldn't stop touching.

Even though we were both fully dressed again, that didn't stop us from finding the soft skin on one another that lay underneath. None of it had been sexual, it was comforting if nothing else.

We'd taken that time to get to know one another even more in a non-physical way. We'd teased and joked with each other so much that I thought I would have a permanent smile on my lips. He'd shared stories of med school and I shared stories about high school and the last few years of college. I'd even shared why I disliked Melonie as much as I did. He vowed that he was on my side in that particular battle.

Now, a couple of hours later, I felt as though we knew each other more than we ever had. Our relationship was going at hyper-speed and had been about the physical aspect. So it was nice to get to know the man underneath the sexual magnetism.

Don't get me wrong, it wasn't instant love with us but it had definitely been instant lust. It would be awesome to get to know him more and more as our relationship grew. Especially now that we knew we were compatible in the bedroom.

When the front door slammed open a couple of hours later, Ian and I resumed our previous positions. I gripped my forgotten book between my hands and thumbed it open to a random spot before pulling my feet from his lap reluctantly. He seemed just as unwilling to release them as he scooted further down the couch. Though we both occupied the big sofa, there was no longer an indication that either of us had touched each other. I immediately felt the lack of his warmth the moment Melonie appeared in the doorway.

I never looked up from my book but tracked her movements as she entered the room. When she came to the center, she stopped in front of the fireplace and stared at Ian. The look on her face screamed sexuality as she slid her coat from her shoulders in front of him. I tried not to let my anger show as she basically eye-fucked him in front of me.

It was actually funny at this point that she was still putting on this show for him. He clearly didn't want her attention in that way. He glanced up from his laptop while she smoothly removed her scarf. She completely ignored me as she all but begged for his attention.

"I missed you today," she pouted and I fought to not roll my eyes. "I was hoping to get to know you a little better before we left Colorado."

Ian looked at his computer with such intensity it was as if the answer to the problem that was Melonie could be found there. "Shame," was all he said.

She shrugged as she eyed the seat between us. I swore that if she sat down there I would kick her in her perfect ass. "Maybe there's still time," she said smoothly as she stepped forward. I looked up from my book then and eyed her cautiously. The jealousy churning in my gut was a new feeling I hated.

"I've been thinking..." she trailed off as she gracefully sank onto the couch, leaving no space between her and Ian. My fingers clenched around my book at the thought of her touching him. Even if Ian visibly leaned away from her, it didn't stop the red rimming around my vision. "I've always been interested in the medical field, maybe I could pick your brain later tonight?" She lifted her hand and trailed it lightly against his thigh. She was being oddly bold tonight, even for her. "Maybe *help* me figure out if it's for me," she asked, her words dripped with innuendo. She was laying it on so thick I nearly gagged in disgust.

Before I could think any better, I slammed my book closed. "You have got to be fucking joking?" I asked harshly. I knew my face was contorted with annoyance but I didn't care anymore. I was so fed up with Melonie and all her bullshit. It was bad enough that she constantly led Ben on but now she needed all the male attention in this house? It was far past the time I spoke my mind.

"Because it sounds like a joke. The thought that you could even make it into medical school is the funniest thing I've heard all year." I huffed a humorless laugh as she scowled at me.

"How about you mind your own business, *Lindsey*?" She hissed my name like a curse word.

"How about you stay in your fucking lane?" I bit right back. "The only reason you're passing most of your classes now is because you're fucking the TAs." I smiled viciously when she gasped as if what I said wasn't the truth.

"You're just jealous!" She stood abruptly and scowled down at me.

I calmly picked my book back up and opened it before replying. "What exactly am I supposed to be jealous of? Everything about you is fake, *Melonie*. And you're so desperate for any kind of male attention that you'll fuck almost anyone with a pulse. On top of that, you're a damn idiot. Go take your bullshit somewhere else because I've had enough," I stated as a matter of fact. I didn't grace her with my attention any longer as I turned my full attention back to my book. My heart was racing a mile a minute but I didn't care. It was far past time I stood up to my bully.

I could practically feel Melonie vibrate with rage as she stared down at me. "You're just a fatass who's jealous that you'll never measure up to someone like me," she spat.

I heard Ian make a sound of disdain and bluster at her comment about my weight. I simply looked up from the page I'd thumbed to before replying calmly, "And thank God for that."

Melanie's face went beet red before she growled in frustration and stomped away toward her room. *Bitch.*

I was still shaking with adrenaline when I glanced over at Ian who was staring at me. I caught his gaze and immediately felt my anger melt into something deeper. He was looking at me like he was about to pounce on me. The dark look in his eyes heated my core and I squeezed my thighs together to ward off the ache. Residual bravado thrummed through my blood, causing me to smirk at him. His eyes flared like he would drag me off to his bed at any moment. He was turned on from watching me tell Melonie off. He liked it when I stood up for myself. *I did too.*

Before I could think of all the ways I wanted him to touch me, Anna rounded the corner. I looked away from Ian quickly and acted like I was still reading my book. The words on the pages blurred together as Anna huffed loudly.

I looked over my shoulder in time to see her enter with an annoyed glaze to her face. She'd kicked off her boots at the front door but had left the rest of her damp snow gear on. I smiled at her and shook my book as if to show her I'd been enjoying the story between the pages. Only Ian and I knew that was a complete lie.

I thought briefly about telling Anna here and now about us. Something about losing my virginity only hours ago made me bolder in what I wanted. And what I wanted was Ian. The only thing holding us back at this point was my need to tell my friend what was happening.

I didn't want to sneak around and pull apart every time we saw Anna. If we were going to give this thing a real shot between us I didn't want to treat him like some dirty little secret.

I watched Anna trudge into the room before she plopped down on the couch between Ian and me, sitting on top of my blanket-covered feet. I could smell the melted snow soaking into her thick winter gear. She looked irritated as she stared at the fire in front of us. I wiggled my toes against her bottom to get her attention.

"Rough night?" I asked.

She scoffed before pulling her stocking from her head with a huff. "Why the fuck did I let Melonie come with us?" she asked.

I snorted as I stole a glance at Ian, who wore a similar smirk on his lips. He stared at the glowing screen of his computer again but I knew he was listening to everything we were saying.

"Because she invited herself and you're too nice of a friend to tell her to fuck off," I answered before closing my book and sitting up against the arm of the couch. I slid my feet out from under her and crossed my legs in front of me. I placed my book on the end table before facing her again. "What happened?"

Anna rolled her eyes and opened her mouth to speak as the front door clicked shut behind me. I looked over my shoulder again in time to see Ben saunter past the living room. He paused when he saw me, making brief eye contact before looking past me. His eyes darkened and flickered with some kind of emotion I couldn't recognize before he stalked past us on his way to his room. When I moved my gaze in the direction he had stared, I found Ian scowling toward the way he'd disappeared. The anger radiating from him was almost palpable before he glanced at me. His eyes immediately softened before returning to his computer.

"Why did I invite Ben to come along?" I muttered under my breath.

It was Anna's turn to snort that time. I noticed Ian's lips twitch behind her as if he found my revelation about Ben funny. "Because you're a good friend and always tend to ignore other people's quarks, even if they are super fucking creepy," she answered as she unzipped her coat.

She pulled her arms out of the wet garment before tossing it at me. I yelped as I caught it. It was cold and wet and I wanted nothing to do with it as I threw it to the floor.

"So what happened?" Ian's deep voice interjected. He closed his laptop and set it on the end table before facing Anna. He genuinely looked interested as he observed her, further reminding me that he was indeed a good dad who was interested in his daughter's life.

Anna shrugged and blew out a huff of annoyance. "Mel and Ben were just a pair to deal with tonight. I think I've come to the conclusion that they did fuck earlier today," she admitted and I winced. I hated that Melonie used Ben like that.

I voiced my opinion but Anna shook her head before continuing. "That's the thing, the way they were acting tonight … I think *Ben* used her." She shuddered as if the thought was unsettling.

I frowned but said nothing, willing her to continue. "I caught them talking to each other multiple times. Melonie was pissed about something and Ben acted like … a fuck toy … like he didn't give a shit that she was mad at him. I overheard him say to her that she was just an easy lay and she needed to get over it because it would never happen again." She shook her head. "I just didn't think he had that in him. I mean, I know I call him a stalker, but I always thought he was, I don't know, harmless." She shrugged.

She did have a point, Ben had always seemed like a harmless flirt. He'd always been respectful to women anytime he was around any. Sure, he and Anna had their little spats, but he was never mean. If he truly did shut Melonie down earlier, that would explain why she suddenly became hot and heavy toward Ian. She was on the prowl for a rebound.

"Maybe I should talk to him," I reasoned and started to uncover my legs.

"No," Anna and Ian said at the same time. I stared between the two of them as they looked my way. Both of their eyes were hard in a way that was not to be argued with. If Anna thought it was weird of her dad to tell me no, she didn't show it as she stood from the sofa.

"Let them figure their own drama out, it's none of our business if he called her the wrong name while he was porking her," she said. She picked up her discarded coat and walked toward her room.

"What?" I asked, shocked.

Anna nodded. "I overheard her say something about it so I assume that's why she was pissed at him. I don't know whose name he said but it was evidently someone she doesn't like." She shrugged again before she turned to walk away. "I'm beat, I'm going to shower and go to bed. Night."

She disappeared down the hall and I was left reeling in her wake. I almost felt bad for how I talked to Melonie now. Even if she did deserve everything I said to her, she had obviously been trying to cope with the disappointment Ben had laid on her. *What's wrong with him?* That was the question that bounced around my head as I stared blankly at the spot Anna had disappeared from.

How he was acting on this trip was … he'd never acted like this. He was my friend but I was beginning to wonder why. I didn't like to surround myself with people who were mean and malicious to others. Maybe I needed to reevaluate our friendship after all.

I was pulled from my thoughts by Ian as he gripped my thigh above the blanket. I swiveled my head in his direction as he stood. He held his hand out for me and helped me stand. I laid my book on top of the discarded blanket before he pulled me to him. He hugged my body flush to his before kissing me lightly.

"Let's go to bed, Bambi," he murmured against me. "We can deal with your friend in the morning," he said as if reading my mind.

I nodded as I went on my tiptoes to capture his lips once more. He pulled away before I wanted to and gripped my hand in his. I let him lead me to my room as I let the rest of my thoughts fall away. I wanted to be with him right now and not think of any drama that would be waiting on me for tomorrow.

Chapter Twenty-One

"Hmm, I could get used to this," a deep voice rumbled over my belly as I stretched. I arched my back sleepily as my eyes fluttered open. Early morning light trickled in through the windows as big soft hands trailed up my sides, climbing higher with each second. The warm palms slid under my top on their ascent, causing the soft fabric to rumple around his wrists.

I smiled and stifled a yawn as I realized whose hands they were. They were none other than the man of my dreams, the star in every fantasy, Dr. Ian Young. I grinned down at my lover with a soft gaze and my breath caught in my chest.

He was between my legs, having already made a place for himself under the thin white sheet that covered us. I could see his naked golden-toned chest underneath. The starkness of his tanned skin against the crisp sheets made my fingers itch to touch him. His hands climbed higher as I watched his sensual mouth crease with a wicked grin. His hair was ruffled from sleep and his features looked softer as he gobbled me up with his hungry stare.

I arched into his hands as they cupped my heavy breasts, his thumbs lightly grazing my tightened peaks. He pushed my shirt up to my neck, exposing me completely to his working fingers. Heat flashed through my body straight to my sex as if his fingers were magical. He strummed me like a finely tuned instrument as his soft lips kissed the swell of my belly.

For once, I didn't stop to compare myself to skinnier girls. I simply laid back and enjoyed his little touches and soft kisses. I reveled in the feel of his rough beard dragging against the sensitive flesh of my belly. I bit my lip to stop the whimper that tried to escape as he lightly pinched my nipples.

His mouth played along my midriff as he worked me into a tizzy. I could feel a solid throb forming in my core that called for some part of him to touch. I wanted his fingers, his mouth, his cock. I wanted it all. I squirmed as his tongue dipped into my navel, the caress mimicking itself lower.

He chuckled against me, eliciting gooseflesh to rise up my whole body. "Do you want to play, Bambi?" he rumbled.

"Yes," I breathed instantaneously. I didn't want to waste any time with pleasantries. I wanted him to keep touching me and so much more.

He chuckled again as I felt his teeth graze the seam of my panties. Thankfully, I'd gone to bed last night in nothing but an oversized t-shirt and panties. The outfit made his early morning exploring all the easier.

I tilted my head up to look over his hands still plucking at me to see his wicked grin. He looked down at my cotton-covered sex with that same appreciative smile before lowering. I jerked as he firmly ran his nose from my center up to my clit. I could feel myself clench as if begging for more.

"I can see how wet you are underneath these," he murmured before he latched his mouth over my thinly covered clit.

I cried out softly as I shoved my hands into the rumpled sheets surrounding me. Just the ghost of his hot mouth on me was about to send me over the edge. I could feel his tongue move against my bundle of nerves through the fabric, causing me to beg for more.

"Please," I whimpered.

He groaned against me and the feeling vibrated up into my core. I could feel another wave of liquid arousal soak my panties. His fingers teased my nipples one last time before he trailed his hands down to my center. He spread my thighs apart with those big hands until I was completely vulnerable to him. When he pulled his mouth away from me I nearly protested before he fingered the inside seam of the undergarment.

"Please, what?" he asked as he pushed the wet fabric to the side. I don't know why I found it so incredibly hot when he didn't take the time to remove them fully. Like he couldn't take the time to properly dispose of them before his need to see me overtook him. "Please kiss this pretty pink cunt?"

I shivered at his dirty words. I nodded as words evaded me. I wanted his kisses, his licks, and his nibbles. I craved everything he could give me.

He grinned before leaning down and placing a chaste kiss right on top of my clitoral hood. I felt my body vibrate with frustration as he lifted his head again. "Was that what you wanted, Bambi?" he asked, his face the picture of innocence I knew to be a lie. He was delectably sinful.

"No," I groaned as I stared down into his darkened eyes. "Touch me, please."

He kept eye contact with me as his hand left my inner thigh. The moment his big fingers slid through my sex I jerked into the touch. I was hyperaware of every little thing he was doing to me as his fingers circled my entrance. He spread my arousal around my pussy in slow tantalizing motions. He made sure to graze over my clit with each move, causing me to pant.

"How's this?" he rumbled.

I could feel my hips undulating themselves, trying to get him to touch me exactly where I wanted him to. I opened my mouth with a sharp breath as one then two of his fingers breached my entrance.

"Or how about when I touch you like this?" he asked before curling those big fingers. The magic button inside of me flared to life and I arched my back further. He pumped into me slowly as he made a *come-hither* motion with his fingers. I could feel an unholy pressure building inside of me with each new movement. But it still wasn't enough.

"Ian, I need your mouth. Please!" I cried as my legs began to tremble.

The growl that ripped from his throat sounded painful before his free hand left my thigh. I didn't have time to comprehend what was happening before he brought his flattened palm back down in a sharp smack. I cried out as the pain radiated from my inner thigh up to my throbbing core. I could feel myself clench down on his fingers with each pulse. His rough treatment stung but it was nothing compared to the deep heat that settled into my bones.

"What are you supposed to call me when I'm fucking you?" his question came out as a growl. His hand arced up again and he delivered another sharp slap slightly above the first. I moaned that time as he curled his fingers at the same time as the slap.

Words evaded me as my orgasm built inside of me. *Was it wrong of me to want him to strike me again? If something felt as good as his punishment then how could it be a bad thing?*

I whimpered as his hand left me again, only this time he landed the smack right onto my splayed pussy. I nearly came out of my skin as he left his hand on the swollen flesh, allowing that sinful heat to sink in fully.

"Sir, Sir, Sir!" I screamed.

"That's right," he said as he pulled the hood of my clit back, revealing the needy bundle of nerves. "I'm your Sir and you're my little fuck toy. Does my little fuck toy want Sir to make her come?" he teased.

I flushed at his dirty talk. How he managed to take something that should be an insult and turn it into a dirty compliment was beyond me. I barely got the yes out of my mouth when he lunged. He leaned down quickly and latched those soft lips against me as he grabbed me around my thighs. He pulled my pussy to his waiting mouth and feasted on me.

I released the sheets at my sides and dug my fingers into his silver and black hair, pulling him to me. He swirled his tongue against me as his fingers continued their assault inside my slick entrance. My orgasm rushed up on me so quickly that it took my breath away. But just when that first wave started to crash down onto me, Ian released my throbbing clit with a naughty smack of his lips.

"You taste so fucking sweet, Bambi. I will wake up and devour this little pussy every morning if you let me," he murmured before giving me a long lick.

I was trembling with the need to release as my fingers played restlessly in his hair. I was so close. "I want that too," I whimpered while moving my hips against him. "Please, Sir," I begged.

"Mmm," he hummed as he watched me writhe under him. I felt his fingers leave my pussy as he dove back down for another taste. His fingers slipped down toward my puckered asshole as his tongue licked from my entrance back up to my clit. I breathed in sharply as his slick fingers rimmed me. "I will take this tight hole too, little Bambi." His deep voice vibrated through my core as he spoke against my wet cleft. "Look at me."

My eyes sprang to him as if I had no choice but to obey his every command. My mouth fell open on a shuddered breath as he pushed one thick finger past my tight hole. It was a strange feeling, not bad, just strange.

"There will be no part of this beautiful body that hasn't been filled with my cock. Your mouth, your pussy, and this…" He pushed further into me and I felt nerves I never knew existed, fire and flare to life. A deep moan rumbled out of my chest at the sensation of being so sinfully filled. "This little asshole will be mine too," he promised before pulling me roughly to meet his thrusting finger. "Eyes on me, Bambi. You look me in the eyes when I'm making you come." With that, he lowered that wicked mouth.

He made sure to show me his tongue lapping up my arousal before sucking my clit into his mouth. I cried out as he fucked his finger into my ass, pulling out hastily just to tunnel back in. The sensation built me higher and higher until all of my consciousness zeroed in on what he was doing to me. My legs shook almost violently as I pulled his hair roughly.

When my orgasm washed over me I tried my hardest to keep my eyes on him, but that was easier said than done. My core clenched almost painfully as I breathlessly cried my release. He groaned against me as my head fell back onto the pillow and my vision dulled around the edges.

Aftershocks wrecked my body as he climbed up onto his knees. He flipped me onto my side before arranging my legs the way he wanted them. One laid straight on the bed between his legs and he curled the other up toward my chest. He gripped my cheeks with one big hand and forced me to look at him as he thrust his big cock into my wet pussy. He didn't even bother removing my panties that time either, he simply tugged them out of the way to make room for himself. I heard the seams pop and tear as he moved the fabric to the spot he needed. He pushed my hips forward at an angle as he fucked into me with the vigor of a desperate man. He held eye contact as he leaned his weight onto me while thrusting hastily.

"What did I say, Bambi?" he gritted out roughly. Though his words seemed harsh, I knew this was for play. Maybe it made me sick but in such a short time I'd grown to love the way he talked roughly to me during sex. It made me hot when he talked to me like this.

"You said to look at you when I came, Sir," I whined. This position made him hit a different place inside of me with each powerful thrust. I could feel how drenched I was with each pull of his thick length.

"You disobeyed your Sir," he said before he moved his hand away from my cheeks. He threaded his hand into the back of my hair and pulled tightly. I moaned as the pain/pleasure crackled over my scalp. He held me tightly, forcing me to look up at him. He moved his hand from my ass and pushed his thumb against my lips. "Open," he demanded coarsely.

I obeyed and he pushed the digit past my lips. I swirled my tongue around it before he pulled it away from me. He moved his now-wet thumb back to my ass, tugged my panties away further, and pushed it into me. I felt deliciously filled as he rubbed into me with the same speed as his cock.

This position caused his head to rub against my G-spot, making me tremble with need. He held me firmly and forced me to take everything he had. He looked like a savage warrior as he fucked into me.

I whimpered as my orgasm loomed over my head. "I'm going to come," I whined.

He groaned as his thrusts became erratic. I could feel his balls tighten against me, getting ready to shoot off. He held eye contact with me as he kept his grip firm on my hair. "Be a good little slut and come on my cock, Lindsey," he ordered as I felt the first hot wash of his orgasm deep inside of me.

My tightly coiled orgasm released at the same time he did. Both of us watched the other as ecstasy coursed through our bodies. The female pride I felt from watching the pleasure on his face was enough to make me want to do a happy dance. *I did that!*

He slowed his thrusts and rubbed out the rest of his release. He released my hair and pulled my leg which was curled in front of me up and around his hip so he could lay down. Both of our rough breaths filled the room as he relaxed on top of me. I felt a euphoric grin crease my lips as he nuzzled his face in my neck.

"You're fucking perfect for me, Lindsey," he muttered as he kissed my shoulder lovingly. I rubbed my hands up his sides until burying one into the hair at his nape. I played with the soft locks as I drank in the moment.

"You're pretty swell yourself," I whispered back. I didn't think there was anything that could ruin the way I felt about him.

His chuckle shook me as he sat up on his elbows. His smile was almost boyish as he kissed my nose. "Swell?" He laughed "And I thought I was the old one in this relationship."

I giggled and flushed. "Maybe I have an old soul," I defended myself.

Ian nodded as he pushed up and away from me. I instantly wanted to recall his heat as he slid from the bed. "Well, you better get your old soul out of bed," he teased as he carefully slid my panties back into place before helping me sit up. My oversized shirt fell back down into place. "Anna will be up soon and we need to figure out what to say to her. I'm done being your dirty little secret." He grinned as he found his pajama pants and began to put them on.

I tried not to flinch at his words. I had indeed treated him like a dirty little secret and it made me feel terrible. I gripped his hand and pulled him to me as he pulled his pants up, taking away my view of his muscled ass. "Y-you know you're more than that, right?" I admitted.

His eyes softened and he crowded me. He wedged himself between my legs and caressed the back of my neck. I craned my neck to look up at him as he lowered his lips to mine. He kissed me softly before pulling away and placing his forehead against mine. "I know that, Bambi."

I nodded and pulled him down for another kiss. It was too short for my liking when he released me and stepped away. "I'm going to shower and then we can figure out how best to tell Anna."

I nodded as he sauntered toward my door, opened it, and closed it behind him. I sat still in my spot as I listened for him in his room. It was quiet this time of the morning so I could hear everything. From him opening his door to digging in his dresser.

When I finally heard his shower turn on, I stood from my spot. My shirt's hem fell to my mid-thigh as I walked over to my suitcase and dug for a clean pair of panties. Even though I'd just changed them last night, they were toast now. I'd packed enough pairs to last me the whole week and being as we were going to be flying back home tomorrow, I should've still had two pairs left.

I frowned as I searched through my bag just to come up with one less pair than anticipated. *What the hell?* I knew damn well that I packed the little red pair with the pink heart on the front. I remembered because it was the last clean pair I'd had because I didn't get a chance to do laundry before we left home. But as I pulled clothes from my bag I saw nothing red.

I wracked my brain as I gripped the other black pair I'd packed. Maybe I was mistaken. I could have sworn I'd packed enough but maybe I didn't. I would have to wear this clean pair today and tomorrow on the ride home, I supposed.

Oh, well. I shrugged to myself and then grinned. I'd just have to tell Ian to not make a mess out of these for the next twenty-four hours. That man wreaked havoc on a girl's panties.

A wicked thought struck me then. I rushed to my door with my clean panties in hand and quietly looked out into the hall. When I deemed the coast was clear I slid out of my room silently and padded over to his closed door before listening.

I could still hear his shower running as I gripped the doorknob. I grinned to myself again as I turned the knob, I was going to surprise him by slipping into the shower with him. *He couldn't ruin any more of my underwear if I wasn't wearing any.*

I snorted at my internal joke. After such a short time of being sexually active, I'd thought of countless ways I wanted him to take me. The shower topped that list right now.

I pushed the door open and heard a rustle from within the room. I frowned as I listened for the spray of water coming from his bathroom. *That's odd.* Was he just letting the water warm up?

My head was turned toward his en suite bathroom when I heard a quiet gasp from the opposite direction. I stepped further into the room and flung my gaze to his dark bed.

"What the fuck are you doing in here?" Melonie's voice carried my way as I watched her cover herself with Ian's blanket. Though she covered her small body quickly, I'd still seen that she was naked underneath the soft bedding.

I stood rooted in place as I stared at my bully currently occupying my boyfriend's bed. I fought for words as she scowled at me. "W-wh—" I stuttered.

Melonie all but snarled at me as she looked me up and down. She halted her gaze on my legs, drawing my attention back to the fact that I had no pants on. And I was still in the same panties that were covered in Ian's release and my arousal. My face flamed at the thought of her knowing exactly what happened between us not moments ago.

"What?" She stuck her nose up in the air at me. "You act surprised that I would be in his bed. He's my lover after all."

My stomach dropped at the thought of her words being true. I knew they were all lies concocted by an attention-seeking bitch, but the thought still stung. Melonie was the type of girl I could picture Ian with. I on the other hand was the opposite.

I heard the water in the bathroom shut off and Melonie snapped her head in that direction. She took a deep breath and let the blanket fall to her lap, exposing her perfect tits. My nostrils flared in anger as I watched her put on a show for when Ian would emerge from the bathroom. She returned her scowl to me and paused her preening. "What are you still doing here, *Lardy Lindsey*? Get. Out," she bit out.

The old nickname was like a shock to my system. *I'm not that girl anymore*. I couldn't allow Melonie to keep having this power over me. I didn't need to compare myself to girls like her anymore because Ian liked the woman I was. He didn't crave someone that looked like Melonie, he craved me.

"You need to get the fuck out of his bed, now." I stood my ground in the doorway even if all I wanted to do was rip her out of his bed by her hair.

Melonie's eyes flared as she sat up straight, further revealing that she was completely naked under all that bedding. We would have to burn those sheets. "*You* get out," she seethed behind clenched teeth.

"No," a deep voice sounded from the opposite side of the room. "*You* get the fuck out."

I swung my gaze to the bulking figure emerging from the bathroom. Steam surrounded him, making him look like an actor in one of those cheesy commercials about bodywash. His towel was slung low on his hips and he was still wet from the shower. As if he'd heard Melonie and me fighting and didn't bother to dry off first.

I grinned at Ian before Melonie pouted from behind me. "I've been waiting for you." I looked over in time to see her pull her leg from under the blanket. I couldn't see from my vantage point but I was sure Ian was getting a full view of her pussy. My vision flashed in and out as rage consumed me.

"I was telling *Lindsey* that she needed to leave so we could have some alone time," she said.

She was laying it on thick and I'd just about had enough. I took a step forward to rip her out of his bed when his voice boomed across the room. If that sound had been directed at me I would've peed down my leg.

"As if I would ever want to fuck one of my daughter's friends." His stern statement pulled at something in my chest. I knew he was saying that just to get it through Melonie's thick skull but it still made me pause. Even though I was his daughter's friend I told myself he didn't truly mean what he said. "And even if that weren't the case, I sure as hell wouldn't want someone who so easily spreads her legs for any man willing to ask for it."

I watched Melonie's face fall at his harsh words. One could almost feel bad for her. *Almost.*

"I suggest you get your bony ass out of my fucking bed, get some clothes on, and get out of my room," he said as he practically vibrated with rage. "Now!" he yelled and I flinched.

That was the only time since I'd known Melonie that I truly believed she had feelings. She looked as though she was about to start crying as she slid from the bed, wrapped her robe around herself, and rushed toward the door. I kept my face down as she brushed past me in her hurry.

I said nothing as I kept my gaze pinned to the floor. I knew Ian didn't mean a word he said about not being with someone who was his daughter's friend, but the statement still hurt. I felt foolish in a way that I'd never felt before. Even if all he'd done this last week is tell me that it didn't matter if I was Anna's friend, that didn't stop the doubt that swirled around my head now.

I didn't notice Ian step in front of me until he gripped my chin. He pulled my face up to meet his. It took me a beat longer than necessary to meet his gaze. I released a shaky breath as tears pricked the back of my eyes.

"Lindsey, I—"

"You sick fuck!" Ian's words were cut off by Anna's voice screaming from across the cabin.

Everything he was about to say fell to the back burner as we both bolted for the den as chaos erupted.

Chapter Twenty-Two

We rounded the corner that led to the den just in time to see Anna with a disgusted look on her face. She still had her sleep shirt and sweats on as if she just rolled out of bed. Her electric-blue hair escaped the two French braids she sometimes slept in. Messy tendrils dangled along her forehead and temples. Aside from the furious expression on her beautiful face, you would have thought she'd only woken up moments ago.

Melonie had been trying to go back to her room when Anna brushed past her, halting her. She turned to face the drama unfolding still clutching her robe to her body.

I rushed closer to her with Ian hot on my heels as Ben appeared from his side of the cabin. He had no shirt on and wore only a pair of boxers, which looked like he'd hastily put on for this occasion. I felt a flush creep up my neck at the sight of him. I'd never seen him in anything other than fully dressed. He was lean and well-built under all those clothes. His tattoos that always disappeared under the sleeve of his shirt continued up to his chest. The whole half of his ripped torso was covered, from the seam of his boxers all the way up to meet the single wilted flower on the side of his neck. I tried not to focus on the intricate designs as I watched him look wildly around the room. His face had panic written all over it as he followed Anna.

"Anna, I'm begging you—" he pled with her before reaching his hand out to grab her arm. The moment his fingers touched her she jerked away from him as if he burned her.

"Don't you fucking touch me!" she yelled and pointed at him. She had something clenched in her hand that he stared at like it held the secret to life itself. "Don't you lay a goddamn finger on me, you sick motherfucker!" Her face turned red as she berated him.

I was painfully aware of the fact that I had no pants on as I stepped up to Anna. I could feel Ian looming closely behind me as he stared Ben down like he was waiting for an excuse to jump him. I felt another flush take over my body as I remembered that he was only wearing a towel and was still very wet from his shower. Both of our states of dress were telling as to what we'd been doing. I cringed at the thought of Anna figuring it out before I got the chance to explain.

"What's going on?" I asked as I gripped Anna's shoulders, turning her to face me. Her expression held a fury I'd never seen before. I'd seen Anna mad before, but this topped all those times.

She opened her mouth to talk when Ben grabbed her hand. As if it happened in hyper-speed, she jerked her hand that clutched something away and Ian moved. Before my brain could fully compute what was happening, Ian pushed Ben backward away from his daughter. Ben stepped back and held his hands up to show he was innocent as Ian crowded him. He stared down at him and clenched his fists like it was taking everything in his power to stop himself from pummeling him.

I gasped at the show of dominance as Ben's eyes flickered wildly from Anna's hand to my face and then to Ian.

"You try that again and you're not going to like how this ends," Ian threatened with a deadly calm.

Ben's nostrils flared before he glanced at me. "Lindsey Bug, please," he begged.

I frowned. *What did this have to do with me?* I looked at Anna and willed her to continue.

She pushed her hair out of her face before speaking. "I woke up this morning and she,"—she pointed at Melonie—"wasn't in bed. So I got up to see if maybe she had gone to speak with Ben. I was going to tell them to give it a rest, I'm done dealing with your drama." She eyed Melonie with a hard gaze as she spoke.

"I went to knock on his door when I heard ... something." She curled her lips in disgust.

"Anna—" Ben's words were cut off as Ian towered over him further. He had the common sense to look up at him with fear as he clamped his mouth closed.

Anna swallowed thickly before continuing. "At first, I thought he and Melonie were fucking again. But then I realized that the only sounds coming from the room were from him. And then his groans turned to words." She shook her head as she relayed her story, like what she was going to say was hard to reiterate. She looked up at me with an odd softness in her gaze. "He said your name."

"You don't know what you heard, you stupid bitch!" Ben yelled as he tried to rush past Ian. It happened so fast, Ian grabbed him around his throat and had him shoved against the wall. The movement was so vicious it made me flinch as I watched him. His back and arm muscles flexed as they held Ben tightly.

"You might want to rethink how you speak to my daughter," he said with a deathly calm.

"Let me go!" Ben gripped Ian's wrists and squirmed to get away from him. Ian held rock still, not bothered by his weak attempts.

I looked back to Anna. "What do you mean he said *my* name?" I asked as a chill snaked down my spine.

Anna shook her head and held her hand out to me. Whatever she held was still concealed as I looked at it. "I thought maybe he finally convinced you to sleep with him. I wasn't about to let that happen so I ... I barged in and I found him with these." She opened her hand and tears clouded my vision. There in her hand sat a pair of red panties with a little pink heart on them. *I knew I packed them.*

"Lindsey, don't listen to her!" Ben yelled but it was background noise.

I zeroed in on the garment in my best friend's hand. I felt myself move before I registered that I was actually doing anything. My fingers brushed over the little embroidered heart before gripping the fabric. I pulled it from her hand and rubbed my fingers over the soft material. That's what he was looking for in my bag the other day. He didn't need any medicine, he wanted something that was mine so he could use them.

"He was ... smelling them while he..." Anna spoke softly and my stomach dropped. *Ben really was a sick fuck.*

"They're not even hers!" Ben lied before Ian put more of his weight on him.

Anna whipped around to face him with a harsh look on her face. "I'm her fucking roommate, you dipshit. We do our laundry together most of the time. I *know* these are hers!" Anna yelled back.

Ben struggled against Ian so hard that his face was turning bright red. Ian looked like he was ready to beat the shit out of him at any moment but held himself back. It must have taken huge restraint because even *I* wanted to beat the shit out of him.

I stepped around Anna, still holding the underwear I would be throwing away later in my hand. I faced Ben whose eyes softened when he looked at me.

"You have to believe me, Lindsey Bug. I would never do something like this to you," he begged.

It was Melonie's turn to scoff from her place off

to the side. She held a nasty look on her face as she stared at me. "That explains why he said *your* name yesterday when he was fucking *me*. What the hell is so special about you?" she asked but I ignored her question.

Ben had said my name when he was with Melonie? All this time I thought we were friends but he had seen me as more than that. Suddenly all the times he showed up seemingly out of nowhere made sense. He was infatuated with me.

I backed up to get further away from him. Ian was looking over his shoulder at me with worry marring his features. If he weren't holding Ben back I knew he would be comforting me. "What's wrong with you?" I asked in a small voice.

Ben stilled his movements and stared at me. I watched his face morph before my very eyes from innocence to malice. He smiled a cruel smile that sent a shiver down my spine. I wasn't going to like what came next.

"What's wrong with me? Don't you mean, what's wrong with you? I don't know many desperate whores that fuck their best friend's dad behind her back," he snarled.

I sucked in a sharp breath right as Ian reared back and punched Ben in the nose. The sickening crunch of his nose breaking reverberated through the room. Ben crumpled to the floor holding his face as Ian turned toward me and Anna. I could feel all the blood rush to my ears as I watched Ben writhe on the floor, blood dripping below him. As if she were shooting lasers at me, I could feel Anna's stare on the side of my face. I slowly faced her as panic laced my blood.

"What's he talking about?" Anna asked me with hurt in her eyes. I could feel tears pricking the back of my eyes as I stared at my best friend.

"Anna, I—" I stumbled over my words as Ian came to my side. He had enough sense to not touch me as Anna's eyes bounced between the two of us.

"Don't even try to lie, you bitch! I saw him in your bathroom," Ben spat toward my back. "I saw the way you let *him* touch you. The way he held you in front of the mirror and you basically let him fuck you! Do you even realize how much that hurt me to see? I'm the one that's been there for you all these years. I saved you from all those losers back home. Showing up on your dates before those fuckers could take advantage of you. And how do you repay me? You let someone you barely know fuck you like a common whore!"

My vision seemed to flicker between hyper-focus and blurry as I let his words sink in. Ian turned back toward Ben at the same time I did. His nose was pouring blood as he smiled up at me. It was like a scene from a horror movie when the heroine finally realizes that the psycho-killer had been her friend all along.

"How—" my voice trembled and then I realized what he was saying. "You watched me through the bathroom window, didn't you?" The flicker of movement I saw that night that I pushed off like it was a deer or something. It had really been Ben watching me all along. "You watched me while I was bathing?" I wrapped my arms around my body as though to shield myself from his prying eyes even though it was too late. I felt more violated than I ever had in my entire life. "How long have you been watching me, Ben?" A surge of adrenaline like I'd never felt before thrummed through my blood. I didn't know if my body was priming itself to run away or beat the shit out of Ben. I watched his face go pasty white as if he just realized what he said.

"This is rich," Melonie mumbled as she watched the scene unfold in front of her, like her own personal soap opera.

"Fuck off, Melonie!" I yelled, I was so done with her shit. Melonie simply scowled at me while I returned my attention to Ben.

"It's not like that, Lindsey Bug. I'm just looking out for you," he said as he got up on his knees.

"By stalking me?" I screeched.

I felt pure rage vibrate from Ian at that moment and I knew if I didn't stop him he would kill Ben. He may be a fucking pervert but he didn't deserve to die. The moment Ian took a step forward I grabbed his arm to stop him.

"Don't," I said as I slid my hand down into his. Ian flexed his jaw as he stared at Ben before lowering his gaze to me. "He isn't worth it," I said as I looked up at him softly. Ian's eyes softened as he held my stare.

"So, it's true then?" Anna's shaky voice sounded beside me, reminding me that she was still there.

I licked my dry lips before facing my friend. I swear my heart cracked in my chest as I watched the hurt on her face. She glanced from my eyes to Ian and my conjoined hands. I refused to let it go under her assessing stare.

"Anna—"

"Are you fucking my dad?" She cut me off as she flicked her gaze back up to my face. My eyes burned as tears flooded me.

"Anna, it's not like that." Ian's deep voice did nothing to draw the angry gaze of his daughter away from me.

"I wasn't talking to you," she said without looking up at Ian. "I was talking to my *best friend*. Are. You. Fucking. My. Dad?" she asked again in a chipped tone.

"Anna, I'm so sorr—"

My words were cut off as Anna reared back and slapped her open palm across my cheek. My head snapped to the side as fiery pain radiated across my face. But that pain had nothing on the heartbreak I felt as I watched tears form and drop from Anna's eyes.

"Anna!" Ian yelled as he held me to him as if he could stop any more of her blows. I had news for him, she could beat the shit out of me and it wouldn't feel half as bad as the guilt that churned in my gut.

"What? You're just as fucking guilty! Neither of you thought to tell me anything? I'm not a fucking child but you guys snuck around behind my back anyway!" she panted and cried at her father.

Ian held me to his chest now but I was numb to it all as tears poured down my cheeks. "It's my fault, not hers! If you want to take it out on someone, then I'm right here," he said.

Anna stared at me with a hatred I never thought I'd see before she released another shaky breath and stepped away. "Fuck this shit," she said as more tears leaked from her eyes. She stomped off toward Melonie and Ben.

Ben now stood on his feet as he stared at me with some dark emotion clouding his eyes. Anna stepped up to him, drawing his attention to her. "Pack your shit and get the fuck out of my house. Melonie, we're leaving, *now*!" she said as she stalked out of the room.

Melonie smiled at me like she thoroughly enjoyed what just happened. Her eyes only left me when she disappeared down the hall. Ben stared after Ian and I stilled. I could feel Ian's muscles priming for another fight if Ben so much as made a move toward me. But he never did, he simply gathered the blood still dripping from his broken nose with the back of his arm, smearing it all over the ink that lay there. He started to walk back toward his room as he kept his stare straight at me. The smile he flashed me before disappearing down the hall caused a chill to race down my spine.

Ian squeezed me to him as my breath left me in shattered puffs. I sobbed in his arms as he rubbed my back and tried to soothe me. I allowed it only because I didn't know what to do anymore. In such a short time I learned that one friend was obsessed with me and I made the other hate me. I'd ruined everything by simply not having the guts to be honest with her.

Ian walked us to the couch, never taking me away from his chest as he did. We sank onto the seat and he cradled me. I allowed him to hold me and gently rock me. I sobbed the whole time while he whispered that everything would be fine. "Anna will come around, she just needs time," he promised.

I wanted to believe him but when everyone except Ian and I walked out the front door and slammed it shut, I had a hard time believing that any of us would be okay ever again.

Chapter Twenty-Three

I'd lost track of time as we sat on the couch. I only knew that the sun was up high in the sky and some time had passed since Anna slammed out of the house. We weren't due to catch our flights until tomorrow but my guess was she wouldn't have a hard time finding a flight a day earlier.

Ian never stopped soothing me even though my tears had dried long ago. I still sat on his lap, though, still in the same ruined panties and oversized shirt I started the day in. It was hard to think I'd started the day in such a great way only to have it all come crashing down moments later.

I wondered how many revelations a person could withstand in one day. Not only did I learn that Melonie was indeed jealous of me, but my other friend had an unhealthy obsession with me as well. I briefly thought that maybe we could find him help when we got back home but if I was honest with myself, I didn't want anything to do with him anymore. There was no salvaging our friendship at this point. He had crossed too many boundaries starting with spying on me while I was in a private moment with Ian.

None of these revelations held a candle to how I felt about Anna, though. I'd betrayed her in such a huge way that I couldn't even blame her if she never forgave me. I'd be surprised if she would even give me the chance to apologize to her.

Her relationship with her dad wasn't like mine. They loved and cared for one another. Unlike mine, I'd be okay if that fucker met the nasty edge of a shank one day. It was different when you actually cared for your dad and then to have your supposed best friend go off and fuck him behind your back. I couldn't even fathom how she must be feeling right now.

I'd cried my last tears long ago and now it was time for me to figure out my next step. It might kill me but I thought one of the ways to get Anna to trust me again was to end things with Ian. Even if it was the last thing I wanted to do and everything in my soul said it was a mistake, I didn't know what else to do. I was so confused as to which relationship was more important to me.

I wanted Anna in my life so badly it hurt, but I also couldn't picture Ian not being in it. I could build our future together so beautifully in my head that it hurt my heart to think about not having just that. It wasn't fair that I had to choose between the two of them, but then again when was life ever fair?

It wasn't fair to the woman who dedicated her life to her husband and kid just to have her husband go off and fuck someone else and then try to kill her. It wasn't fair to be a young carefree college student and then have one night ruin the rest of her life. It wasn't fair for a girl to have to grow up with neglectful parents just to marry an equally abusive husband. Life wasn't fair to those people deserving something much better.

Yet, they still got a second chance. They just had to make the right decisions for themselves to mold their lives into something they deserved. So the question was, what decision was the right one for me?

Did I choose the friendship I'd always wanted? Or did I choose the passionate relationship I'd always dreamed about?

I blinked and swallowed thickly as I seemed to come out of my daze. I peeled my cheek away from Ian's chest and sat in his arms. He helped but seemed hesitant to let me stand. I said nothing as I stood in front of him and looked down at his worried expression. He studied me as I did him.

Just like I hadn't changed since shit hit the fan, he was still in the soft white towel and nothing else. His hair was mused and looked just as haggard as I felt. Looking at him wasn't making the decisions I had to make any easier.

I tried to swallow again only to realize how dry I was. I'd cried everything out of me and was becoming dehydrated. Without looking back at Ian, I turned and headed toward the kitchen. Maybe if I got away from him I would have a better time figuring out where to go from here. If only it were that easy.

I didn't have to look behind me to know that he followed me into the kitchen. I ignored him as I stepped up to the cupboard and grabbed a glass. I walked on numb legs to the fridge and filled the glass with cold water. I could feel Ian standing at my back as I brought the liquid to my parched lips. I downed half the contents before filling it again. I said nothing still as I drank again.

Ian's hands found their way under the hem of my shirt and circled my waist. He knelt down and nuzzled his nose against my neck. "Don't do this," he grumbled against me, sending shivers down my spine.

I pulled my shoulder up as I stepped away from him. I couldn't do what I needed to do if he was touching me. "Do what?" I asked numbly as I brought my glass back up to my lips. I wasn't thirsty anymore but I needed something to distract me from his all-encompassing self.

Ian used his finger to latch onto the rim of the glass and pulled it down from my mouth. I flashed him a glare when I finally looked up at him. "You're pulling away from me," he said as he stepped into my space.

I thrust my hand out and placed it on his warm chest, stopping his advance. I couldn't deal with him being so close. "I don't see that I have any other choice in the matter," I mumbled and averted my gaze. I could feel my eyes burning all over again but I refused to let him see me cry anymore.

"That's bullshit and you know it," he growled as he towered over me. I could feel his frustration radiating off of him and I tried to act like it had no effect on me. Like *he* had no effect on me.

I shrugged as if nothing about this was bothering me as I raised the glass to my lips again. "Not like it mattered much anyway. We both knew this would never work," I lied even though everything in me screamed for him. I wanted him more than I wanted my next breath.

I almost had the glass up to my mouth when Ian swung his hand out, swatting the glass away from me. The glass shattered on the hard-tiled floor and water splashed my legs. I scowled up at Ian as he caged me between his hard body and the counter. "What the fuck is your problem?" I gritted behind clenched teeth.

Ian pulled me to him as his hand wound into my hair. He clenched his fist and tugged until there was no room for escape. I bit back my whimper of pleasure as the sensation radiated along my scalp.

"You're my fucking problem," he growled. I felt my already ruined panties become wet again as his fingers pulled the hem of my shirt up. He grabbed my hip bone in a punishing grip that I was sure I'd get a bruise from. I ignored the excitement that flooded my body at the thought of wearing his mark.

"If you're upset, then you can cry to me. If you're confused about our next steps, then you can talk to me. If you're angry, then you can fight with me. But I will not allow you to just walk away from me. You acting like none of this bothers you and you could just end this without a fight pisses me off," he seethed as his fingers pulled my panties down.

This time he wasted no time with teasing me as he pushed through my folds. I sucked in a sharp breath as he plunged his thick fingers into my soaked center. He groaned as he pumped into me and I clenched down onto him. He then pulled his fingers out and rubbed my wetness and his earlier release around my clit.

"You can't leave me when my cum is still inside of you, Bambi," he murmured before pulling me over to the bar. He was careful to avoid the broken glass as he turned me around and pushed me onto my belly. I had to go on my tiptoes to be comfortable. He continued to hold my hair as he forced me to push my ass out for him. I felt a tug and heard the rip of my panties as he pulled the tattered remains away from my body, exposing everything to his hot gaze.

I didn't feel like fighting him before. I thought if I just acted like I didn't care about us, then maybe he would get pissed off and walk away from me. That would make my decision easier. But I could see now that that would have never worked. But now, as I lay splayed on the bar, I wanted to fight.

I kicked back toward him and came up empty as he stepped out of range. Before I could kick again he stepped between my legs, pushing his towel-covered cock against the seam of my ass. "Let me go!" I growled, knowing full well I didn't want him to let me go. I wanted him to take his towel off and fuck me from behind. I wanted him to punish me like I felt I deserved.

"Not until you talk to me," he growled right back before I felt the hard smack of his hand against my ass. I yelped as the sting settled across my flesh. He gave me no time to adjust to the pain as he delivered another one right under the first.

Yess. This is what I wanted. I didn't want to talk,

I simply wanted to feel.

I arched my back and pushed my ass out for him as he struck me again. He held my hair so tightly that I had no choice but to lay with my cheek against the cold countertop as he delivered his punishment to my achy ass. He peppered me with harsh succession and I sank into each strike. I lost count of each land as they became slower and fewer. He'd rub me and soothe the reddened skin between each one like he knew exactly what I needed. He always knew what I needed.

I felt tears leaking from my eyes as he halted his punishment. It wasn't from the pain as that was becoming something I craved. It was almost cathartic in a way, like I had so many emotions building inside me and this was the only way they would come out.

"Talk to me, baby," he pleaded softly as his hand kneaded my sore backside.

I opened my mouth to speak and then closed it as if deciding what to say. "I—" I whined. "I don't know what to do. Anna hates me and I feel like the only way to get back into her good graces is to end things with you but that's the last thing I want to do. How I feel for you..." I trailed off as I thought of my next words carefully. "I don't think I want to live a life without you in it."

Ian paused his kneading and released my hair. He pulled my hips back to his and that's when I felt that his towel was no longer covering him. He must have lost it while he was spanking me and not bothered to pick it back up. I allowed him to pull my upper body up against his front. He pulled away long enough to pull my shirt up and over my head before hugging me. *Nothing between us.*

"I don't think I could let you go even if you asked for it, Lindsey. I need you too much. I know you don't want to believe me right now, but things with Anna *will* work out. We need to give her time to cool down and then we'll talk to her." His hand roamed my torso as he spoke. It was like he couldn't stop touching me, he needed to have his hands on me.

His big hand climbed up between my breasts before he clamped it around my throat. A surge of arousal leaked down my thighs as he turned my face up to his. He leaned down and took my lips like a starved man. He shoved his tongue past my lips and danced with mine. My nipples puckered painfully as my sex throbbed for him. I could feel his thick cock between my ass cheeks and I wanted nothing more than for him to fill me. I needed him now more than ever.

His other hand slid down my body and nudged between my folds. I whimpered into his mouth as his fingers circled my clit. I was wound painfully tight after my erotic spanking. My hips moved with his fingers as he spread my slickness around. I pulled my lips away long enough to beg.

"Please, Sir."

My words urged him on as he groaned and took my mouth again. He gripped my throat tighter before pinching my clit between his fingers. I sucked in a huge breath as my orgasm exploded from me.

"Fuck, yes, Bambi. Keep going," he ordered against my lips as his fingers moved hastily against me.

I swear the orgasm started over before the first had stopped as he rubbed me from clit to entrance. I cried my release and gripped his wrist holding my neck like a lifeline. I could feel wave after wave of scorching arousal leak from me as he brought me the most pleasure I've ever felt.

"Oh, God, Ian! Fuck me!" I screamed as the orgasm started to fade into another.

Ian growled before pushing me back onto my belly. He released my neck and pussy just to grab my hips and slam his big dick inside of me. The power from his thrust drove me up the countertop. My toes barely touched the floor as he fucked into me.

"I can feel that greedy little cunt sucking at my cock, begging for my cum," he roared behind me.

Sounds of wet smacking flesh filled the kitchen as he pulled me back thrust for thrust. This position made him go deeper than before and he knocked my G-spot with each pull of his glorious cock.

"Yes, Sir! Come for me!" I cried as I tightened around him. My core spazzed as yet another climax wracked my body. I didn't know it was possible for a person to come this many times with the same intensity.

Ian's thrusts became erratic before he pulled me back to his chest. He wrapped his hand around my throat again. I looked up at him as the last of my orgasm faded enough to feel the first spurt of his cum shoot out of him.

"This is for you, only for you," he groaned as his climax contorted his face into something akin to euphoria.

I threaded my hands into his hair as he rubbed the rest of his release into me. His pumping had turned languid long ago as if feeling every little quiver I had left within me.

When we were both spent, he carefully slid us to the floor, not caring that it was covered with my earlier water. "We'll clean it up later," Ian promised but I wasn't sure if he was talking about the water or Anna. He pushed my hair away from my face as he held me to him lovingly. I allowed him to pull me under his big body and he made a place for himself between my legs.

"I promise we will figure this out, just don't leave me." His voice was smaller than I'd ever heard it before.

My heart stuttered in my chest as I realized I would never be able to walk away from this man. I nodded and leaned up to take his lips with mine. His hands roamed all over me as he kissed me with everything he had.

I allowed myself to accept what he said wholeheartedly. I needed to give Anna time, I had to believe she would come around when all the dust settled. At least, I had to hope so. I didn't want to picture my life without either of them.

Chapter Twenty-Four

"Look at me, Bambi." Ian's voice sounded in the otherwise quiet interior of his car effectively pulling me from my scattered thoughts. I pulled my gaze from the passenger window where I'd been staring silently for the last half hour. I didn't even know when we pulled up outside of my dorm building but I could tell he'd been waiting for me to say anything for a while now.

The light pitter-patter of rain tapped on the windshield in a steady beat as if making a mockery of my steadily rising heartbeat. We were back home now but I still wasn't sure what I was going to say to Anna.

We'd stayed at the cabin just us two for the last day of our trip. When Anna and everyone else left the day before, Ian convinced me to stay and not chase after her like I desperately felt I should.

"I know my daughter, we need to give her a little space and time to calm down," he'd said as he soothed my uneasy soul. As much as I wanted to fly back the same day she did and beg at her feet for forgiveness, Ian was right. I knew Anna too and she was as stubborn as they came. Most of the time when someone pissed her off, it took a few days for her to even say their name out loud, let alone speak to them again. The truth was, she was the first person to drop someone who did her wrong without a second glance. I envied that about her most days. That was until I was on the receiving end of her wrath.

I would find out in a few short moments if I too would be on the short list of people she no longer gave a damn about.

I tried, *really tried*, to let Ian's words of confidence sink in these last twenty-four hours. He told me over and over again that Anna would forgive me. That she really didn't care if I was dating her dad, she was just hurt that we felt the need to sneak around behind her back. We'd inadvertently treated her like a child and tried to hide what we were doing like she wouldn't have been able to handle the revelation that we were indeed crazy about one another.

I tried not to cringe at the thought of someone doing to me what we'd done to Anna. I would be just as pissed off and hurt as she was if someone treated me with kid gloves and didn't think I was mature enough to handle two adults doing adult things. *I'm the worst type of friend.*

"Are you hearing me?" Ian's voice broke through my internal struggle. I fluttered my eyes a few times to escape my fog as Ian stared at me. The corner of his lip twitched in a smirk before sobering. I leaned into him as he brushed his hand along the side of my cheek before dragging his thumb along my lower lip. "I said, are you sure you don't want me to go in with you? You're not the only one of us at fault here, I didn't confess what we were doing either."

I tried not to melt into a puddle at his feet. It wasn't every day you met a man willing to accept blame and make up for his wrongdoings immediately. Just one more attribute to add to the ever-growing list of reasons I was falling for this man more and more each day.

I stared up into his eyes before I cupped the outside of his hand, holding it to me before turning and kissing his palm. I then pulled his hand to my lap and traced my fingers along his. I kept my gaze trained on our hands as I spoke. "No, I think this is something I need to do. I'm supposed to be her best friend and I royally fucked up. I broke rule number one of being someone's best friend."

I glanced up at Ian's face in time to see him quirk a brow at me. I flashed him a sad smile. "You're supposed to tell your best friend everything, no matter what," I squeaked in a small voice.

Ian nodded before leaning forward. His lips pressed against mine softly in a too-quick kiss. "You don't need to take this on by yourself. Even though I know she will forgive us, Anna's temper can be—"

"Believe me, I know," I cut him off before raising my hand to my cheek. I could still feel the place she slapped me yesterday. She hadn't left a physical mark on me past the redness that marred the skin right after, but that didn't stop the memory of the sting left behind.

Ian's jaw tightened and released as he ran his thumb over my knuckles. "She shouldn't have hit you like that." I could hear the anger in the way his voice trembled. I could see how this would be hard for him. If it had been anyone else that hit me, I knew without a doubt he would've dragged them. But it wasn't a random person that hit me, it was his own daughter. I could see where he would be conflicted about defending me in that way.

Nonetheless, I felt as though I didn't deserve to be defended. "I deserved it," I mumbled before returning my gaze out the window. The rain had let up some since we arrived back home but it was still coming down in a somewhat steady beat. It stood as a reminder of my shitty mood.

"I think we'll agree to disagree," Ian muttered under his breath. "All right, if you really need to do this on your own, I'll wait in the car." He sounded so pouty about it that I couldn't help the grin that split my lips.

I turned back to him and kissed him swiftly before opening my door. "I'll let you know when it's safe to venture in," I teased as I pushed the door open and stepped out of the car. I closed the door behind me with a soft push as my adrenaline spiked.

I shivered as the chilled rain bounced off my exposed arms and walked on heavy feet away from Ian and toward the front entrance of my dormitory with determination. I was going to make Anna forgive me come hell or high water. I needed her to be in my life and I would be damned if I let her out of it that easily.

I briefly feared that her stipulation for forgiveness would be for me to stop seeing her dad. That topped the list of things I would *not* do in order to win her back. She could ask me to deliver her the Loch Ness Monster and I would book my flight to Scotland at the earliest opportunity. She could beg for the Heart Of The Ocean and I would rent a ship and dive crew immediately. But if she asked me to end things with Ian, that was a non-starter.

Being with Ian taught me a lot over this last week. From watching the way he treated me I'd learned that I'm just fine the way I am. It sounds ridiculous to think that it took the circumstances I went through to see that I *am* enough. Sometimes you have to be treated like you're precious in order to see you were worth it all along.

It was funny to think that just yesterday I thought I was willing to walk away from Ian if that meant I would win Anna's favor. In such a short time he had silenced almost every single inner voice I had that told me I wasn't good enough. That I was too overweight, too awkward, too inexperienced, too … *much*.

I'd always made myself smaller for other people to be comfortable. I never expressed how I felt in certain situations because I didn't want to make a fuss. But I was done living for other people's comfort. It was far past time I started taking up space for myself and demanding what I needed for a change.

I'd learned that it's okay to tell people what I need or take it for myself when nobody was willing to give it to me. I wanted to be with Ian, and I was going to be with Ian. He made me happy and made me feel like I was the smartest, sexiest, most intriguing person in the world. He made me feel safe, cherished, and loved.

I loved Anna, but I wouldn't let her take what I'd discovered with Ian away from me. And if she was really my friend, she wouldn't want to.

The walk from the front entrance to my dorm was shorter than I realized. The halls were so quiet you could hear a pin drop. Most of the students were still away on spring break and wouldn't be back for a few more days.

I came to a stop in front of my door and started to dig my key card out of my bag but then stopped myself. Maybe it wasn't the best idea to just barge in. Anna was more than likely on the other side of this door and I felt the need to let her give me permission to come in. Even if it was my dorm too.

I raised my fist to knock on the door and paused as I looked over the colorful decorations stuck on the corkboard mounted there. Memories caught in the form of pictures filled my vision. Still frames of Anna and I sitting at one of the football games she'd dragged me to. I begrudged the fact that she made me go until we got there and I realized how much fun I was having. Another photo was a selfie taken at a screening of a fellow student's work in the art department. Anna loathed the idea of sitting through the three-hour documentary but she went with me anyway and we ended up having the best time. Even doing things that the other didn't care for, we always ended up having a great time because we did it together.

The back of my eyes burned from unhashed tears

as I stared at the artful display that depicted two best friends in the best years of their lives. It would hurt so fucking much if this was all I had left after this was over. A headful of memories and a heart full of hurt were all I would have to look back on.

I sniffed and straightened my spine. *I'm not going to let that happen.* I raised my fist with renewed determination and knocked against the heavy wooden door.

I stood rooted in that spot for what felt like hours as I listened for movement on the other side of the door. I heard nothing and saw little else as I watched for shadows at my feet. *Maybe she isn't here.* I stared up at the peephole and silently begged for her not only to be home but to answer my call of desperation.

I released a shuddered breath and raised my fist again, poised to knock once more when the door flung open. I sucked in harshly and held my breath as Anna appeared on the other side.

Her blue hair was pulled up in a messy bun with wild tendrils hanging out everywhere. She didn't have an ounce of makeup on her naturally beautiful face. Her normally expressive light-brown eyes were puffy and red-rimmed like she'd been crying. The thought made my chest hurt. She held a flat expression on her lips as she stared at me with some indiscernible emotion flickering across her face.

"What do you want?" Her harsh question made me flinch. So that answered the question of whether she was still angry with me. One day to come to terms with my betrayal was evidently not long enough.

"I—" I choked as if that were the first word I'd uttered all day. I cleared my throat before continuing. "I need to talk to you."

Anna said nothing as she released the side of the

door and ventured back into the dark room, not bothering to turn on the light as she did. I stepped inside the room, shut the door, and flipped the switch, bathing the room in artificial light. Anna walked back toward her bed and flopped down heavily. I noticed then that she only wore a ratty old oversized shirt with some band's logo on the front and underwear, her normal sleepwear. It was past noon and I wondered if she'd even left her bed at all today.

My worried expression must have been screaming out loud because she looked down at herself and then at me before shrugging. "I slept in," she mumbled and then a sour look crossed her lips. "Actually, I don't owe you any explanations. I'm not the one that lied."

I nodded and bit back my need to defend myself. I deserved everything she was going to throw in my face. I walked to my bed adjacent to hers and sat down carefully. I looked at her and willed her to meet my eyes, but she kept her gaze trained above my head.

"You're right, I lied to you," I admitted. Her watery eyes flickered to mine briefly before looking away again. She was stubborn but I was willing to grovel. "You asked me when we were shopping if I was seeing anyone and I flat-out avoided the question. That's as good as lying." I swallowed thickly.

Anna still said nothing as she stared at the same spot on the wall behind me. I could see moisture gathering in her eyes as she tried to wrangle in her emotions.

"I'm a liar and a backstabber and a shitty friend." I felt the tears I'd held onto for so long leak down my cheeks. "I'm a fucking coward because I couldn't tell you that I had feelings for your dad, that I was messing around with him. I couldn't bring myself to admit that I wanted him more than I've ever wanted anyone in my life."

My tears clouded my vision and I quickly wiped them away as Anna finally looked at me. Her tears were freely falling now but she didn't swipe them away. The fact that I was the one responsible for those tears sat like a ball of lead in my gut.

I rubbed my palms down my jean-clad thighs as I continued. "I wanted to tell you from the moment it started happening. It all just happened so fast and before I knew it we were in a full-blown relationship. You're my best friend, Anna. I'm so sorry I didn't tell you, we didn't mean to sneak around as we did. I didn't know what to say to you and didn't want you to hate me." I didn't bother to wipe away my tears now. There was no point in hiding how I felt anymore. "I didn't mean to hurt you like I did, you have to believe me. I didn't mean to fall for him but it just happened!" I sobbed.

Anna's face was watery through my own tear-soaked vision. Her nostrils flared and her lips tightened but she remained silent as she held herself around her middle.

"I love him, Anna. I love him and I love you and I don't know what to do. Tell me what I can do! I can't lose you. Just please tell me what to do." Fat tears fell from my cheeks as I all but begged at her feet.

Anna released a pent-up breath and moved then. "Goddammit, Lyns," she cried before sitting beside me. She pulled me into her arms and I leaned against her. She coiled her arms around my shoulders and placed her chin on top of my head as she held me. I held onto her forearm like she was my last lifeline to this reality.

We both shook with our sobs as she spoke. "I want to hate you so fucking much," she admitted and I started to pull away from her. I was not above getting on my knees and begging for forgiveness. But as I pulled away she tightened her grip on me. "I want to hate you for lying to me and for sneaking around. At first, I was so fucking mad at you. I wanted to scream in your face and beat the shit out of you guys. I hated that you felt the need to hide it. Like you couldn't trust me to realize that you guys were into each other."

"Anna, it's not li—"

"I know," she silenced my protest. "I understand why you thought you needed to hide. I'm still pissed off but not at you. It pisses me off that I'm not even mad at you anymore."

I sucked in a sharp breath at her admission. "What?" I asked in a shaky voice as she loosened her grip and then dropped her hands. She rolled her eyes and wiped her face as she looked at the ceiling. When she finally dropped her gaze to me it wasn't hate I saw reflecting back at me.

"I don't care that you're with my dad, I just..." she said and I held my breath. She sniffled as she grabbed my hands in hers. I moved so I was fully facing her on the bed. "You are both adults and I don't care that you're sleeping with each other." Her lips twisted as the words came out as if they tasted weird on her tongue. I couldn't help the snorted laugh that bubbled up. She gave me a half smile then. "Just don't lie to me, I don't want secrets. You're my best friend, Lyns, and I need you to be in my life too."

I nearly sobbed again when she finished speaking. Words evaded me as more tears leaked down my cheeks. I flung my arms around her neck and pulled her to me in a bear hug. Her arms surrounded my ribs and she hugged me back just as fiercely.

"I swear, no more lies or secrets," I promised against her neck.

I felt her nod against me but neither of us released the other. "Good, and I'm sorry I slapped you," she said.

I shook my head against her. "I deserved it."

"No, you didn't." She was the first to loosen her grip. She gripped my shoulders as she sat up and searched my eyes seriously for a moment. I worried what would come out of her mouth next.

"I'm not gonna call you Mom, though," she said so seriously.

The noise that left my mouth was a cross between a choke and a laugh. She smiled then and we both burst into unstoppable giggles. We laughed so hard that my side started hurting and I laid back on the bed. Anna flopped over with me, still holding her stomach.

"That's not something I would ever ask you to do!" I howled as we faced each other again.

"Good." Her cackles turned into light chuckles as the moment passed.

"I love you, Anna," I admitted quietly.

She smiled at me and I swear I saw her eyes flicker with new light. "I love you too, Lyns."

A knock sounded at the door and broke us both from our little bubble. Anna rolled her eyes before smiling. "Let me guess, he wanted to come in here with you?" she asked and I nodded. She scoffed but it was an endearing sound. "Rule number one, he will always try to fight your battles for you. He's always been super-protective," she said as she stood from the bed.

The knock sounded again as she approached the door. She smiled over her shoulder as she gripped the door handle. "And persistent."

I smiled back at her, I knew all about his persistence. Anna shook her head as she opened the door. "Don't worry, we made u—"

Anna's words were cut off as Ben, not Ian,

pushed into the room past her. I sucked in a sharp breath as he rushed into the room with a wild look in his eyes. Fear slithered up my spine when he locked those black-and-blue-rimmed hazel eyes on me. He had a bandage on the bridge of his nose as a reminder of what Ian had done to him yesterday. His nose was broken for sure and it looked like it hurt like hell.

"Lindsey, please, you have to listen to me," he begged.

"What are you doing here? Get the fuck out!" Anna yelled as she grabbed his arm. The sheer violence in the way he ripped his arm away from her had me cowering toward the wall at my back.

"No! I'm here for Lindsey, back the fuck off!" he screamed at her. The amount of malice in his words had my pulse thumping in my veins so much I feared they would burst soon.

"Fuck you!" Anna screamed right back as she grabbed for him again.

It seemed to happen in slow motion. One moment Ben was pleading with me to hear him out and the next his face mirrored the look of pure volatile rage. It was a true Dr. Jekyll and Mr. Hyde moment. I didn't usually believe that people could be entirely evil, but the way Ben scowled at Anna told me I was so very wrong. I didn't even have time to try and stop him as he flung around faster than I'd ever seen him move and hit Anna across the face.

Chapter Twenty-Five

"Ben!" I screamed as Anna's head snapped to the side and she crumpled to the floor, knocked out cold. I scrambled up from my cowering spot and rushed to my friend lying motionless on the cold floor.

Before I could reach her, Ben turned to face me and caught me around my middle. My feet left the floor briefly as he hauled me around. "Stop!" I screamed as he pushed me back toward my side of the room. I kicked and thrashed like a wildcat until he put me back down. I was still facing away from him as he sat me down but I turned on a dime and rushed back for Anna.

He grabbed me again and pulled me to him roughly. His fingers bit into the flesh of my biceps, making me wince in pain. "No, *you* stop!" his voice boomed through the room and I wanted to hide inside of myself. Aside from him acting out at the cabin, I'd never seen this anger from him before and it scared me.

My chest heaved as I stared from his crazy eyes to Anna softly breathing on the floor. I glanced up at the door Ben hadn't bothered to close when he barged in. I could only hope that someone was around and they would call campus security because I feared that would be the only way I would get out of this situation.

"What are you doing? Let me go!" I yelled, hoping someone was out in the hall.

Ben seemed to be having a hard time with his emotions as his expression flickered from sadness to anger then to empathy and back to anger. It was like watching some sort of sick picture show. He shook me a little and squeezed my arms tighter.

"Can't you see that I can't let you go, Lindsey Bug?" His nickname for me slid off his tongue so easily and left me feeling queasy. He meant it as endearing when it really sounded like the sick hopefulness of a delusional person. His eyes were mad as I stared up into them but his tone was sugary sweet.

My heart thumped in my chest so heavily I could hear it in my ears. I kept replaying Anna's words over and over in my head about Ian coming to fight my battles. I only hoped it was true that he would show up any moment now. I kept darting my gaze from the open door to Anna lying on the floor. I should have known better, really. Because the moment he noticed I was looking for someone to come rushing through the door his head snapped in that direction.

"Ben, no." I tried to calm him but it was no use. He brought his stare back to me and the menacing look I found there had me cowering back.

"Are you waiting for *him* to come save you?" His voice was a lot calmer than it should have been. The tone frightened me even more than if he would have screamed it. He jerked me to him roughly and that time I couldn't help the whimper of pain as he squeezed me so tightly it felt like my arms would break. Ben wasn't a huge guy by any means but hc was bigger than me, a point that was obvious right now.

"Ben, you're hurting me," I whimpered as I tried to pull away from him again. He simply held tight as he walked up to the door.

Once he was close enough, he released one of my arms and grabbed the door. Taking that as my one and only shot, I reared back and punched him as hard as I could. Pain exploded across my knuckles the moment I made contact with his cheekbone but I didn't let that stop me. He grunted and cursed as I kicked, clawed, and punched until he was forced to let me go. I pushed him far enough away from me so I could make a move toward the still-open door.

Victory was short-lived as he rushed me again and shoved me back. I lost my footing as he slammed the door and went careening into my work desk. My back slammed into the corner before I fell against it. I cried out as sharp pain radiated from the place of impact straight up to my neck. I didn't give my body time to ease the pain, though, as I pushed away and got back to my feet.

Ben locked the door before facing me again, but I didn't give him time to speak as I grabbed the first heavy thing I could find, which happened to be a stapler. I gripped my fingers around it and threw it as hard as I could at him. I hit my mark dead on as it smacked him in the mouth. Satisfaction surged through me when I saw blood dribble from his split lip. But that joy was quickly vanquished when he gathered the blood with a swipe of his thumb and his eyes darkened with fury.

My breath left me in labored puffs as he stalked toward me and I grabbed all the things I could to defend myself. I threw pencil holders, Trapper Keepers, books, anything and everything, but nothing slowed him down. He simply swiped everything away from him as if nothing would stop him from getting to me.

The moment he grabbed me again I gripped a pair of scissors in my hand and thrust it forward as hard as I could. His eyes dilated in surprise before I saw a flicker of fear. I screamed as I stabbed him in his belly with the scissors. He sucked in a harsh breath as he released me and staggered back.

I gripped the side of the desk to hold myself up as I stared at them sticking out of his gut. Nausea rose as blood trickled out and dripped to the floor. Panic still thrummed thickly through me as Ben stared down at what I'd done to him. His eyes mirrored everything from pain to anger as he flicked his gaze back up toward me.

I'd never known true fear for my life until that moment. He kept his hateful eyes on mine as he gripped the handle of the scissors. "All I ever wanted to do was love you, Lindsey," he seethed as he pulled the scissors slowly out of his belly. His shirt was covered in thick red blood and more leaked out as he pulled the scissors completely free.

I could feel my entire body shake with fear as he held the bloody weapon in his hand and scowled at me. "Ben—"

My words were cut off as he rushed me again. I had no time to fight as he yanked me to him with even rougher hands. I tried to hit and scream but it was no use. I was no match for his sheer size as he twisted me around and slammed the front of my body to the wall next to the door. My head hit the wall with a thud and my vision dimmed around the edges. He gripped my wrists behind my back and tugged them so harshly it felt like my shoulders might dislocate.

"Ah, please!" I shouted out in pain.

He crowded me from behind and I could feel his blood seeping into the back of my shirt, making my back sticky and warm. *I'm going to be sick.* He pushed me against the wall so tightly I couldn't get a full breath. I tried to think of my next move but it was impossible to move in this position.

"You think this is how I wanted this to go?" he breathed in my ear. He was so close I could almost feel his teeth against me. "I just wanted to talk to you and explain why I was watching you. But you and that bitch"—he snarled in Anna's direction—"made that impossible."

"Ben, I can't breathe," I wheezed. My breath was fast and short as I tried to get the air I so desperately needed.

"No! *I* can't breathe, Lindsey! You left me for someone else and took all my air with you. I just need you to see that I'm the one for you. Not some old fucker who had his chance. Me!" he yelled into my ear so loudly I winced as far away from him as I could.

I wanted to thrash and fight as if my life depended on it because it did, but I could feel the scissors he still held in his hand. Though they weren't pointed at me, they were still a threat. "Okay, let's talk," I whimpered, still trying to find a full breath while compressed against the wall.

Ben made a sound I could only describe as a wounded animal on its last breath. I felt wetness splash against my neck as he buried his face there. *Was he crying?* I held stock still as he inhaled deeply and nuzzled my hair that was trapped between my neck and his face. "I just want you so much, Lindsey. Do you know what I've done for you? How many people I've hurt just to protect you?" I quivered as his words sank in. *Who did he hurt?* Had he done something I didn't know about? Did he hurt someone to keep them away from me? Suddenly all the times I'd never heard from the guys I went out on dates with made sense now. "Why won't you love me like I love you?" he sobbed against me.

If I wasn't in fear for my life I may have felt saddened by this desperate ploy for affection. But as it was, I didn't give two-tenths of a fuck how he felt right now. He'd knocked out Anna and was now holding me captive. There was no redemption for him in my eyes. *But he doesn't know that.*

"I do love you, Ben," I lied and tensed as he stilled against me.

He lifted his face from my now-wet neck before he spoke quietly. His breath puffed across my hair, making the ruffled curls move against me. "You're lying." He didn't seem to believe his words even as they parted from his lips.

"No, I'm not." I let the lie roll smoothly from my tongue. I was amazed at my ability to lie so well but when the situation was either lie or get stabbed to death, a person tended to learn to lie well.

"But, Anna's da—"

"I knew you were watching me, I just wanted to get your attention." I tried not to cringe at myself as I wiggled against him. I needed to get him onboard with the idea that I wanted him. Even if that meant making myself do something I'd never done before, act seductive.

I tried as best as I could to push my ass out against him. It was easier said than done as he held me tightly but I managed to move against his groin enough to show him I was *interested*. He released a pent-up breath as he felt me move against him.

"Lindsey," he groaned my name like a prayer before I felt him loosen his hold on me the slightest bit. I tramped down the thrill of excitement that surged through me. It was working. This could work. I could distract him long enough to get away. I just hoped I could look at myself in the mirror after.

"I wanted you too but I needed you to be jealous. I needed you to fight for me so I teased you with Ian." I hated the words that left my mouth. I wanted to call them back immediately and tell him I really hated him. I loathed this person I didn't even recognize as my friend behind me. He was never my friend, he just wanted the one thing I'd never allowed him to have—*me*.

"Fuck, I love you so much," he mumbled as he pressed his lips to my neck. I felt tears burn the back of my eyes as he kissed and nipped the sensitive flesh he found there. I squelched down the urge to push him away, the need to scream that I would never be his. The only thing that kept me from doing just that was when he released one of my wrists, moving it to be held with the other in his one hand, and snaked his arm around my belly. I could feel the scissors tap against my hip as if he hung the handle from his thumb.

I licked my dry lips and tried to calm myself as best I could as his fingers moved to the button of my jeans. He continued to kiss me up my neck until he reached my ear. I felt the button release and a little part of me wanted to die as he spoke. "I can make you forget all about him," he whispered as he pressed his excitement against my ass.

I played along with him just so he would release me but I didn't know what I'd do if he took me right here against the wall. He still held me tight enough that there was no chance I would escape. *Would Ian forgive me if this went any further?* I had to believe he would want me to do anything I could to get out of this situation.

"I want to touch you." I hoped playing that card would win me his favor but I wasn't sure at this point. After all, what person in their right state of mind would believe anything from a girl who just stabbed them? He was showing how truly unhinged he was.

I sucked in a sharp breath as he ignored my words and pushed his hand into my pants. I had to bite my lip to smother my cry as he fumbled around my panties. I didn't know if I could keep this act up much longer.

"Ladies, is it safe to come in yet?" Ian's voice sounded from the other side of the door. Ben snapped his head up and removed his hand from me in a split second. I would've breathed a sigh of relief if I felt like I could breathe at all. His hand at my back gripped my wrists tighter but I wasn't thinking of the pain anymore.

I sucked in as large a breath as my containment allowed and screamed for my freedom. "Ian!" My voice sounded just as fearful as I felt as Ben jerked me away from the wall only to slam me against it again.

That time when my head hit, my vision swam. His roughness was effective in the way of silencing me but not in getting Ian to go away. My scream coupled with the thunk against the wall only made it blatantly obvious that something was amiss.

"Lindsey!" Ian roared on the other side of the door before a loud bang sounded. I could feel the hard kick against the door from the vibration along the wall. Ben pulled me away roughly and walked us backward further into the room.

"Fuck!" he hissed as he knew the game was over. Tears washed unabashedly down my cheeks as I stared at the door.

"Hey! Over here!" I heard Ian's muffled yell as he kicked the door again. That time a swell of triumph rose in my body as I heard the door crack at the handle. A few more kicks and I knew he would be through to me.

"Tell him you're fine!" Ben yelled at me as if Ian wouldn't hear him. I simply shook my head as Ian kicked the door again. I could practically feel his wrath as the door splintered further. "*Tell him!*" Ben screamed again only this time he brought those bloody scissors up to my neck.

I turned my head slowly to face him. The look of pure terror I saw in his eyes was almost enough to make me smile. "No," I spat just as Ian's final kick landed against the door and it busted open.

I swung my gaze around just as Ian hurried into the room followed by campus security. His eyes flared with fury as he caught my gaze before finding Anna on the floor. I watched as he quickly assessed her and saw the moment he realized she was breathing. The security guard spotted the bloody scissors still pointed at my neck and immediately released his gun from the holster before speaking into the radio at his shoulder.

"Goddammit!" Ben roared behind me and pressed the weapon against me harder. I craned my neck as far as I could away from him as the sharp scissors stabbed against me. "You couldn't just leave us alone? She doesn't want you, she wants me!" he screamed so loudly his voice broke.

Ian held his hands up to show he had nothing to harm Ben as he stepped forward. His body moved gracefully and he seemed calmer than his eyes let on. I could tell by the dark look in his eyes that he would kill Ben the moment he could.

"Let her go," he said in a calm voice.

I trembled as Ben shifted nervously behind me. I wiggled my hands against him as his grip seemed to loosen. If he noticed I was inches away from freedom, he didn't let on. He was too focused on Ian moving closer and closer with each passing second.

"No, she was mine first," Ben seethed as if I were a toy on the playground to be fought over. As if he remembered he was supposed to be holding me hostage, his grip clamped down on my wrists again. Though I couldn't see his face, I knew by the way his muscles twitched he was looking wildly from Ian to the security guard holding the gun pointed toward him.

I desperately looked for a way out and only one thing came to mind. It would hurt like a motherfucker, but it would give Ian the opportunity he needed to subdue Ben. Before I could talk myself out of it, I glanced at Ian and caught his gaze. He held my stare and I tried like hell to convey what I was about to do with my eyes before I nodded. He seemed to get the message as he readied himself to pounce.

Without another thought, I took a deep breath and dropped all my body weight against Ben. He held only my wrists tightly but it did him no good as I let myself drop to the floor. My shoulders screamed in pain as they jerked in an awkward position before he was forced to release me, unable to hold onto them anymore. I felt the scissors drag against my neck up my cheek and narrowly miss my eye but I forced myself to ignore the pain as I rolled away from my captor.

Ian lunged into action then. He grabbed for the scissors as he punched Ben across the face for the second time in the last two days. The crunch of his already broken nose breaking further caused bile to rise in my throat. Ben howled in pain as his grip on the scissors released completely.

Ian moved with the speed of a predator as he gripped Ben around the top of his head and held him in the same position he'd held me in moments ago. Ben yelped in pain as Ian pressed the sharp scissors against his strained neck, drawing blood. Ian looked barbaric as he bared his teeth and held Ben still.

"Stop!" the guard commanded as I heard the stomps of more people running down the hall. I found myself a little bloodthirsty as I begrudged the fact that Ian took the guard's warning and stopped himself from sinking the scissors in further.

"You're lucky that man with the gun is here to save you. Because if he wasn't watching, I would slit your fucking throat for hurting what is *mine*." He leaned in toward his ear then and whispered so quietly there was no way anyone else could hear him besides Ben and me. "You ever come near these two again and I will gut you like a fucking fish and make you watch while I do it."

He dropped the scissors then, turned Ben in his

arms, and rammed his knee into his groin. Ben groaned in pain before crumpling to the ground at his feet. Two more campus security guards rushed into the room then and all three detained him. I tried to hide my joy at the fact that they weren't being gentle with him even though he was now bleeding from his gut and his face. He probably tasted his balls too as far as Ian kneed them into his throat.

Ian rushed and knelt down for me as they dragged Ben out into the hallway to finish cuffing him. I scrambled from my spot and slid over to Anna as soon as he was gone. She was still in the same position she'd fallen in as Ian came to my side.

"Anna," I cried as I pushed her hair away from her face. I could already see the faint purple under her skin of the bruise that would soon be there. Ian turned into the doctor I knew him to be before my very eyes as he assessed his daughter. I could hear sirens in the distance, I was sure the guards had called the police.

I watched Anna's eyes flutter and then she winced and groaned. She picked her head up from the floor, saw me and Ian sitting there, and then laid back down with a moan of pain. "Fuck, that hurts," she whimpered.

"I know, the ambulance is on the way," I said, almost to reassure myself more than her. Ian helped her roll over onto her back and placed a pillow under her head then.

When he was finished tending to her I tackled him with a sob. I slung my arms around his neck and buried my face into his chest. He pulled me to him and roamed his hands over my body, looking for signs of damage.

"Hey," he said as his hands grazed over the sticky wetness of Ben's blood on my shirt. I shook my head against him as more tears leaked from my eyes. "Not mine," I managed.

As if the mention of his blood was funny, I heard Ben's quiet chuckle coming from the hallway. I glanced over to see him laying on his belly with the three security officers holding him down. My stomach rolled and revolted at the smile he held on his bloody face. He caught me looking at him and tilted his head up off the ground and sucked at his teeth. I flinched as he spat a mouthful of blood onto the floor below him before he smiled broadly once again. I wanted to throw up as he started laughing like this was all a big joke to him.

I always laughed and brushed it off anytime Anna had made fun of him in the past. When she constantly called him a psycho or mocked him with some famous serial killer's name. But as I sat there with him staring into my eyes covered in blood and smiling, it solidified every inkling feeling that he truly was deranged.

As if he knew I couldn't look away from the psychopath in the hallway, Ian gripped my head and turned me to lie on his chest. I gripped him fiercely and all but crawled into his skin. "Okay, it's all right, shh. I'm here." He soothed me as we sat on the ground and waited for the authorities to take over.

Chapter Twenty-Six

Three Weeks Later

"You sure you don't want a ride to the restaurant?" Ian's voice sounded in my bedroom doorway just as I exited the bathroom. I would've jumped, frightened that he was here at all if it weren't for the fact that he was always here. I smiled as I loosened my grip on the towel wrapped around me.

"And what would you do while I'm at brunch? Sit in your car and wait for us to finish eating?" I smiled up at him as I brushed past him on my way into my room. That was weird to think, *my room.* I hadn't had my own room since moving from Mom's house to college. But here I was once more, in a room I didn't have to share with anyone. Well, except for Ian when he stayed the night, which seemed like almost every night.

I was still getting used to not having to share sleeping space with a roommate, even if said roommate was just down the hall now, it still felt odd. I hadn't realized how accustomed I'd become to sleeping in the same room as someone else until the first week in our new apartment. It was rough the first couple of nights when I realized I'd come to rely on Anna's steady breathing a few feet away to help lull me to sleep. Luckily, Ian had stayed with us more often than not and him being next to me every night helped a lot.

After everything that happened with Ben, Anna and I decided we no longer wanted to stay in our dorm. The place where we'd spent the last few years building our friendship had become quickly tainted by the memory of what he put us through.

Thoughts of Ben caused my chest to clench as I dried my hair. It was too soon to know what was going to happen to him. All I knew was that he was still being held in jail until his court hearing later that month. The police were working with the college on an open investigation. So far, a lot of the case was still hush-hush but being as Damon was married to my aunt, I knew more than most about what was happening.

Apparently, not a lot of people realized just how depraved Ben really was. Some students, mostly guys that I'd gone on a couple of dates with, were now coming forward and speaking up about the threats they'd received. I was disgusted to learn about the multitude of death threats they'd gotten simply from going out with me once or twice. It was no wonder to me now as to why they ghosted me. I still couldn't believe how blind I'd been to not see what was happening right under my nose.

I didn't know enough about Ben's family to know if he would be getting any legal help from them or not. I still didn't know how I felt about the whole situation. It was weird to go from being someone's close friend and then to worst enemy so quickly. I felt uneasy anytime his name was spoken like I should've done something to help him in the end.

When I opened up to Ian about it, he'd helped me sort through the feelings I was having. He made me see that there was more than likely nothing I could've done for him. I didn't know what his past was like but Ian's thoughts from a professional standpoint were that he must have had some kind of past trauma that made him compulsive and obsessive with women. I guess we all have issues and he just chose a poor way of coping with his.

Nonetheless, Jill and Mom helped me find a lawyer that would take on my case against him. Jill, being herself, was ready to cut Ben's balls off at the earliest opportunity and I think my mom was ready to help hold him down. I still felt bad for him but my hope was when all the dust was settled he would get the help he clearly needed. I don't know what would have happened to me if Ian hadn't shown up when he did. I liked to think that I knew Ben enough that he wouldn't have forced himself on me but we would never really know.

Even if he wouldn't have tried anything sexual with me, what Ben did to Anna and me in our dorm caused us to be on the fast track out of there. Ian was all too happy to help us find an affordable apartment near the college and coincidentally closer to his condo.

I smiled at the memory of moving day. Anna and I hadn't had to lift a single finger that day. Ian, Heath, and Reid had all come to help us move what little we had in our dorm into our new two-bedroom apartment. Watching all the men together with my mom and Anna next to me had been amusing. I hadn't missed the way Anna's eyes tracked Mom's husbands but then again she hadn't tried to hide her obvious attraction. I couldn't blame her really, if they weren't my stepdads they would totally be hot in all senses of the word.

I teased her about having a starry-eyed crush on my stepdads. That was until she pointed out that I not only had a crush on *her* dad but I was actively fucking him. I still felt the hot flush that rose to my face at the mention of him. It was taking us a little time to get used to the fact that I was with her dad. I was just glad we chose an apartment with soundproof walls and bedrooms on opposite sides of the space. The last thing I needed was for Anna to know how much I thoroughly enjoyed being with her dad.

Who just so happened to be staring at me from the doorway like he was about to eat me up. I brought myself out of my thoughts and watched him carefully as

I finished drying my hair. I smiled to myself as I thought of all the ways I'd like him to have his way with me. It was funny really, I'd noticed things about myself these last few weeks. I'd clearly gone through a sexual awakening since my first time with Ian.

In the past, if he would've looked at me like he was now I would've blushed and looked the other way. Not stood up straight and met his searing gaze with one of my own. The smile that creased his lips emboldened me as he gripped the doorway. I felt confidence rise in me as I dropped the towel I'd been drying my still-damp hair with.

"I think I can manage to get myself to brunch, Dr. Young," I answered his earlier question. I loved the way his eyes flared at the mention of his official title. I nearly melted into a puddle as he crossed his arms and leaned against the doorframe.

"Do you want to play *Doctor*, Bambi?" he grumbled. It was clear he could feel the same sexual tension I was feeling.

I bit my lip as I ran my fingers along the top edge of my towel, teasing the top swells of my breasts. His eyes flickered there and watched my movements. He made no other move toward me, though, seemingly content to just watch the show.

I nodded as I played with the part of the towel I'd tucked to hold it in place. "I have about an hour until I have to meet the others. Anna isn't here either, we have the whole place to ourselves," I said as I gripped the plush fabric.

It took no effort at all to release the towel and let it drop to the floor around my feet. I stood completely naked in front of him. I wasn't sure if it was the A/C or the intense way he stared at me that caused gooseflesh to rush over my body. The dampness between my thighs had nothing to do with my shower and everything to do with the man currently gaping at me. My nipples puckered painfully and I didn't stop myself as my hands climbed my body in search of the tightened peaks.

I kept my sights trained on him as I pinched myself. His eyes darkened and he clenched his jaw as if holding himself back. *That just won't do.* Along with my sexual awakening, I learned that I'm undoubtedly an instant gratification kinda gal. I didn't like waiting for all the delicious things this man would do to my body.

I released my breasts and sauntered over to my bed. It didn't even cross my mind anymore about how my body looked. I knew Ian loved my body for all its flaws and I did too. I kept my gaze on him as I laid down on top of the freshly made bed. I pointed my legs in his direction and bent them at the knees. He watched me like a wolf observing its prey as I parted for him.

He finally pushed away from the doorway and stalked my way then. I trailed my hand down my belly until reaching my mound. I wasted no time pushing my fingers through my slick folds, finding the place that begged for his attention. My breath caught as I grazed over my clit and swirled my fingers around the thumping nerve.

Ian knelt at the end of the bed so he was at eye level with my most intimate area. "That is a beautiful pussy, Bambi. Spread yourself wide so I can see how wet you are. Are you ready for my cock yet?" he asked.

I obeyed immediately and kept working my fingers in tight circles. "I'm always ready for you," I moaned as I dipped down, gathered my arousal, and swirled it around. We'd both grown to love this. He liked watching me bring myself pleasure as much as I enjoyed doing it. His groan of appreciation drove me higher as I continued to work myself. I was already so close to the edge, all I needed was a little extra push.

I kept my gaze pinned on his as I swirled my hips in time with my fingers. I liked watching him watch me as if I were the sexiest creature on the planet. He focused his whole being on what I was doing to myself as his hands snaked around my thighs. He gripped me firmly before drawing me closer to the edge of the bed. I knew what was about to happen before it did, but that didn't make me any less eager.

"Do you taste as good as you look?" he growled right before his mouth descended onto me. He didn't even bother moving my fingers as he lapped at me. I cried out as I moved them further up for him to perform his unique brand of magic with that sinful tongue. I splayed myself wide with my fingers and pulled up so my clit poked completely out of its hood.

I could feel his grin against me as his mouth latched around the throbbing nub. My legs shook and my muscles convulsed as he ate at me. My orgasm hung over my head like an appending storm I couldn't escape and as soon as I felt him suck my clit past his teeth I was a goner.

I cried my release as he pulled me closer to him. He held onto both of my thighs so tightly there was no hope for escape as ecstasy washed over me in waves. My only option was to thrust my hands into his peppered hair and hold on for dear life. I pulled at the silky strands, extracting a deep groan from him that sent vibrations into my core. Just as I loved when he was rough with me, he also liked when I gave as good as I got. Just when I thought I couldn't possibly take any more, he loosened his grip and pulled away.

I writhed in post-orgasmic bliss as I listened to the rustle of clothing hit the floor. Lucky for me, Ian was just as much into instant gratification as I was.

Warm hands caressed my sides as he descended on top of me. I watched him as he kissed, licked, and nipped his way up my body before settling between my splayed thighs. "I will never get tired of the taste of your cream on my tongue," he murmured as he nudged the head of his cock against my entrance.

I arched my back as he stretched me inch by inch. "Fuck me, Sir," I whimpered and trailed my hands up his taut back.

He chuckled above me and I couldn't stop the smile that formed on my lips. "Demanding little Bambi. You want this cock?" he teased as he slowly pumped into me. He was working me up just so I could crash back down. "Tell me, how did you go from being so innocent to such a filthy little slut so quickly?" he asked as his fingers found my breasts. He teased and tweaked me, eliciting sharp gasps from my parted lips.

I tilted my head up toward his lips as he finally plunged fully inside of me. My core quivered and spasmed around him, begging wordlessly for him to fuck me. I could feel every throb of his heavy length inside of me and I craved everything he would ever give me. He met me halfway and kissed me softly. I licked the seam of his lips before nipping at him. He grunted at the sensation and pulled his hips away just to slide back in. I wrapped my legs around his slowly pumping hips and urged him on.

"Well, my friend's dad caught me watching him masturbate and then he taught me how to give myself the most pleasure I'd ever felt." I smiled as he twisted his hips with each solid thrust, knocking my engorged clit each time. His grin turned devious as I told him the story he lived through. "He taught me how to love my body and take what I needed for a change." I gasped as he increased his speed little by little. I could hear how wet I was with each pull of his glorious cock. "Fuck, I'm going to come again," I moaned and then turned a mischievous smile toward him. "Will you make me come on your cock, Sir?" I pouted prettily.

He smiled down at me so genuinely that it made my chest swell. "How can I deny you when you asked so nicely? I believe I've created a sex-crazed monster out of you," he teased.

I grinned up at him as I wrapped my leg around his. Before I gave him time to realize what I was doing, I pushed at him and flipped him over onto his back. His cock never left me as I rolled us. The look of surprise written in his eyes was priceless and I would have laughed if not for the pleasure this position gave me. I moaned as I sat completely onto him. I rocked against him as his hands found my hips. He groaned as pure lust clouded his eyes.

Euphoria mixed with pride for myself swirled in my gut as I leaned down over him. I grazed my lips against him as I gently fucked him up and down. "You have no idea," I muttered before he threaded his fingers into my hair and pulled me to him. When his lips sealed to mine I didn't question the feeling of perfection. I was finally right where I was meant to be.

****

"So, how's Dr. Hottie?" Jill asked as she raised her mimosa to her lips. I couldn't stop the grin that formed on my lips at the thought of Ian. I'd left him naked in my bed, his hair still rumpled and skin flush from our earlier romp. We'd almost taken too long and I was a little late to brunch, but I didn't mind. When you started your day with really great sex, little things like running late didn't seem to bother you.

"Shit, you don't even have to answer. We can all see that he's hittin' it right," Emily muttered from behind her menu. I smothered my laugh as my mom smacked her on her biceps.

"Do we have to talk about my daughter's sex life?" she complained but even I could see the grin she tried to hide. She was happy for me even if she didn't want to hear about how well he was "hittin' it."

"Oh pu-lease. You fuck two guys at the same time and you want to act like a prude when it comes to Lindsey finally knocking the cobwebs out?" Jill arched an eyebrow at her best friend and Emily snorted. I held my hand over my mouth to hide my smile as the table next to ours tried their hardest to ignore us.

"I don't think that table across the restaurant heard you, you should probably yell a little louder," Mom whispered harshly but I could see the endearment for her friend sparkling in her eyes.

Jill waved her off. "Don't even act like you're ashamed of nabbing those two hotties. We all know your new book is all about the filthy things they do to you behind closed doors," she said as she glanced at her menu.

"When inspiration strikes, you have to write it down," Emily piped up as she grabbed her champagne flute. "I've definitely had to get out my notes after Leo and I had gotten done before." She fanned herself as if remembering a particular time when "inspiration" struck.

"So, back to you," Jill turned back toward me and put her elbows on the table. Her eyes twinkled with mischief as she clasped her hands on her cheeks and stared at me. I couldn't stop the giggle that bubbled up at the look she gave me. She looked like I was about to drop the juiciest bit of tea for her to gobble up. "Does Dr. Silver Fox know what he's doing down south? I bet he does. I tell you what, the first time I saw that man I may have been high on pain meds but I could tell he knew exactly how to treat a woman. Does he make you come until you almost black out? Damon does this thing with his tongue—"

"Do you ladies mind keeping it down? This is my grandma's eighty-ninth birthday brunch and what you're talking about is making her uncomfortable," the middle-aged man at the table next to ours spoke. His face held the same distaste that could be heard in his sneering words.

Jill's face soured as we looked over at said grandma. She didn't look fazed at all as she enjoyed her blueberry muffin.

I winced as Jill bristled. "Seriously? She can't even hear us. If anything I'm sure she would like to sit at our table and talk about how Grandpa used to rail her back in th—"

"What my aunt is trying to say is, we will try to keep it down," I interrupted Jill before she got us thrown out of the restaurant. The man eyed Jill warily before returning to his meal. Jill glared at the back of his head and stuck her tongue out in a very juvenile move before turning her gaze back to me.

"They are going to stop letting us come back here soon." Mom laughed.

"We're just here to enrich these stuck-up brunch-goers with our tales of whoredom. I mean, really, they should thank us, anytime we eat here everyone else gets a free soap opera with their meal." Emily shrugged.

"Mental breakdowns and all." Jill brought her flute up in a mock toast before downing the contents. We all followed suit and laughed lightly.

We set down our empty glasses before my mom patted my hand. "We really are happy for you though, sweety." She smiled.

"Yeah, Jill is just like our horny teenage boy of

the group. I, for one, knew from the moment you guys bumped into each other in the hospital that there would be a juicy story there," Emily admitted.

"I was surprised when he didn't fuck you on the floor at my reception, what with you looking at him with stars in your eyes. What was it you said to him?" I knew what was coming next as Jill clasped her chest in an overdramatic display. She pushed the back of her free hand to her forehead and acted as if she would faint. "*I could think of a better place I would like you to take me.*" She breathed in a southern accent.

Everyone busted up laughing as I pushed her shoulder. I couldn't even stop myself from laughing with them. "I swear to God, you and Anna are cut from the same cloth." I laughed.

Our waitress stopped by at that moment and refilled our glasses again before moving on to the next table. When our howls finally quieted I gripped my glass and lifted it in a real toast that time.

"Seriously, though, I'm happy for all of us." I smiled to myself before continuing. "To the ones who had to fight back against lies and deceit for the love you should have gotten in the first place." I tilted my head toward Emily who returned the motion. "To the ones who had to go through hell and back and still found the love you were forever worthy of." I nodded at Jill who flashed me a small smile. "And to the ones that put themselves first for the first time and finally got what they always deserved." I flashed Mom a watery smile and she emulated the same back. "I'm over the moon grateful that my life has been composed of strong badass women who know their self-worth and are willing to fight for the things that matter most in this world. I love all of you so much and I wouldn't want to be anywhere else than where I am right now."

"I'll drink to that," Emily said as she raised her glass to mine. Mom and Jill were next as we all clinked glasses before sipping the sweet drink. No matter what the future may hold for us, I was glad I got to experience it with them by my side.

"So, you're really not going to tell us how big his cock is then?" Jill asked and I choked on my drink.

"For fuck's sake, Jill." Mom laughed. Emily was too busy coughing up mimosa to say anything at all.

"What? I thought that's what we were all here for in the first place." She shrugged and winked my way.

I smiled back. *So grateful for these women.*

The End

Keep reading for a prologue to my new book coming soon, *Crawl for Me*:

They say obsession is a conscious thought that continually preoccupies or intrudes on a person's mind. Whoever the fuck *they* are, they don't realize how fucked up a person truly is to be obsessed with another person. Could you imagine having an unhealthy obsession with a living, breathing thing? The unruliness that consumes your every waking thought when you're not able to keep that person under your control. You feel what they feel, you hate what they hate. You have the visceral need to see that obsession become a permanent staple in your life. You would do anything for that person, *be* anything to make them a reality. The trials and tribulations of being obsessed with someone so far out of your control would put a toll on anyone's mind I would think.

Don't even get me started on the limits of depravity it has on you when your love is simply overlooked or tossed aside. I never really knew why I found it so easy to cross that line drawn in the sand of morality, but it was something I'd done long ago. I thought it was easy because I was doing it for the person I loved most. The things I did to keep her safe from predators would make a serial killer quake in his blood-soaked boots.

She'd never know what I did for her. Who I threatened, who I killed. I smiled to myself as I sat on the hard slab of rock they called a bed in this godforsaken place. If Lindsey only knew how red my hands truly were. Maybe it made me a sick fuck to feel joy course through my veins when I remembered the way it felt to have warm blood dripping from my fingertips. I used to think something was wrong with me because I felt no remorse for my actions. Now I realized it was the rest of the world that was fucked up.

I wasn't so far out of touch with reality to not know what I was. I was the bastard son that nobody wanted. I didn't know my sperm donor, though my mother once said he was some rich dude living high in his ivory tower. He was willingly blind to the fact that he was the cock that impregnated a common whore. Not a dime nor a birthday card ever came in the mail from dear ol' Dad.

My harlot of a mother wasn't much further down on the list of piece of shit adults I'd known growing up. The revolving door that was my mother's bedroom swung so freely that it'd taken a long time to be able to sleep without the screeching of that door signaling that I was no longer alone. No longer forgotten.

Lily was her name, the whore that birthed me. I'd say *raised* but that would be a damned lie. The system raised me more than she ever did. Maybe that's why I was so fucked up. Abandoned by my father, neglected by my wilted-like-a-flower, mother, beaten by the constant stream of foster parents that were just in it for that monthly check.

My court-appointed psychiatrist had been taking deep dives into why I was the way I was. Educated idiot didn't realize my past is laid out like a goddamn blueprint for the way my mind worked. As if my "Mommy issues" weren't an obvious diagnosis, that prick still requested I see him more than once a week. As if he could cure what he called my *God Complex* by forcing me to talk about my past. He thinks he knows everything about me but he hasn't even scratched the fucking surface.

He doesn't know about Heather. Doesn't know what I did to her when I was all but fourteen years old. Or Amber, freshman year at my old college. I could still see the way her eyes flared as I slid my blade across her porcelain skin while I sank into her for the last time. He thinks this was a one-time offense as if my life hasn't been slowly building toward this moment. He thinks I'm able to be redeemed, that I'll somehow be able to become a normal upstanding citizen. What he doesn't know is that I'd already been redeemed. This place was liberating me every single day. Teaching me all the ways to improve my art. Did I know I was a vile, wretched human being for the impure thoughts I had on a daily basis? Yes. Did I care or was I willing to change? Absolutely not.

You see, the main lesson this whole situation with Lindsey taught me was that I'm right. Women like her needed men like me. They needed someone to teach them not to be whores. Not to spread their legs for just anyone that asks for it. To put *them* on the path of redemption or end them if they couldn't be redeemed. They needed a guiding hand. One that would help them overcome the obstacles they may face. Someone who wasn't afraid to slit some throats in order to help them be who they were always meant to be.

Lindsey could have her doctor, I'd made up my mind. Just like Heather and Amber, she ended up not being worth it in the end. I'd serve my time, I'd follow their misguided rules. And then I'd leave this place a new man. A *better* man.

I stood from my cot and walked to the mirror mounted to the wall above the foul-smelling steel toilet. The filth of this place didn't bother me anymore, it was the fallacious souls that walk these halls that made my stomach turn. I glanced at the deep-crusted scab marring the chiseled face that had gotten me far in this life. The number of sluts willing to spread their legs for a face like this one was astounding to me still. Though I'd sunk my cock into those willing to open their bodies to the oblivion I offered, it was the ones that were harder to get that called to my specific tastes. The ones that acted like they didn't want what I had to offer but begged me with their eyes to fuck them. Those are the ones I craved. The ones I could save.

Lindsey may think she was the first and last but there are always more. Always others who would crawl for me just to have the small slice of euphoria I could offer them. Some would embrace the type of protection I could give them.

I briefly wondered if my new scar would ruin that instant appeal most females experience when they saw me. I ran my fingers over the puckered skin a little too harshly and watched as the scab broke open, blood pooled before dripping down into the sink below. I'd received the gift my first week in this fine state penitentiary when I was held down in the shower room by three skinheads. They sliced me from hairline to cheekbone, trying to get me to shout for the guard. My cellmate interrupted their fun, though, allowing both of us to get our hands a little bloody before the pigs that watched us broke up the brawl. Cade thought he'd saved me from the pain those scumbags were inflicting, but he hadn't realized that I welcomed the pain. Sometimes I dreamt about the pain just so I could feel *something* again. The scar I was sure to carry forever would be a constant reminder in the future. Every time I would look at it I would remind myself not to get caught again.

I watched my hazel eyes in the mirror as my blood thumped a steady beat into the bowl below me.

Resolve darkened them as a smile creased my lips.

I would never be back in a place like this. Cade had told me that his family was well-connected and could set us up when we get out. Once I did my time, I would leave this town, this state. I would leave myself behind as well. Ben may have been the person that walked through those cell doors months ago, but he wouldn't be walking out. It was far past time I gave over to that voice in my head. *He'd* always been with me, in the deep recesses of my mind. Quietly whispering all the dark, maniacal things I ended up doing. I blinked and it was as if a switch flipped in my mind, allowing *him* to take control. Permanently this time.

Ben was dead, and all that was left was Ryker.

End of sample chapter

EVERNIGHT PUBLISHING ®

www.evernightpublishing.com